WITH MALICE

EILEEN COOK

HOT KEY BOOKS

First published in Great Britain in 2016 by
HOT KEY BOOKS
80–81 Wimpole St, London W1G 9RE
www.hotkeybooks.com

A CIP catalogue record for this book is available from the British Library.

ISBN: 978-1-4714-0585-3
also available as an ebook

This book is typeset in 10.5 Berling LT Std using Atomik ePublisher

Printed and bound by Clays Ltd, St Ives Plc

Hot Key Books is an imprint of Bonnier Publishing Fiction,
a Bonnier Publishing company
www.bonnierpublishingfiction.co.uk
www.bonnierpublishing.co.uk

WITH
MALICE

To my grandparents, who taught me to love a good story

Chapter One

Beep. Beep. Beep. Beep.

I'm not a morning person. Understatement.

My hand couldn't seem to muster the energy to turn off the alarm. It picked at the covers. The blanket felt wrong. Scratchy. Thin.

This isn't my bed.

The realization made me uneasy. I must have crashed somewhere else. I hoped I'd remembered to call my mom. I felt a ripple of worry. If not, I was going to be in deep shit for not coming home. She was already mad about . . .

My brain was blank. I couldn't remember why she was ticked at me. I remembered fighting about it. I'd slammed my door, and Mom threatened if I did that again, she'd take it off the hinges, but the reason why we'd argued was gone.

It felt like the reason was right at the tip of my tongue, but I couldn't pin it down. Every time I tried to concentrate, it slipped away.

Beep. Beep. Beep. Beep.

Most annoying alarm ever. It sounded only half awake, a slow quiet beeping, just loud enough to make it impossible to ignore. All I wanted was to go back to sleep.

I was exhausted. Even my skin was tired, like I was stretched too thin.

I swallowed and winced at how dry my throat was. *I don't remember partying last night. What the hell did I drink?* My stomach did a slow barrel roll. I made myself concentrate on not throwing up. Simone must have talked me into doing shots. She was the captain of bad decisions. I told myself I wasn't scared, but it was weird that I couldn't remember. What if someone had slipped me something? My mom had sent me an article on roofies, and I'd rolled my eyes, thinking she worried about stuff that was never going to happen, but now it didn't seem so stupid.

Don't freak out. You're fine. Just figure out where you are.

I forced my eyes open. They felt gritty, like I'd rolled them in sand before popping them into my skull. It was too bright in the room. It was hard to make anything out clearly. There was a window with the blinds up and bright sunshine blasting in. Like it was afternoon instead of early morning.

Beep. Beep. Beep. Beep.

I turned my head to see the alarm, but as soon as I moved, there was a shot of pain, sharp, like a dental drill, driving into my brain. I moaned and my vision blurred.

I blinked and realized it wasn't a clock. It was some kind of machine. Plastic tubing connected it to me, pooling over the rail of the bed, leading to a needle that was stuck to the back of my hand with clear medical tape that made my skin look wrinkled and old.

I was in a hospital.

My heart skipped a few beats. Something bad had happened. Hospital bad.

"Are you going to stay with us this time?"

I turned very slowly, trying to avoid a repeat of the pain in my head. A woman leaned over. She was wearing bright yellow scrubs. A stethoscope draped around her neck. It looked almost like a . . . The word skipped out of my head. Gone. I tried to focus. It was like a . . . serpent. That wasn't the right word, but I couldn't think of it. Thinking about it was making my headache worse. I opened my mouth to ask her what the right word was, but nothing came out. My heart raced and I clenched my hands into fists over and over.

"Just relax," she said. She pressed the back of her cool hand to my forehead. "You're okay."

I could tell nothing about this situation was okay, but I didn't want to be difficult. She seemed really nice. You could tell by her eyes. That's one of my abilities. To judge someone's character by their eyes. The window to the soul, as Big Bill Shakespeare would say. I wrote an essay on that quote last year and won a writing contest from the school district. It had only a fifty-buck award, along with a certificate "suitable for framing." I acted like it was no big deal, but I was actually really proud.

". . . you are?"

I blinked. I'd missed what she said. She was going to think I was rude. She stared at me, waiting for an answer. I swallowed again. I would have sold my soul for one of those cold, sweaty bottles of Dasani from the vending machine by the gym.

"Okay, let's try something else. Do you know your name?" she asked.

Was she kidding? Did I know my name. Didn't she know who she was talking to? National Merit Scholar. Perfect score

3

in Ms. Harmer's chemistry class, first time in school history. State debate champion *and* an almost certain shoo-in for our class valedictorian, as long as Eugene Choo doesn't pull ahead. Not that I'm rooting for the guy to fail, but if he got an occasional 89 instead of 100 on a paper, I wouldn't weep a thousand tears.

Know my own name? This one I got.

"Jill," I croaked. My voice sounded like I smoked a few packs a day and gargled with gravel.

She smiled widely and I felt the absurd rush of pride I always experienced when I got a question right. I really had to work on my need to be such a pleaser. You'd think I wouldn't always demand validation. Simone's always on me for that.

Simone was going to freak when she heard I was in the hospital. She'd bring me new PJs from Pink so I wouldn't have to wear this disgusting hospital gown that was probably last worn by some incontinent old man. Or someone who died in it.

Gross.

Simone would also bring a stack of her favorite trashy magazines. She'd make me move over so she could sit on the edge of the bed, and we'd take a photo she could put online. Things would be better when she got here. Simone had that effect on people. She'd make this an adventure. My throat seized, and I was suddenly sure I was about to start crying. I wanted her there so badly my chest ached.

"I'm going to get the doctor," the nurse said. "A lot of people are going to be glad to see you back with us."

I started to nod, but the pain came again when I moved my

head so I stopped. I closed my eyes when she left the room. It was good to be back.

I just wished I knew where I'd been.

***

"Knock-knock."

There was a sharp prick of pain in my foot. My eyes snapped open. A guy in a white lab coat stood at the end of my bed. Before I could say anything, he jabbed the arch of my foot with a large pin.

WTF?

"Do you feel that?" He reached for my foot and I pulled it away. *Back off, Dr. Mengele.*

He smiled and laughed. He was a happy sadist. "Looks like you felt it. Do you remember meeting me?" He moved closer so he was standing at the side of the bed. His hair was curly and stuck up like dandelion fluff. He looked a bit like a clown, or somebody's goofy Uncle Dwight, who could be counted on to make lame jokes and wear one of those holiday sweaters with a reindeer on the front to Christmas dinner in a nonironic kind of way.

Creep alert. I shook my head slowly. I'd never seen this guy before in my life. The sheets tangled underneath me as I scootched to the far side of the bed.

"We've met a couple of times. I'm Dr. Ruckman." He stared down at me.

"Hi," I said. My voice still didn't sound like my own. "Where's my m-m-mom?" The words snagged in my throat,

5

forcing me to push them out. I couldn't understand why she wasn't there. Normally my problem was getting rid of my mom. I'd never been in the hospital before. Well, once in second grade. I fell off the— *Dammit. Now I can't think of what they're called. The ladder thing, suspended above the playground. Lion bars? No. Elephant bars. That's not it either, but that's like it. You swing across them.* I'd had to get stitches, but I'd never *stayed* in the hospital before. Maybe she didn't even know I was here. She could be sitting up, waiting for me to come home, getting worried. Guilt bloomed in my chest. I didn't want her to worry.

"Your mom went down to get some coffee. She was here all night, hoping you'd wake back up," he said.

All night? I'd only closed my eyes for a second. The light in the room was different. I turned; it was dark outside the window, the sky just starting to lighten to a dark purple bruise blue at the horizon. Sunrise. Where the hell had the rest of yesterday gone? Panic rippled through my stomach, threatening to take over.

"You think you're up for trying something to drink?" the doctor asked. He reached for the plastic pitcher on the table.

My mouth watered. I'd never wanted anything that badly. There were crack addicts who were less needy. I nodded.

The doctor pressed a button and the bed cranked up a bit higher. I was barely sitting up and it still made me lightheaded. He guided the straw between my lips. I wanted to tell him I could do it, but I wasn't actually sure I could. I took a sip of the water and almost cried at how good it tasted. I tried to take another, but he pulled the glass away.

6

"Let's take it easy. See how that sits for a minute or two," Dr. Ruckman said. "Can you do something else for me? Can you raise your right hand?"

I reached up with my right hand and wiped my mouth. I cringed. My lips had moved beyond chapped. It was like I'd run them through a cheese grater. *Jesus, when is the last time I used some lip balm?*

"Where's the—" My brain scrambled to find the right word. "Health professional who was here. The, uh, caregiver." That wasn't right. "RN!" I spat out, but that wasn't what I meant to say either.

"The nurse?" Dr. Ruckman suggested.

"Nurse," I repeated. Nurse.

"Tish works evenings. She'll be back at three. She'll be glad to hear you're more alert." The doctor was scribbling something on a chart.

I licked my disgusting mouth. I bet when Tish came on she'd find me some ChapStick. She looked like the kind of person who would have an extra tube in her bag, along with gum, Kleenex, or an Advil if you had a headache. I felt like crying, but I wasn't sure if it was because everything hurt, because I wanted more water so badly, or because I was scared and didn't know why.

"Do you know what day it is?" Dr. Ruckman asked.

I opened my mouth to answer and then closed it. What day was it? They must have given me some kind of painkiller that was messing with my head. "Tuesday?" I could tell from his look I'd gotten it wrong. "Wednesday?" A buzzing sound filled my ears, like my head was full of angry bees. I wanted

7

to get out of the bed and run away, but I suspected my legs wouldn't carry me far.

"Take a deep breath. You're okay," Dr. Ruckman said. He patted my shoulder like I was a puppy who was at risk of peeing on the rug because someone had set off a bunch of firecrackers.

I shrugged off his hand. Clearly I wasn't okay. I didn't even know what day it was. The door squeaked as it opened, and when I looked over, I knew I was in really bad shape. My parents were there.

Both of them.

I hadn't seen them together in the same room in years. They hated each other. They didn't even try to pretend to get along "for the sake of the child." Now they were standing side by side.

My mom gasped when she saw me sitting up in bed.

"Mommy," I said, and started to cry. I couldn't remember the last time I'd called her Mommy, but it had slipped out. It felt so good to see her, like she could still make everything better by giving me a kiss. She pushed past Dr. Ruckman and pulled me to her chest. Her familiar smell, a Jo Malone perfume of lavender and amber, filled my head, and I buried my face in her sweater, crying harder.

"Shhh, baby. You're okay," she mumbled into my hair. I could feel the moist heat from her breath, and I wanted to crawl out of the bed and into her lap like I was six and afraid of something under the bed. She started to gently prise my fingers off her cardigan. "You need to calm down, Jill. It's not good for you to be worked up." She held my right hand sandwiched between hers.

"Hey, kiddo," Dad said. He squeezed my foot. I could see him swallowing over and over, like he was about to start crying himself. There was no sign of his new wife and the replacements. My stepbrothers. Twins, no less. My stepmom insisted on dressing them alike, as if they'd just popped off a Ralph Lauren billboard. When they were around, I acted like I couldn't tell them apart. Mostly because I knew it drove her nuts.

I took a hitching breath and tried to pull myself together. Mom passed me a tissue, and I wiped my nose. Dad pulled a chair closer to the bed for her, and she sat next to me, all without letting go of my hand. He stood right behind her.

"What happened?" I asked.

"You were in a car accident," Mom said. Her lower lip shook.

I waited for her words to wake something up in me, but there was still nothing, just a void.

"Do you remember the accident, Jill?" Dr. Ruckman had his pen poised over the chart.

They stared at me intently. "I think so," I lied. How could I not remember? An accident so serious I'd ended up in a hospital. No way was I admitting the huge gap in my memory. "I remember tires squealing and glass breaking," I added, figuring that was general enough to cover all the bases.

Mom squeezed my hand. Her expression was brittle. The accident must have been really bad. I hoped the car wasn't totaled. My dad wasn't exactly generous with child support, and she didn't make that much at her job. She loved that stupid Mercedes, even though it was ten years old.

"What's the last thing you remember well?" Dr. Ruckman clicked his ballpoint pen. On off, on off, on off. It was making my headache worse.

I fished about, trying to remember something that stood out clearly. Then it came to me in a flash. "I remember being over at Simone's. Tara was there too. We were celebrating the end of the play. We did *Grease*. Simone was Sandy." It was all really vivid. I felt the band of tension around my chest loosen as the memories flooded in. The feel of the worn corduroy sofa in her family rec room. Simone standing on the cracked faux leather ottoman singing "Look at Me, I'm Sandra Dee" at the top of her lungs while doing a bump-and-grind number. Tara and me laughing so hard I'd been sure I'd pee my pants. "We sold out all of the performances. Everyone came." I glanced over at my dad. "Almost everyone."

He looked away. The show had run for four nights, and he couldn't manage to make a single one. The replacements had a cold.

Simone, Tara, and I had lounged around, dissecting everyone else's performance. I left out the part about how we toasted our victory with some of Simone's dad's beer that we stole from the fridge in the garage. I was almost sure I had planned to spend the night. I remembered wearing sweats. My stomach clenched. I wouldn't have driven drunk. I was capable of doing stupid things, but I was pretty sure I wouldn't have done anything that dumb.

"How long have I been out?"

"Your accident was just over three days ago, Thursday. This is Sunday morning," Dr. Ruckman said. "What you're experiencing is retrograde amnesia. It means you forgot not only the accident, but some time before and after too. It's pretty common with head injuries. That's also why you're having some trouble with

10

word finding. It's called aphasia. I would expect both of these to get better with some time. Do you remember the ambulance?"

"No," I said.

"How about the flight?"

I blinked. I could understand the words he was saying, but it was almost as if he were speaking a different language. They must have flown me to a bigger hospital, maybe in Detroit. There was a sense that I did remember something about flying, but when I reached for it, it skittered out of reach. Like a spider bolting for a corner. Gone.

"It's okay if you don't recall. You've been in and out since you were brought here. Your Glasgow scale score—that's how we measure the impact of a head injury—was pretty low, but you've been doing well, coming up and out of it."

"What's a perfect score?" I asked.

"Fifteen," he said.

"What am I?"

"Today I'd say you were a fourteen or fifteen." Dr. Ruckman smiled.

I smiled back, relieved. Nailed it. I needed an account of what else was wrong with me. "My leg's messed up," I said, stating the obvious, since it was hanging from a sling suspended above the bed.

Dr. Ruckman lightly tapped my knee. "You've fractured your left femur. When you were admitted, we used external fixation to keep things stable, but now that you're doing better, we're going to schedule you for surgery, and they'll put in some pins."

"Oh." My stomach sank through the bed. This was bad. I was supposed to leave in a couple of weeks. Surgery and pins

11

sounded serious. I'd been planning the trip forever. "Can I still go to Italy?"

My parents exchanged a look. A thick fog of tension filled the room. *Oh, shit.* My heart felt like a hummingbird trapped in my chest. They had to let me go.

"I can see a doctor over there," I said. "And I'll do whatever exercises I need to. Or I could use a wheelchair," I suggested, knowing there was no way a school trip was going to let me go in a chair.

"Sweetheart," Mom said.

"I'll do anything," I pleaded. "Don't say no now. I might be better in a day or two, and we can decide then."

"The trip is over," my dad said.

"Keith," Mom said, her voice tense.

"But—that's not fair," I said. "You can't decide now. I haven't even had the surgery yet. I might be okay—"

"No," my dad cut me off. "I mean you already went. The car accident was in Italy."

It felt as if someone had ripped the air out of my lungs. I'd been in Italy, and I couldn't remember a thing. It was one thing to miss some memories, but I'd blacked out the entire trip. That couldn't be possible.

"Sweetheart?" Mom patted my hand. A wave of clammy sweat broke out across my forehead and down my back.

"This is a lot for Jill to take in. We might want to give her some time," Dr. Ruckman suggested.

"No, I need to know," I said. The beeping from my monitor picked up speed.

"Don't be upset," Mom said.

12

My mouth fell open. Was she kidding?

Dr. Ruckman picked up a syringe and injected something into the tubing that led to my arm.

"Hey," I protested.

"Why don't you rest for a bit, and we can talk more later." Dr. Ruckman patted my arm.

I wanted to yank away from his touch and tell him to keep his patronizing tone to himself, but my head began to fill with thick bubbles, and it seemed I could feel the cold medicine sliding into my veins, traveling through my body. I could almost trace its progress. I sank back down on the pillows.

Mom squeezed my hand. "You're going to be okay, Jill."

"That's right," Dad added. "You're going to be just fine."

They smiled, but I had the sense they were trying to convince themselves more than me.

Chapter Two

When I opened my eyes, I could tell the light in the room had changed again. More time lost. The second thing I noticed was that my headache was still there, a tight vice around my skull. On the upside, my thinking was a bit clearer. There was still a big hole where my memory was supposed to be, but it no longer felt like I was trying to think through a thick haze.

My mom was sitting next to my bed doing one of her needlepoint kits. She'd done them since I was little, initially kits from Hobby Lobby, but at some point she graduated to hand-painted canvases from England that she stitched up in silk floss and adorned with tiny glass beads. The odd thing was that as soon as she was done, she would either give it as a present or put it in the bag for the Salvation Army. She didn't actually like finished needlepoint. The whole process seemed pointless to me.

"Hey," I croaked.

Her head jerked up. She stood and came over to the bed. "How are you feeling?"

"Thirsty."

Mom grabbed the yellow plastic pitcher on the table and poured a glass for me, sliding the bendy straw between my lips. She brushed my hair out of my face.

"Where's Dad?"

"Lydia needed him at home."

For a second, I didn't know who she was talking about. Usually my mom called my dad's new wife "that woman," and I didn't call her anything if I could avoid it. Mom and I were pretty united in our shared loathing of my dad's new family.

Mom must have seen something on my face. "He had to go. He stayed here at the hospital for the last two nights."

I picked at the blanket. My nails were long. Longer than I'd had them in a long time. There was still some chipped polish on them. Pink. "I really went to Italy?"

"Mmm-hmm. You were there when the accident happened. In a small town in Tuscany."

"How did I get here?"

"Your dad had you flown back as soon as the hospital in Florence was able to get your condition stabilized."

"They couldn't treat me there?"

Mom rolled her eyes, and I could picture how it went down, my dad huffing and puffing about how he insisted on the top tier of care. That was classic for my dad. He had to have the best of everything. A Rolex, an Audi, a house in the West End. Almost more important than having the best was the idea that everyone *knew* my dad had the best.

"He chartered a private medical flight." Her hands twisted around the metal rail of my bed. "The plane belonged to some friend of his and then he paid one of those mobile health teams to escort you back."

My mind raced. Then a fact clunked into place. "But if I was in Italy and the last thing I remember is the play closing, that means I'm missing weeks. At least a month." The idea of all that time just being gone made me feel like I'd jumped from a plane without a parachute.

"The best I can guess is that you're missing about six weeks." Mom took a deep breath. "The doctor says it's not unexpected, given your injuries."

Six weeks. It seemed an impossibly long time. "What happens now?"

"Well, in addition to your head injury and your leg, you broke a couple of ribs and have some soft-tissue injuries to your neck and back. They've set up some physiotherapy for you to address those, but Dr. Ruckman says soft-tissue injuries usually take care of themselves."

"How long do I have to be here?" I wanted to go home.

"They're going to do the surgery on your leg and then they'll transfer you from here to the rehab hospital. You'll be there for a couple of weeks."

"I can't be gone that long. I've got—" Once again, the word was missing. It had been there and then, just before I spoke, it disappeared. "I've got, you know, with the teachers and everything."

Mom's forehead scrunched up. "School?"

I nodded. How the hell had I forgotten that word?

"Don't worry about your classes. Your teachers will understand. I'm sure we can work something out."

"Has Simone been by?" I wanted to talk to my best friend. I could ask her things that I couldn't ask my parents. I was close to my mom, but there were still things I didn't tell her. Simone would fill me in on the missing time. I would have texted her every day from Italy. She could make sense of things. She'd even make a joke out of it so it didn't feel so scary. One thing that was awesome about Simone, and occasionally annoying, is that she always seemed to know what to do. She didn't waste time second-guessing everything she did.

Mom turned her back and filled up my water. "The hospital is only letting family visit."

"Can't you talk to them? Tell them Simone is family."

"The hospital has rules."

"But I'm closer to Simone than I am to some cousin—"

My mom dropped the glass. The plastic bounced off the tile floor, spraying water everywhere. "Dammit!" Her eyes darted around the room, looking for something to wipe up the water, and then she yanked her scarf off the back of the chair. She dropped to her knees and started blotting it up. She looked almost ready to cry. She stood and grabbed the pitcher. "I'll ask the nurse to refill it for us."

"It's okay," I said. The way she was acting made me nervous.

She sat back in the chair with the pitcher in her lap. The makeup around her eyes was smudged, and her skin looked sallow in the dim light.

"Have you been here since I got here?" I asked. She nodded. "Maybe you should go home too. Take a break."

Mom sat up straighter, as if she'd been caught dozing on the job. "Don't be silly."

"Go home, Mom. Get some sleep. The nurse will likely give me something that puts me back out in a minute or two anyway. I won't even know if you're here or not."

She fidgeted with her hands. "I don't want you to be alone."

I raised an eyebrow. "I'm pretty sure I won't be alone. Hospitals frown on just locking up the patients at night and leaving them to fend for themselves."

"Are you sure?"

"Just come back in the morning."

She shifted in her seat again. I could tell she wanted to go. She was practically holding herself back from bolting out the door. "If it won't bother you, I wouldn't mind a long hot shower."

"Just go," I said.

Mom stood and shoved her needlepoint into her Coach tote. "If you want me to return, even if it's the middle of the night, ask one of the nurses to give me a buzz."

I rolled my eyes like she was being absurd, although now that she was actually pulling on her spring coat, I didn't want her to leave. "I think I can make it until morning." I hoped I sounded more confident than I felt.

She leaned over and kissed my forehead. "I'm glad you're awake."

"Me too." My throat felt tight, like I might start crying. "Hey, do you know where my—" Another hole opened up, swallowing a word. When I closed my eyes, I could picture it. The screen lighting up, the chirping sound it made when a text came in. I held my pinkie finger to my mouth and my thumb to my ear. "My call-y thing."

"Your phone?"

I nodded, filing the word away. *Phone.*

"Sorry, honey, it was broken in the accident."

"Can you pick up another one for me?"

18

Her mouth pinched. "A phone isn't our big priority right now," she said.

"I just want to text a couple of people," I said. I prayed I wasn't going to get a lecture on how, if I couldn't take care of my stuff, maybe I didn't deserve nice things, or how everyone was addicted to their technology.

Mom pulled the belt on her coat tight. "Focus on getting better first." She leaned down and pecked me on the forehead, then swept out of the door.

As soon as she was gone, I had to clench my mouth shut to keep from calling her back. It was totally silent except for the beep and clicking of the IV machine by my side. I knew it was absurd, but I was suddenly certain that there was nothing outside of the room. That if I'd been able to get up and make it to the door, there would have been just some kind of void where the hallway was supposed to be.

I swallowed. I felt panicky and knew I had to get control. Last summer, when my mom was out of town visiting her sister, Simone came over. We watched a bunch of horror movies and ended up freaking ourselves out. When a raccoon tripped the motion sensor light on the patio outside, the two of us had started screaming like a guy with a chainsaw had been beating on the door. We'd scared ourselves over nothing, and this was the same thing. I was perfectly safe.

I still left the light on.

Chapter Three

What the heck is in Jell-O, anyway? I poked it with my spoon, and it jiggled in its assigned slot on the tray like a blob of cherry-flavored cellulite. The hospital kitchen didn't do much to inspire patients to be a part of the clean-plate club. That was saying a lot, because I was starving. I hadn't been allowed any solid food the day before the surgery, and post-surgery I'd been allowed only clear liquids. Today was my first real food day, and so far I wasn't impressed. Tish, my favorite nurse, had promised to sneak me a mint chocolate-chip milk shake from 31 Flavors when her shift started. I'd have lost my mind if it weren't for her. She was the only one who acted remotely normal around me. Everyone else was either freakishly cult-like perky or treated me like I was part of the furniture.

My door swished open, and Lisa, the day nurse, came in. I was pretty sure she liked me better when I was unconscious. I'd tried everything to charm her, but she hardly even spoke to me. She bustled over and checked my IV and changed the bag with a smooth, practiced movement.

"Dumping rain, huh?" I said.

She glanced over at the window as if she were just noticing there was an outdoors. Who knew? Maybe she lived in the supply closet on the ward. She made a noncommittal noise, which I took to mean *Why, yes, it is raining. Now that we've discussed the weather, let's have a nice girly chat about movies or the world geopolitical situation.*

"Any news about the TV?" I asked. The hospital rooms didn't come with one; you had to order it for an extra fee. I was desperate for some bad TV to pass the time.

She stiffened. Great, now I'd offended her. She probably felt like she had enough to do saving lives without having to track down my entertainment.

"I know it's not your fault. I bet this stuff takes . . . a long time." I snorted like we were in this together, having to deal with slow hospital bureaucracy, as if I hadn't forgotten the word I wanted to use.

"You should ask your mother about the television," Lisa said. She left without another word. Yet another fail in my effort to win her over.

I flopped back on the pillows. I was bored. Beyond bored. My mom had brought a couple books and a stack of magazines, but reading, even for a few minutes, gave me a raging headache. If I kept trying to read despite the headache, I got nauseous too. I still didn't have a phone either. Mom said there would be time for me to talk to everyone when I was transferred to the rehab hospital. Until then, she would update everyone for me. She didn't want me to wear myself out. We'd fought about it yesterday, and she'd won with the parental favorite: *because I'm your mother, that's why.*

I was a bit ticked at my friends. There might be rules about who could visit, but it seemed like they should try. Sneak in if they had to. I would have done it for Simone. Considering she'd once broken into the school through a small window in the bathroom to get a pair of shoes she'd left in her locker and just *had* to wear on the weekend, it seemed like she could slink past a nurse and see me. She and Tara could come up with some kind of scheme and make it work.

My leg itched under the cast. I wanted to dig my nails in and scratch, but that wasn't allowed either. The list of things I couldn't do was long. I knew I should be glad that I was mostly okay, but I felt sorry for myself. My dad had come by only once since I'd woken up. He sent flowers. Some weird orange and purple things that looked like they belonged in a sci-fi movie instead of a vase. I was willing to bet they were expensive. Nothing common like roses from him. I was also willing to bet his admin assistant had ordered them for me.

"Hello!" Two of the care aides bustled in, breaking me out of my funk. They didn't speak the best English, but they were really nice. They seemed impossibly tiny, but their size was deceptive. They were freakishly strong. One of them filled my water pitcher while the other started bustling around the room.

"We change your linens," the aide announced. She pulled a wheelchair up next to my bed and dropped the armrest on one side. She patted for me to move to the edge. "Okay, put your good foot on the ground, then you lean on me. I swing you over. Leave your leg with cast on the bed." My stomach rolled with unease. If I jostled my leg, it was going to really hurt.

"I'm not sure—" I sat up, and in one swoop, she had my butt in the wheelchair. She put up the side with a click and then raised the leg rest so it was even with the seat and moved my

22

casted leg over. The IV bag clipped to the pole on the chair. If she wanted, she probably could have bench pressed me over her head without breaking a sweat.

She clapped her hands together, and her shiny black hair swayed back and forth like a curtain. "There. Done. You wait two minutes, we get you right back." The aide pulled the sheets from the bed with a swoosh, like a magician removing a tablecloth. They were like a tiny Asian version of Penn and Teller. They chattered back and forth to each other in a language I didn't understand.

That's when I got the idea. I rolled the chair slightly forward. I looked out of the open door. Just down the hall, there was a waiting room, no doubt full of uncomfortable furniture and outdated magazines. I could see a vending machine down there. Non-Jell-O snacks. I could hear a TV. Then I saw it hanging on the wall—a phone with a giant LOCAL CALLS ONLY sign above it. That was it. I was calling Simone. If she wouldn't reach out to me, I'd get in touch with her.

"I'm just going to get some air," I said. Neither of the aides looked up from what they were doing. I pushed the wheels forward. My heart was pounding like I was sneaking out for a wild weekend, instead of going down the corridor. I stopped just outside the room. Everyone moved around at what seemed like a thousand miles an hour.

Pull your shit together, I admonished myself. If I stayed there much longer gawping at everything, Lisa or another nurse was going to notice and roll me right back into my room. I pushed myself down the hall. My leg on the raised footrest stuck straight out from the chair, like the prow of a ship. I said a quick prayer that no one would run into it, because I was certain I would end up writhing on the floor in pain while Lisa and my mom stood over me telling me they'd told me so.

There was a metal cart parked halfway down the hall. I paused. I could see a distorted reflection of myself in it. At least I hoped it was distorted. I touched my swollen forehead, my finger tracing the stitches that made a black line down to my eyebrow. *Let's hope InStyle calls for the Frankenstein look for summer.* My lower lip was also puffy, and my hair hung lifeless and greasy. Maybe my mom was right about not having a lot of visitors for a while. I pressed a bit on my swollen bruised lip, wanting to feel something. I knew I'd been in an accident, but it almost felt like it had happened to someone else. It was like pain was the only thing grounding me in the here and now.

Time to get moving. I pushed the chair along. My arms were already tired, and my shoulders sore. There were deep scratches down both of my forearms as if I'd taken a swan dive through a window. Simone had better be grateful for this call. I was going to need a nap by the time I was done. Clearly, I hadn't been doing enough cardio before the accident. I was in crap shape.

The TV in the lounge was showing *Judge Judy*. She was eviscerating some white trash guy who'd stiffed his girlfriend on a giant cell phone bill. Then she turned on the girlfriend for being stupid enough to buy him the phone in the first place. Beauty fades; stupid is forever. Sing it, sister.

I stopped in front of the vending machine, my mouth watering. SunChips, Doritos, Reese's Peanut Butter Cups, packages of artificial-ingredient-stuffed oatmeal cookies, Mounds bars. *Oh, coconut-filled Mounds. Only you understand me.* My hand pressed against the glass. Then it hit me. I didn't have any money. Not a cent. My bag wasn't in my hospital room either. My mom must have it. *Shit.* I glanced around to see if there was anyone who might lend a girl a dollar for a snack treat. The waiting room was empty. I couldn't get a break.

It didn't matter. Simone would bring food when she came to visit. It was a mystery how she stayed so thin. My mom called her the locust. She could clean out a pantry in no time straight. I only had to look at a cupcake, and my butt would start getting larger. Simone said I was curvy, but everyone knows that's best-friend-speak for pushing chunky.

I picked up the phone and dialed. Thank God, Simone's number was still in my head and hadn't fallen into one of the black holes. I clutched the receiver and waited for her to pick up, but the number just rang and rang. Her voicemail didn't pick up. Shit. I couldn't text her without my phone. I hung up and decided to leave a message for her on her home landline.

I was shocked when her mom picked up. She was never home in the middle of the day. "Hey, Ms. M," I said.

"Jill? Why are you calling here?" Her voice was ragged.

There was a loud rustle and then Simone's dad got on the phone. "Jill, you shouldn't have called. We have nothing to say. I made that very clear to your mother." He slammed the phone down.

I pulled the receiver back and stared at it. I waited for something in my head to click into place and explain what had just happened, but there was the same empty black space. It was possible Simone had blamed me for something to get out of trouble. Her parents could be freakishly strict. Last year they'd found a bottle of vodka hidden in her closet, and she'd convinced them it was mine and she was only hiding it for me. And she wondered why they didn't like me much. She was the wild one, but as far as her parents knew, every bad decision we'd ever made had been my idea. The truth was Simone was the one who double dared me to do everything from stealing lip gloss from Walmart in seventh grade to drawing mustaches on Heidi Villers's student council election posters.

"It looks like you're up and about," a voice said behind me.

I spun the chair around, and a guy in a suit stood there. He had almost a military look: short hair and one of those superhero jawlines. *Figures a good-looking guy would approach me the one time I look like something the cat hacked up on the rug.*

"Jill Charron, isn't it?"

Was this someone else I'd met and forgotten? How those dimples could have disappeared from my mind was a mystery. I smiled at him and tucked a lank piece of hair behind my ear.

"How are you feeling?" He leaned against the wall.

"Getting . . ." The word vanished. "Getting improved." I winced. That was the wrong word. What were the odds he was into dirty hair, stitches, *and* someone who was inarticulate?

"Glad to hear it." He graciously ignored my screw-up. "Are you game to answering a few questions?"

"I'm not really supposed to be out of bed," I admitted.

"C'mon. I'll buy you a Mountain Dew," he offered, motioning to the vending machine.

"How about a Mounds bar?" I countered. My mouth started to water.

"Done." He reached into his pockets and pulled out some change.

Good-looking *and* willing to buy chocolate. Simone would die when she saw him. If he was the promised physiotherapist, she would make a crack about how he could lay hands on her anytime he wanted. He was totally her type, with the dark hair and smoldering eyes. Simone had a thing for good boys who acted like they were bad. Ryan, her last conquest, was always quoting the poet Kahlil Gibran because he thought it made him sound deep, but he spelled the guy's name wrong and he wore Lands' End polo shirts. The vending machine whirred and dropped the candy. He passed me the chocolate.

"I want to ask you about the accident," he said.

"Are you the physiotherapist?" I asked. I tore the wrapper open. The smell of the chocolate was enough to make me sigh with pleasure. I took a big bite.

"I'm your lawyer, Evan Stanley."

The bite of candy bar stuck in my throat and seemed to swell. I forced it down. "Lawyer?"

"I want to get your statement about what happened. While things are still fresh in your mind."

"I don't know," I hedged. The hair on the back of my neck lifted like antennae reading the signals in the air.

"I know it's hard, but this situation isn't going to go away on its own. We'll have to talk sometime."

I stared at him blankly. What situation was he talking about?

"What are you doing?" Tish said, grabbing the handles of my wheelchair and lurching me back so that I almost fell forward. She glared at Evan. "She's barely twenty-four hours post-surgery. She is not up to answering questions, and she certainly shouldn't be doing it without her mother present."

27

He raised both hands as if he were surrendering. "I just took a chance stopping by and ran into Ms. Charron. I thought I'd see if she was ready to talk. I'm not the enemy here. Her father hired me to watch out for her interests."

Tish pushed me back toward my room. She was mad at him, but I felt like I was the one who had screwed up. "That's fine, but I still don't think you should be talking to her without one of her parents with her."

"The young lady is eighteen," Mr. Stanley said.

I decided he was no longer good-looking. Now I wanted to get far away from him. I wished I'd never left my room. The chocolate bar in my hand was starting to melt. The smell of the waxy chocolate with sticky sweet coconut was making me nauseous. I didn't want it anymore, but there was no place to put it. Dropping it on the floor seemed rude, so I was stuck holding it as it began to ooze.

"We don't have a lot of time to waste. That girl's parents are demanding answers, and we're going to want to get in front of the story," Mr. Stanley said.

My hands grabbed the wheels of the chair and brought it to a hard stop. The muscles in my shoulder felt as though they were tearing free from the bone. I stared up at him. His face was expressionless. I told myself I was being ridiculous—the accident had happened in Italy.

"What girl?" I whispered.

He raised his eyebrows as if he couldn't figure out why I was playing dumb. "You know anyone else who died in the accident? Who else would it be? Simone McIvory."

Chapter Four

Everyone was treating me as if at any moment I might explode into a thousand shards. Evan Stanley kept apologizing over and over, but I ignored him. I couldn't believe I'd thought he was attractive, even for an instant. The sight of him made me want to hurl. After Tish banished him from my room, she tipped the blinds so it was half lit and tucked me back into bed. The hospital staff slipped in and out of my room to do what they had to, but mostly they left me alone. I knew everyone expected me to be crushed and crying my eyes out.

I wasn't.

When I was around eight, I saw the movie *Dumbo*. A theater in town was showing it on the big screen, and my parents had taken me as a treat. It made me sob uncontrollably. I cried until I threw up, thinking about how unfair it all was. How Dumbo was alone and how everyone made fun of him. How his mother was locked up for just trying to help. For weeks after seeing the movie, I'd start crying if I saw anything that reminded me of the story. I couldn't eat animal crackers without breaking down. My mom decided I was too sensitive for Disney. She was pretty sure seeing *Bambi* would kill me. It wasn't until my dad left that I learned that there are more painful things than cartoon animals having a bad day, but crying about those doesn't change reality either.

I lay in the hospital bed and stared up at the ceiling. In the far-right corner, there was a tiny water stain shaped like an elephant. I'd been focusing on it, willing myself to let go, but everything inside me was locked in place.

Simone's dead.

Dead.

Gone.

Passed away.

I could even say it in French, thanks to the two-year language requirement at our school. *Simone est morte.* It didn't matter how I said it. The words just rolled around in my head like pool balls bouncing off the sides of the table, nothing sinking.

Simone couldn't be dead. It wasn't possible, like saying the sun was blue or that fish lived in the desert. Simone couldn't be dead, because she was my best friend. We'd been friends since fourth grade. When we were ten, she fell off her bike and broke her arm, and I rode her all the way home on the back of my red Schwinn. She was the one who walked me through how to get a tampon in the first time and calmed me down when I was pretty sure I'd somehow managed to lose it up inside myself. She was who I told when I had my first kiss, and I was the only one who knew her dad had affairs and her mom put up with them. When my parents said they were getting divorced, Simone came over that night and held me while I cried. We were closer than sisters. We hung out with other people, but they were just extras. We were the core.

I couldn't imagine my life without Simone in it. Of the two of us, Simone was the fun one. She made everything a party. Simone was Batman, I was Robin. Simone was Shrek, I was Donkey. Simone was Sherlock, I was Watson. The truth is no one wants Robin without Batman.

I could hardly remember a time before we were best friends. The idea that she was gone was incomprehensible and terrifying. I couldn't fathom why she had even been in Italy. The trip had been expensive, and her parents didn't have the money to send her. What had she been doing there?

The door squeaked open. "Jill?" My mom's voice was tentative, as if she was afraid of me. Tish must have called. My dad was behind her. This was enough of a crisis that it merited even his attention.

"Why didn't you tell me?" I kept staring at the ceiling. They'd let me believe she was alive. They'd lied.

"We were going to," Mom said.

"When?"

She touched my arm, and I yanked it away, sending a fresh spasm of pain into my shoulder. Mom sighed. "We didn't want to overwhelm you with too much, too fast."

"I was driving, wasn't I?" I asked.

"Yes," my dad said.

My stomach dropped. I'd known in my heart I must have been the driver, but I'd still wanted them to tell me something different. That explained why there was a lawyer involved. Now it wasn't just that Simone was gone; it was that somehow this was my fault. Maybe her family was going to sue me.

"What happened?" I picked at the blanket. I'd worked free

31

a loose thread and wound it tightly around my finger, feeling the tip go cold and bloodless.

"Have you remembered any more about the accident?" Mom asked.

"If I remembered I wouldn't have to—" The word disappeared. I grunted in frustration and hit the rail of the bed with my fist. I wanted to force the word out, but it wouldn't come. I raised my arm again.

"Easy." She put her hand on the rail, and before I could stop myself, my fist slammed down onto hers. She sucked in a gasp, yanking her hand back.

"I'm sorry," I said. Guilt pressed down on my chest.

Mom had her hand cradled in her lap. "It's fine."

"This is why you didn't want me to have a TV," I said, putting the pieces together.

"There's been a bit about the accident on the news." She twisted her hands together in her lap.

"Why was I driving in Italy?"

"We don't know," Dad said. "The program doesn't let kids drive over there. We're not even sure how you got the car. Supposedly it was a rental car some idiot left the keys in. That was something we hoped you might remember, how it came to happen. You lost control. It went over a city wall."

His words didn't bring any images into my head. There was still a blank space where the past weeks had been. How could I forget something like that? The clock ticked on the wall. Each second moving from the present to the past. Moving Simone farther away.

I finally asked, "Was I drunk?"

"No, of course not." My mom sounded horrified, which made me feel better. "They tested you when you were admitted to the hospital in Italy. They don't know why the accident happened." Her voice was strained, and I realized she was trying not to cry.

I wanted to tell her everything was going to be okay, but both of us knew that was a lie. This was something that couldn't be fixed. Sure, my leg would get better, and I'd get out of the hospital, the cuts would heal—but Simone would still be dead. I felt dizzy. This had never happened to me before. Something bad that couldn't be undone. The permanence of it made me angry.

"I want to go to Simone's funeral," I said. Suddenly the decision seemed crystal clear. I pulled myself up in bed. It felt good to have a purpose. "I need to go." I was her friend; everyone would expect me to be there. I owed her that. I needed to say goodbye.

"Sweetie, the funeral is planned for tomorrow. You're not ready—"

I cut her off. "I'm her best friend. I have to go." I didn't care how bad I felt. In fact, I wanted to feel bad. I needed to sit at the funeral with every bone in my body throbbing in pain. Mentally I started going through my closet to figure out what I could wear that would go over the cast on my leg. I wondered if Simone's parents would let me say anything, and if they did, what could I say that would be worthy of Simone? She deserved a speech that was more than a regurgitated song lyric or bad poem. "You have to talk to Dr. Ruckman," I said. "Tell him I need to go."

"It's not that," she said. She took a deep breath, as if she were about to dive into a deep icy pool.

"Simone's family doesn't want us there," Dad said.

His words were like a slap in the face. "Oh." It wasn't that they didn't want us there; they didn't want *me* there.

"I called her parents. They hung up on me," I said. My heart folded in on itself, getting smaller and harder.

My parents exchanged a look. "They're struggling," Mom said. "They'll come around. You're family to them the same way Simone was a daughter to us." Her voice caught and she started to cry.

I watched the tears fall from her eyes and waited for my own eyes to water, but I still couldn't believe it. Or I didn't want to believe it. There was no one in the world I was closer to than Simone. In eighth grade, Richard Slater started a rumor that Simone and I were lesbians. I'd gotten upset, but it rolled off Simone's back. She said he was jealous that no one loved him even a fraction of the amount she cared for me. That her love for me went beyond sex, that our friendship was stronger than any guy. Simone said we were a part of each other. Like Siamese twins who share a heart and can't ever be separated or one would die.

I looked back up at the ceiling and searched out the small elephant. I pictured his trunk curled around a feather. He believed that the feather was magic and made it possible for him to fly.

I don't believe in magic.

Simone's gone.

I started to cry.

My dad stood there looking uncomfortable with all the tears. He grabbed a box of tissues from the windowsill and passed them over to my mom and me. They were a hospital industrial brand and felt rough and harsh on my skin.

"It's a tragedy, but that's all it is. I'm not going to let her family turn this into some kind of drama," he said.

"Keith," my mom said.

My dad had never liked Simone or her family. The truth is he's a snob. He didn't like that her mom was a cashier at the grocery store and her dad sold cars. Like it reflected badly on him that I didn't have a Hilton or a Rockefeller as a best friend. My dad didn't see the point in a relationship unless he could get something from it. My mom had learned that lesson the hard way.

"All I'm saying is that Evan doesn't think we should have anything to do with their family until this is all resolved," Dad said.

I felt a flare of annoyance. "Do we really need a lawyer?"

My parents traded glances again, and the uneasy feeling in my belly grew heavier. I was having a stress baby.

My mom patted my shoulder.

Dad tucked his shirt into his pants with sharp jabs. "We're making sure that we look out for you. You need to be able to focus on getting better, not jetting back off to Italy so that a bunch of trumped-up know-it-alls can feel important."

My headache increased. "Italy?"

"The police there have to figure out what happened in the accident. They want to ask you some questions."

I sat up straighter. "I should go." This was something I could do. "If I can help in any way, then I should do that."

"Sweetheart, I don't think it's a good idea. You've just had surgery. You still have a lot of recovery ahead of you."

"I wasn't planning to fly out tomorrow," I said. "But we can talk to Dr. Ruckman, maybe let the Italian police know I could come in a week or two." An idea popped into my head. "Or we could do an interview on—" The word zapped out of my head. "The computer thing, the online talking."

Mom's forehead was scrunched up as she tried to figure out what I meant. I wanted to push the word out, but it was stuck somewhere in my brain. I could picture the swooshing S logo on my laptop and the burbling sound it made when it fired up, but the name was gone.

"This is ridiculous. You're not talking to the police. This is why we have a lawyer. If we have any information, then Evan will pass it on to them," my dad said.

"But if there is anything I can do to help them figure out what happened with Simone, I need to do that."

"What are you going to tell them? You don't remember the accident. Hell, you don't even remember being in Italy," Dad snapped.

I pulled back, his words like punches on my bruised ribs.

Mom fluttered closer. "I think what your dad is trying to say"—she shot him an angry glance across my bed—"is that until you're feeling better, you shouldn't worry about any of this."

Dad closed his eyes like he wanted to pretend neither my mom nor I was in front of him. "I need you to promise that you won't call Simone's family again," he said finally.

"I get that they're upset with me, but—"

"No buts," Dad said. "You need to trust your mom and me on this one and know that we're doing the best for you. Okay, kiddo?" He looked down at his Rolex. "I've got to get going. Are we covered here?" He didn't wait for an answer, but instead kissed my forehead. The smell of his Tom Ford cologne filled my head, like leather and cigars. "I'll be back tomorrow for your move over to the rehab center." He nodded at my mom and left.

Mom sighed and slumped into the seat next to my bed.

"Dad's making it worse by getting a lawyer," I said. My headache ratcheted up a notch as I tried to force myself to remember the accident. I was there. I had to know. I had been with Simone when she died. I owed it to her to at least remember her last moments.

Mom's mouth was pressed into a tight line, and she looked on the verge of crying again. She patted my hand absently. "We're going to sort it out together. Don't you worry."

But I was worried. Simone was dead, and I had no idea how it happened.

Chapter Five

Taken from the Junior Yearbook of Simone McIvory

To my best friend Si—
If I could choose you as a sister I would. Here's to an awesome
summer and a kick ass senior year!
XOXOXO Jill

Taken from the Junior Yearbook of Jill Charron

Jilly my sister from another mister! We are going to RULE this
school next year. Always remember Peach Schnapps at Formal,
dancing at Turner Field, ragers at the spot, and you carrying me
home (ha!). BESTIES BEFORE TESTIES!
Love you—Simone

***

Excerpt from Police Interview with Natalie McIvory

Date: 30 April
Time: 13:00

Present: Natalie McIvory, Detective Linda Winston, Detective Jonathon Reid
Transcript to be provided to Italian police

Continued from page 2

Natalie McIvory: I don't think Jill wanted Simone to go to Italy. It bothered Simone that Jill didn't seem excited she was going. Simone had expected Jill to be over the moon that they would be able to travel together, and it hurt her feelings when Jill didn't act happy.

Detective Reid: Did Simone say why she didn't think Jill wanted her to go?

Natalie McIvory: No. She went over to Jill's house to tell her just a few weeks before the trip. She'd finally talked her grandparents into letting her use the money they'd saved for her college for this program. She wasn't planning to go to college in the fall, not that she couldn't have gone, of course, but she wanted to work instead. No one in our family is afraid of a little hard work. She knew her grandparents would like the idea that the money was being used for an educational opportunity, and they couldn't say no to her when she put on the charm. Almost everyone found it impossible not to give in to Simone when she really wanted something.

Simone shouldn't have been able to go on the trip. The program had all these requirements, and you had to apply in the fall. One of those jump-through-a-million-hoop things.

Simone just kept calling them. Over and over. She was like that when she got an idea in her head. Stubborn as a donkey, just like her dad. The program had a last-minute cancellation, and they'd already put down deposits on everything, so they accepted her. To be honest, I think they were just bowled over by her. Simone was thrilled. It wasn't so much that she cared about going to Italy. I remember she used to call everything over there "Europe-land." (*Chuckles*) She was a beach vacation kind of girl, not so much into museums and old buildings. Simone wanted to go on this trip because Jill was going. She wanted them to have the experience together. When she got in, I was happy for her. (*Pause*) If I had told her she couldn't go, she'd still be alive. (*Cries. Tape is turned off.*)

TAPE RESUMES 13:08

Natalie McIvory: Sorry. I'm okay now. What I was trying to say is that Simone wanted to go because of Jill, but Simone said that when she told Jill she was going, Jill didn't seem that excited. If you ask me, it was because she was jealous. Jill was always jealous of Simone. You could tell, even when they were young. Jill hated that Simone was prettier, a cheerleader, popular. Our family doesn't have a bunch of money like hers, but there are some things money can't buy, and I think it ate Jill up.

Ask anyone—everyone loved Simone. Back when the girls were fourteen, we took Jill with us on vacation to Kentucky to see some family on my side. The girls were hanging out at the hotel pool, and you could tell the boys who worked at the restaurant were flirting with Simone. I saw Jill push Simone

40

into the pool. She *pushed* her. She acted like it was a joke, but I could tell there was anger there. I never thought things would end up like this.

Detective Reid: Would you say that Simone was the leader in their friendship?

Natalie McIvory: Simone was always a leader. I remember when I went back to work when she was still a toddler, the daycare told me that she used to organize the other kids. She was the one who picked the activities and who could use what crayon. Not that she was bossy; Simone just always knew what she wanted. She was incredibly confident for someone her age. She was cheer captain at school. They made her captain in her junior year. (*Pause*) You might not know it, but that's a pretty big deal.

Jill comes from a broken family. Her dad left a few years ago. Took off and started another family. Now that was a big hot mess. I'd overhear Jill and Simone talking about it. You could tell it just gutted the girl. Then she had two parents without consistent rules and, if you ask me, way too much freedom. I'm not a counselor or anything, but I watch Dr. Phil every day, and you know, girls who lose their dads' attention early on will go out of their way to get approval from others—especially other guys. Running after boys to feel loved.

Detective Winston: Was Jill sexually active?

Natalie McIvory: Well, I couldn't really say. It wasn't something the girls talked about with me, but I wouldn't be surprised. Jill was always looking for attention. We raised Simone to know her worth. She didn't need to chase after boys. There were plenty who were happy to do the pursuing, but she stayed true to the values we raised her with. It might sound old-fashioned, but her father and I believe that sex before marriage is a sin.

Transcript to continue on next page

Transcript to continue on next page

***

Excerpt from Police Interview with Tara Ingells

Date: 2 May
Time: 08:05
Present: Tara Ingells, Jennifer Ingells (Tara's mother), Detective Linda Winston, Detective Jonathon Reid
Transcript to be provided to Italian police

Tara Ingells: Simone, old-fashioned? Who told you that? The girl was a total slut! (*Laughs, then stops suddenly*) I don't mean that in a bad way—that came out wrong. Simone just loved to party. You aren't going to tell her folks I said that, are you? They'd be really PO'd.

Detective Reid: (*Tape is unintelligible*)

Tara Ingells: No, not Jill. It was sorta like she wasn't that interested in guys. She was kinda a bookworm. I think if she hadn't been Simone's friend, then she would have been, like, nerdy. She was really into school. Jill could be shy sometimes, but she was super funny.

Detective Reid: How did you come to know Jill and Simone?

Tara Ingells: Simone and I were in cheer together. I was friends with her first and then the more time I spent with her, the more I got to know Jill. We hung out all together, like the Three Musketeers. Simone was in charge of good times, Jill was the one you went to when you needed to talk something out, and I was . . . I don't know, I guess you'd have to ask them why they liked me. We had a good time together. We were all in drama. We were just in the school play together a few months ago. (*Sniffles.*)

Detective Winston: Would you say you were best friends?

Tara Ingells: Totally. I probably spent more time with Simone because of cheer and stuff, but Jill's awesome. If it weren't for her, I totally would have failed chem. Seriously, Gagnon, who teaches that class, like, lives for failing people. Simone and Jill were extra close—the two of them had been friends since something like second grade, like, forever. I was their friend, but they were, like, a whole different level of friends. I can't believe Jill would ever do anything to Simone. They were like sisters. Seriously, the whole thing has to be a huge mistake.

Detective Reid: Did Jill ever tell you how she felt about Simone going with her to Italy?

43

Tara Ingells: Jill was psyched. Jill loved all that stuff—art, history, that kinda thing. I remember her talking at lunch one day about how she and Simone would be walking in the steps of Galileo and Roman emperors. She was always saying that kind of smart sh—stuff. Simone and I were totally rolling our eyes because, um, hello, Italy? Shopping, hot guys. You have to know Jill. That's just her. Jill was beyond excited to go; she planned it for over a year. The trip was all they talked about for the weeks before they went. What they were going to bring, clothes, stuff like that. Jill was really worried about what to pack. They were only allowed to bring one small suitcase. It was weird, because normally Simone is the one who is totally fashion obsessed, but this time it was Jill. I think Jill wanted to have a whole new wardrobe for the trip, so she could sort of reinvent herself. (*Pauses*)

Detective Winston: Is there something else you want to add? Maybe a comment one of them made to you?

Tara Ingells: Um . . . well, it's probably nothing. Jill was worried that Simone used the money her grandparents gave her for college to pay for the trip. Simone was always saying that she was a terrible student, but she wasn't, really. She just preferred to spend her time on doing stuff that was fun, you know. Simone was always joking about how she was going to end up going to hairdresser school or something, but as it got closer to graduation, you could tell it bugged her. Of course Jill wanted Simone to go—but she thought Simone should use the cash to take some classes at the community college.

(Sniffles) Jill's going to Yale, you know. She got early acceptance and everything. It's a pretty big deal. She wanted Simone to be smart. Think all long term and stuff. Simone's family isn't exactly rolling in cash. She was looking out for Simone. It was like her brain was already a grownup.

It's really sad, because they were both so excited to go. They were both so sweet. Honestly, they were the nicest people in our class. They deserved to have this epic time.

***

The Record Eagle, "School Trip Ends in Tragedy", dated 3 May

Two local girls, Jill Charron and Simone McIvory, were involved in an automobile accident in Montepulciano, Italy. The girls were on a school trip through the Adventures Abroad Program, designed to expose promising high school students to new cultures. Ms. McIvory was declared dead at the scene. Ms. Charron sustained significant injuries and was flown from Italy to a local hospital for further care. Italian police have reported the cause of the accident is unknown.

Comments:

Lissamum: Prayers for the family.

Gymratt: Why would anyone let their kids go all the way to Europe without them? Shame on the family.

CooperE: How can you blame the family? The accident could have happened anywhere—it's a tragedy.

Billy42: I went to school with them and they were a bunch of stuck-up bitches. Save your tears for someone who matters.

***

From the Eulogy for Simone McIvory, 5 May

Tara Ingells, Speaker

I know everyone here today is really sad, but I'm choosing to focus on all the people in heaven who must be really happy. It was impossible not to be happy when Simone was around. We could just be sitting at the beach, and Simone would find a way to make it fun. She even made things like remedial math halfway decent. (*Laughter*)

It's no wonder people wanted to be around Simone. She was nice to everyone. She had a way of making you feel special. She wouldn't want us to be sad now.

I remember when I first met Simone in cheer. We were learning a new routine, and I was, like, nervous to go out on the field and do it in front of the whole school. Simone told me to put a smile on my face and just do it. She didn't waste time second-guessing things or being afraid. She just did it. And that's what she would want us to do too. Live fearless.

Chapter Six

I said a silent prayer I was seeing double.

"Why is there an extra bed?" I asked.

"That's your roommate's side. Her name is Anna."

Inside my head, I said, *Oh, hell no*, but even with a head injury, I knew that wasn't the right way to respond. "Is there a way for me to have my own room?" I asked instead. I don't have any siblings. I don't share well. "Please," I added, using my adult suck-up voice. The nurse was already unpacking my things and putting them in a small closet next to the bed by the door. The room looked like it belonged in a hospital. Worn brown linoleum that was faded from years of being washed with harsh cleaners, hospital bed complete with rail and plastic mattress coating, and industrial-grade chairs parked at the side for a visitor. The other bed was surrounded by a hoarder's amount of crap—empty water bottles, magazines, a couple paperbacks, a sweatshirt, and a tangled set of earphones. For all I knew, there was a flattened mummified cat buried at the bottom.

I didn't know how I would cope with someone in the room. I was having trouble sleeping. This was an understatement. I would be wide awake in the middle of the night and then, in the afternoon, suddenly be taken out by a wave of exhaustion. I'd fallen asleep in the middle of dinner last night. Drooled all over the front of my PJs. This was one of many reasons I wasn't interested in sharing with a roomie. That and the fact I was having nightmares. Nothing I could remember in the morning, but I'd wake with the sense that a memory of Italy had just dodged out of sight. That they were sneaking up on me.

"Most people love having a roommate. We'll get you settled today, and you'll start your program tomorrow." The nurse picked up a few things around the other bed, tucking them away, and tossed out an empty chip bag.

My dad's lips pursed together. "How much would it cost to get a private room for my daughter?" he asked.

I winced at his tone.

"A lot of patients find it nice to have someone who is going through the same experience," the nurse said. She yanked the curtain back so the view of the treetops could be seen from the window.

There was a flush, and the bathroom door opened. A girl wheeled out. Her hair was dyed a flat black, but there was a wide strip of dark brown where it was growing out. That's what I noticed first. The second thing was that she wasn't wearing any pants, just a pair of baggy granny panties. She had a pierced nose and huge silver hoop earrings. Beyond huge—you could have lobbed a baseball through her earring like at one of those carnival games. I wasn't sure what about her I found most disturbing.

"My catheter was leaking," she announced to our group as if it was no big deal. "I threw my stuff in the hamper." She didn't seem remotely embarrassed to be half naked in front of a bunch of strangers. She looked at me. "I'm Anna Lopez."

I nodded and did my best not to stare as she wheeled herself over to the bed by the window and then grabbed the triangle that hung from the ceiling and swung up and onto the mattress. She was like a circus performer. A pantsless performer who used entirely too much eyeliner.

"Can you get yourself dressed?" the nurse asked. Anna was already doing a weird shimmy into a pair of flannel pajama bottoms that were covered with penguins wearing sunglasses. I would not have guessed she was the whimsical jammie type. Her legs were thin, wasted. She picked them up and moved them around as if they were things instead of an extension of her body. The sight of her legs made me vaguely nauseous, and I was glad when they were covered again. I rubbed my cast like it was a genie lamp and said a silent prayer of thanks I hadn't broken my back.

I used to play that game with Simone. Which would you choose—to be blind or to be deaf? To be paralyzed or to lose an arm? To be burned or to have your leg caught in a bear trap? Now that it was real life, the game didn't seem that much fun.

My dad was staring at Anna as if he'd never seen anything like her. Anyone who looked like they didn't spring from the pages of *Forbes* magazine gave him the hives.

"I'm Helen," my mom said. "And this is Jill, your new roommate, and of course Keith, her dad." My mom smiled. She was the master of social situations. If we were ever in a bank robbery, my mom would be the one passing out snacks from her handbag to the other hostages while making small talk.

"I'm going to have to ask you to check into getting a private room for Jill." Dad ignored Anna and focused on the nurse. "As I'm sure you can imagine, this is a special situation. I think Jill would be more comfortable on her own."

I wished I could melt into the floor.

"This ward is full of special situations," the nurse said. "Besides, there aren't any other options. We don't have any single rooms. They're all doubles."

"Well then, I'll pay the difference so my daughter can have a double room to herself," Dad said.

"This might be fine," my mom said. "Jill, what do you think?"

Before I could even open my mouth, my dad cut in. "Don't be ridiculous. You know as well as I do how interested everyone is in her story. Is that really a temptation you want to put in front of someone like—" He motioned to Anna.

"Keith," my mom said through clenched teeth. Apparently my dad had confused paraplegia with being deaf.

Anna waved off my mom's concern for her feelings. She seemed thrilled to have a front-row seat for this drama.

"I'll be fine," I said, my face flushed.

My dad stared upward and sighed. "For once would it kill you to take my side? I am trying to give you what you wanted."

"I don't want to cause a problem," I said.

The nurse shut the closet door. "Perfect. I'll let you two girls get to know each other. Anna, I'll leave it to you to show Jill down to the cafeteria for dinner." The nurse patted me on the back and turned to my parents. "There is an orientation meeting for family downstairs. If you have more questions about Jill's treatment, or the housing situation, you're welcome to talk it over with her team leader. That's Dr. Weeks."

"Don't bother to unpack," my dad said. He yanked out his iPhone and started firing off texts to various people. He bustled out without waiting for my mom, who trailed after him.

Anna watched the door swing shut.

"So, what's wrong?" Anna asked, pointing at my leg.

"Fracture—they put in pins," I offered. "I guess you have a spinal—a back—a spine thing," I finally pushed out.

Anna smiled. "Is your head fucked up too, or is talking just not your strongest skill?"

"My doctor says I have word-finding issues," I said, slightly offended. "It's called aphasia. It's already gotten better, and I lose fewer words every day. I have a brain injury."

"Sure it's a brain injury," she said.

"It is," I insisted. "Before this I got A's in English. My verbal test on the SAT was in the high 700s."

Anna threw her hand over her chest as if she were overcome. "Oooh, impressive." She waved off whatever I was about to say. "Calm down, Einstein. I'm sure you were plenty smart. I was just yanking your chain."

I wanted to tell her I was still smart, but I wasn't completely sure. "Do you go to Lincoln?" I asked.

She cocked her head to the side. "Why would you guess that?

I flushed again. Lincoln was the east side of town. There's no nice way to tell someone that they look like the kind of person who goes to school someplace with metal detectors. "I just haven't seen you around my school," I said.

Anna paused long enough for us both to realize she knew I was lying and she was going to ignore it for now.

"I was in a car accident," I said to fill the space. "What are you in for? Same thing?" I felt like I was in one of those prison documentaries.

"Me? No. My boyfriend pushed me down a flight of stairs. Bastard." She inspected the split ends on a chunk of her hair. She noticed I was staring at her. "I mean, he's not my boyfriend anymore."

I blinked. "Well, that's good."

"You got a boyfriend?"

"No." I had the sense I was boring her. Maybe I wouldn't be up to her roommate standards. "Actually, I guess I don't know if I'm dating anyone. I'm missing the last six weeks."

She turned to face me. "Really? You don't remember stuff before the accident. Not at all?"

"Nope. I remember things from way before. For me, it was the end of March last week, and now it's May. Everything in between is just gone."

"That's fucked up."

Anna seemed to have summarized my situation better than anyone else. "Yep." I picked at my pajama bottoms. My mom had gotten some at Nordstrom and then slit the one leg up the side so my cast would fit. I kept pulling loose threads off. If I kept this up, I'd end up pantsless too. "My best friend died in the accident," I added.

I kept finding times to bring up Simone's death in conversation. Maybe if I said it often enough, it would finally sink in.

"Yeah," Anna said. "Sorry."

"It's worse, because there was, like, another six weeks that I had with her, and I don't remember it at all." I swallowed hard. "I'm missing that time."

"Maybe it will come back to you," Anna offered.

"Maybe," I said.

Anna sighed. "I wish I could forget some stuff."

"The fight?"

"Nah. What I wish I could forget is how much I still like him." She looked over at me. "I know. I know. I don't even have the excuse of hitting my head."

"There's still time," I offered.

She laughed. "How long are you in for?"

I shrugged. "They told me at least two—" The word was gone. "Two, not months, not days either," I said, hoping she could figure out what unit of time I meant. "Then I'll do outpatient stuff for a while."

"Do you know who your physical therapist is?"

I shook my head.

"You should hope it isn't Sam. Everyone calls him the Sergeant, a real physical terrorist as they say." Anna looked up at the clock. She reached up and swung herself back down into her chair. "C'mon, we've got an hour before dinner. I'll show you around. Tell you all the stuff the staff never shares with you. By the way, no matter how they try to sell it, never choose the veggie casserole for dinner. That shit is nasty. And what they call tacos is an abomination of my cultural history."

I felt like crying again, because she was being nice. I desperately wanted her to like me. I couldn't help but wonder what Simone would have thought of Anna. There have always been other people who hung around the two of us, but the truth was, no matter how many other friends we had, each of us always knew that the other came first. Everyone else was there to fill out the group. They weren't required. Just supporting actors whose names you couldn't always remember.

"You okay?" Anna asked.

I shrugged. "I guess. I'm just a little emotional." I willed my eyes to stop tearing up. Anna didn't look like the kind of person who would have a friend who cried at the drop of a hat. She looked like a person who could be stabbed and then would wrap the wound with duct tape and go out dancing, all on the same night.

"Look at the bright side," she told me. "If life didn't toughen you up, this place will." She sped down the hallway, pointing out a small kitchenette as she rolled by. I pushed the wheels of my own chair and tried to keep up. For someone who was so skinny, she was hiding muscle in there somewhere.

"I'm sorry my dad was such a dick," I said to her back. "He's not coping well with all of this. Emotions aren't exactly his thing."

Anna shrugged. She gestured to a sign by the elevator. "We'll head downstairs later, but if you ever get lost, just find one of these. They've got the whole place color-coded. Our ward is yellow. We've got a TV lounge down here, but we share it with another ward. There's some guy who watches baseball non-freaking-stop. The Chicago Cubs too, so what's the point? They never win. No matter what he says, he doesn't own the TV. You can ask him to change it after an hour." The muscles in my arms burned as I pushed the wheels. She looked over her shoulder. "Don't worry about your dad. He's just looking out for you."

"I'm not sure what he thinks is going to happen. It's a rehab hospital. How much trouble can I get in?"

"I'm betting he worries that I'm going to sell you out to the media." Anna stuck a dramatic pose over her shoulder. "Sexy Latina, fellow rehab patient of Jill Charron, tells all. Tune in at ten to hear the full story."

"I don't think that's a story that's going to make you much—" The word dropped into one of my brain's black holes. I could picture it. Stacks of bills and coins. "Much cash," I settled for.

Anna stopped her chair and spun it around so we were facing. "You joking?"

I couldn't stop fast enough, so my leg, which was extended out in front of my chair, ran into hers. It wasn't hard, but it was enough to send a lightning flash of pain from my foot to my hip.

"Are you playing dumb?" Anna asked.

I stared at her. This must be some kind of rehab initiation prank, messing with the brain-injured kid. "I don't know what you're talking about."

Anna's eyebrows shot up to her hairline. "Whoa. You're serious. You have no idea why your dad thinks I might sell you out?"

I wanted to spin my chair around and leave. Find my parents and tell my dad he was right—I didn't want to stay with Anna, after all. Whatever she was about to tell me wasn't going to be good.

"Jesus, they left you in the dark. Come with me. There's a computer in here we can use." Anna wheeled into the lounge. The room wasn't big. There was a round table in the corner next to a bookcase filled with abandoned, well-thumbed paperbacks and board games likely missing pieces. In the front of the room there was a group of chairs covered in some kind of stain-resistant industrial fabric. There was one person sitting and watching some reality TV show with heavily Botoxed women screaming at one another. Anna pulled up to a table on the far wall, where three computer stations were set up.

The computers looked like they had been donated around the time when Madonna wasn't a living mummy and people wore neon not ironically. Anna flicked a computer on, and it heated up, giving off a vaguely toxic burning-plastic smell. There was a sign taped to the wall in a page protector stating that patients had to sign up for a time to use them and were limited to thirty minutes unless there was no one waiting.

"What are you looking for?" I asked.

"No way you're going to believe me. You better see for yourself." She looked over her shoulder at me. "You're famous."

As she clicked through, a photo of a tiny red car crunched almost beyond belief flashed on the screen. My stomach lurched. Was that the car? Why was a car crash in Italy a big news story? I figured when I flew home, our local TV station would do something, but I never imagined it would be all over the Internet.

"You sure you want to know all of this?" Anna asked.

I nodded, and Anna turned the giant box monitor to face me. The headline ripped the air out of my lungs.

CHEERLEADER ABROAD KILLED IN JEALOUS RAGE?

I wheeled my chair closer to the table. I skimmed the article, each word detonating like a bomb, shattering my reality. I kept trying to rearrange the sentences to say something else, but it was clear.

People thought I'd killed Simone on purpose.

Chapter Seven

Adventures Abroad Program Application, 21 November

Name: Jill Charron
High School: Jefferson High

Please explain to the selection committee what you feel you will gain from this experience in 300 words or less.

My reasons for applying to the program include supporting my long-term academic goals, as well as my desire for personal growth. I feel this trip to Italy accomplishes both objectives and better prepares me for my future while also giving me the opportunity to be a better world citizen.

I have a long-standing interest in history and look forward to having the opportunity to walk in the steps of Galileo, Caesar, and Michelangelo. I've read that over ten million tourists visit Rome each year, so imagining the millions and millions of people who will have stood in the same places I will be standing is awe inspiring. It makes me feel insignificant in the shadow of all this history. At the same time, being connected to all that went before makes me feel a vital part of it. As I will be leaving for Yale in the fall, I know this experience will raise my awareness of art and history and leave me better prepared for college.

Almost more important is the chance for personal growth. Saint Augustine said, "The world is a book, and those who do not travel read only one page." I was born and grew up in a small community. I've been fortunate enough to have supportive family and friends. However, I feel the opportunity to go somewhere on my own without this structure will allow me to grow. How will I know who I can become if I don't give myself a chance to try new things, to push myself beyond my normal boundaries? Who might I be if I am away from the things that I currently use to define myself?

I hope you give my application serious consideration. Thank you.

Applicant meets all requirements. Approved. Liz Ochoa, Program Director

***

TransEurope Airlines
Employee Incident Report
Flight 4727, 12 April
Crew Member: Ian Bovery, First Class Steward

This occurred at approximately 22:30 on the Chicago-to-Rome leg. Dinner service had been completed roughly one hour previous, and cabin lights had been dimmed in the plane. The majority of passengers were sleeping or watching the in-flight entertainment system.

I noted a passenger, later identified as Simone McIvory, had left her seat in coach and snuck into the first-class section. After a period of time (approximately five minutes), she encouraged another passenger, Jill Charron, to join her. I observed they had a brief argument over the idea, and Ms. McIvory pulled the other girl into first class. They sat in the two seats that were empty as a result of the assigned passengers having missed their connection.

I approached the girls and pointed out that they were not in their designated seats. I was aware they were part of a large school group that was on the flight. They stated that the rest of their group had gone to sleep and that they wanted to see what it was like in first class. Although I know it is against company policy, I allowed them to remain, as they indicated they would behave and that this was a "once-in-a-lifetime opportunity." They were quiet, the seats were empty, and it seemed a positive experience for two high school students, so it did not seem to me to be a problem. I stated they could remain for a few hours, but would need to return to their seats prior to breakfast service, and they agreed. They were not disruptive to the other passengers. They seemed focused on talking about their upcoming travels.

Approximately thirty minutes later, my co-worker Jessica LaPointe noticed the girls and demanded to know why I hadn't asked them to move. She said that this was company policy and a possible safety risk. Ms. LaPointe, as the senior crew member, escorted the girls back to their seats and indicated that she would be writing me up for disciplinary action.

This is my statement of the event. I have read Ms. LaPointe's statement and note that she accuses the girls of taking two small individual wine bottles from the beverage cart. I did not observe this, nor were any bottles found when the seats were cleaned. I do not believe there were any safety violations, as the two girls did use their seat belts and were not "skipping back and forth" between coach and first class as Ms. LaPointe reported. While I am aware company policy does not allow passengers to change seats without approval of the senior officer, I do not feel that my violation was significant, and it was done as an attempt to improve customer satisfaction.

**

Email
From: jillycharron@gmail.com
To: hcharron@winstonubc.com
Subject: Trip
12 April 22:38

Mom—

I am on the actual plane! This is HAPPENING! I know you won't get this email until we land and I get some Wi-Fi, but I wanted to say—thanks so much for helping me convince Dad to let me take this trip. I know you think I'm being overly dramatic—but I honestly feel like this adventure is going to change my life. There's something about going someplace where I don't know anyone (except for Simone!) and can sort of do anything or be anyone. You're the best mom ever for letting me go.

And yes, before you say it again—I'll be safe. I won't carry too much cash. I won't take drinks from anyone I don't know. I will make sure to stay with the group, blah, blah, blah. :) And I'll take a million pictures so I can share everything with you, and I won't change so much that you don't know me anymore. Ha!

Love

J

***

Simone McIvory's Facebook Page

Date: 2 May

Kelly Connors: RIP You will never be forgotten!

Mandi Ogden: I will always remember grade 11 geography with Simone and her jokes about dinos and world end. She will be missed.

Casey LaForde: Only the good die young.

Kana Sa: Beautiful girl is with the angels.

Michael Caul: Our class will not be the same without Simone. I can't believe she's gone.

Additional 100 comments on next page.

Chapter Eight

The laminated card had a list of colors—red, blue, green, yellow—but the ink color didn't match the word. The word *blue* might be printed in green, for example, or the word *red* was in bright yellow. Dr. Weeks would have me read each word on the page and then suddenly switch and have me instead list out what color the words were printed in. It shouldn't have been that complicated, but I kept getting confused. It took all my energy to stay focused. This didn't bode well for a future career in law.

I clenched my jaw. I wanted to rip the card in half, but it was encased in thick plastic. That would be the only thing more frustrating than doing the test, being unable to destroy it.

"You doing okay?" Dr. Weeks asked. She had a tiny mouth, like the tied end of a balloon. It annoyed me for some reason, then I was irritated at myself for being annoyed over such a stupid thing.

I put the card down. "I don't see the point of all of this." I motioned to the table behind her that held a whole bunch of tests. Blocks I had to put together. Pictures I was supposed to copy. Lists of words she would tell me and then ask me to recall a few minutes later. Endless stacks of bubble sheets. I was buried under bubble sheets.

Dr. Weeks leaned back. She was wearing reading glasses with another pair perched on top of her head. This was not exactly instilling a lot of confidence. "The Stroop is a frustrating test. But all of this will help us get a baseline of how your brain is working."

"It's not working," I said. "I can't read for more than a few minutes without getting a migraine. Three times this morning, I forgot the name of the nurse who brought me breakfast. I can't talk without forgetting the most basic—" Gone. Again. "Fuck!" I shoved my hand across the table, and the papers on it went flying to the floor.

"Well, that's one word that's still there."

Great. I had just lobbed an f-bomb at my neuropsychologist. This wasn't like me. I'd never even had a detention in school. "Sorry." It was a good thing I could remember that. It was a word I needed to use frequently.

"Getting frustrated is normal. So is feeling like your emotions are on a roller coaster," Dr. Weeks said.

"I've been through a hard time, blah, blah, blah," I said.

"That too, but I meant it's more than that." She spun around in her chair and took a plastic model of the brain off her desk. "This is your brain," she said. "Well, not yours, but you know what I mean." She winked.

She pointed at parts of the model. "Here we have the frontal lobe, this part here is the occipital lobe, the temporal, the parietal, and here at the bottom, we've got the stem." She smiled at my expression. "Don't worry, there's no test. Think

65

of the brain like a company. Different parts are in charge of different things, like departments. The frontal lobe is the executive office. That's the part that does the problem solving, keeps your impulses under control, things like that. The parietal looks over things to do with movement and orientation—think of it like the transportation department. The brain stem looks over all the basics. It's the facilities department. They keep the air moving, heat regulated, that kind of thing. You with me?"

"Yeah," I said.

"So the kind of trouble a person might have depends on where the injury happened. As if there were layoffs in a certain department. The bigger the injury, the more layoffs and the more difficulty performing that task."

I traced the ridges on the model. Braille brain. "Where was my injury?"

"You had some shearing in the frontal lobe area. That basically means your brain, which is sloshing around in your head in a bunch of fluid, slammed into your skull." She slapped the front of the model with the palm of her hand. "That means you're going to have some challenges with problem solving, regulating your mood, things like that."

"Great." I wanted to rub my forehead.

"You also had some bleeding in the temporal lobe." She tapped another section with her pencil. "That's why you're having memory trouble and language issues. You've got some amnesia of events leading up to the accident, but otherwise your long-term memory looks pretty good. You're having a bit of trouble getting things from your short term into your long term. That's like the brain's filing system. It doesn't mean the information is gone, just that your brain can't remember where it filed that piece away. That's why you'll have trouble with recalling people's names, or what you just read. It's going to take a while for it to either get better or for you to learn some strategies to manage it."

"So there's a chance it might not get better."

"Yes. The brain sometimes makes a workaround, transfers staff to the department that's short, but sometimes the brain just has to learn to work with what it's got. There are some good signs. You're young. Teen brains tend to bounce back pretty well as compared to really small kids or elderly adults. And we've already seen some improvement with your word finding. However, you need to know that this may be as good as it gets."

I liked that she didn't soft-pedal the truth, but it still made me tear up. She handed me a tissue from the box on her desk. I bet she went through Kleenex by the case lot. I took a deep breath. Her office smelled like freshly sharpened pencils, which I found oddly comforting.

"I'm not crying. It's just a frontal lobe thing," I said.

She smiled and slid a bowl of Hershey's Kisses across her desk in my direction. "Chocolate. Best medicine out there."

I peeled the foil off and popped it into my mouth. "I feel like I could live with the—talking thing now that it's better, but I hate that I can't remember anything from the past few weeks. It's like the truth is inside my head, but I don't have any way to get it out."

Dr. Weeks shrugged. "It's possible your memory isn't related to your injury." She pulled the bowl back and grabbed a chocolate for herself. "It could be that your brain doesn't want you to remember."

I swallowed. "You mean because I can't face what I did. That the accident was my fault." The online articles I'd read about the accident made me sick. They painted me as if I was this crazy loser who finally snapped after years of having a prettier, smarter, sexier best friend and decided to take us both out. Murder suicide. It didn't make sense. Simone was better than me with some things, but I was better than her in others. It evened out. She was my best friend. Sure, she annoyed me, but I knew I annoyed her too. It didn't mean that either of us would *kill* the other. It was absurd, but everyone acted like it was a perfectly reasonable thing to have happened.

And I couldn't understand why so many people cared about the accident at all. My lawyer, Evan, said it was because the story had legs. Two pretty girls, an exotic foreign location, mystery as to why I did it, and the potential for revenge and jealousy to be the cause. It didn't matter what the truth was—what mattered was that it was fun to talk about.

The whole case seemed to be based on how the one eyewitness didn't see any brake lights before the car hit a stone wall that went around the town. She told police that I aimed straight for it. Anna had pointed out that it was possible there had been something wrong with the car. Maybe the brakes or steering were busted. When she'd come up with the theory, I'd experienced a huge wave of relief. It explained everything. All I needed was for someone in Italy to look more closely at the car, and it would clear things up.

"I'm not saying the accident is anyone's fault, but what happened, however it happened, had to be extremely upsetting. It's not uncommon when there's trauma, emotional or physical, for the brain to shut down. It goes into emergency-only systems as a way of protecting itself. Your brain may be giving you some space to recover."

I looked out her window onto the parking lot. The rehab hospital was directly behind a strip mall, complete with a grocery, a coffee shop, and one of those everything-for-a-buck stores. It was weird to see people coming and going, doing everyday stuff. It made me feel like I'd gotten stuck in the wardrobe of Narnia, peering out, with no idea how to get back to the real world.

"I think not remembering is worse than anything that could have happened. I keep imagining different scenarios. There has to be something I can—" The word disappeared from my head.

"Do?" Dr. Weeks finished my sentence. "You can't force yourself to remember, and there's no pill or treatment that can zap your memory back into place. However, you can help it along."

I leaned forward. This was way better than putting together block puzzles. "What?"

"Do you have a phone?"

I nodded and pulled the replacement my mom had finally given me out of the bag that hung from the handles on my wheelchair. Now that there wasn't anyone to text, it seemed pointless, but I still took it. It was like a lucky rabbit's foot, my reminder that life could be normal again. I'd find myself compulsively checking online to see how everyone else's life was progressing without me. I stalked Simone's Facebook page every day to see what people were saying about her. I wasn't allowed to post anything on social media. No selfies. No nothing. My dad and Evan had forbidden me to text or email anyone from school. Not even Tara. Just in case. Neither of them clarified in case of what. I was cut off from everybody. I passed it over to Dr. Weeks, and she began to click around. Who knew? There really is an app for everything. It hadn't even occurred to me that there would be some kind of memory aid I could download.

Dr. Weeks slid the phone back over to me. "I put the memo section on your first home screen. Anytime there is something you need to remember, either type it in, or there's a voice record function. If you're getting headaches, it may be better to use the record. You can transfer it later from speech to text."

The excitement in my chest slowly deflated like a deserted party balloon. "That's it?" I'd been hoping for something more impressive.

"Don't look so disappointed. In the old days, when I was still taking my horse and buggy to work, we had people use notebooks and a pencil. At least this way you can play games and take a call too." She smiled. "It isn't very glamorous, but it works. Memory is a funny thing. Did you ever do one of those hedge mazes that you can walk through?"

"When I was a kid, my mom took Simone and me to a corn maze."

Dr. Weeks pointed at me. "Bingo. Those mazes are complicated because you can't see the whole picture. If you get up high, it's easy to see how one way will lead you to the next until you get out, but when you are in the middle of them, you can't tell."

"So my brain is a cornfield."

She raised a finger in triumph. "Not just any cornfield, a sculpted maze of a field. Write down what you remember, even if it's just a tiny flash. Often one memory will lead to another. Like a trail. Right now you can't see the full image of what happened. All you have are pieces, but if you write down enough of the clues, snap the puzzle pieces in place, you may get the big picture."

I tucked the phone back into my bag. It was worth trying. I didn't have a lot of other options, and it would be nice to use the phone for something other than playing games.

"Tell you what, let's call it a day with the testing." Dr. Weeks cleared her desk and leaned back. "That will give us some time to chat. I wanted to see how you feel about things with your lawyer. You mentioned last time you found him stressful."

I shrugged. I didn't like talking to Evan Stanley. He was my lawyer, which should have meant he was on my side, but it didn't feel that way. He looked at me like he thought I was guilty. That I was someone who had to be managed. I picked at the skin on my thumb and then made myself stop. "I don't know what he wants from me. I don't remember the accident. I can't tell him—"

I realized my hands were clenching the side of the chair, so I relaxed them. And tried to find another word to replace the one that was gone. "I can't tell him what happened. He wouldn't let me go to Simone's funeral. I want to talk to Simone's parents, apologize or explain or something, but Evan said I shouldn't

71

speak to them. That it might hurt my case somehow, or give them something they could use if they decide to sue us."

"And you don't agree."

"They lost their daughter, but she was my best friend. She was like my sister. We were both only children, so we used to say all the time that we were sisters by choice. I lost something too. It's not right that they don't seem to get that." I bit my tongue, stopping myself from saying more. Blaming her parents wasn't fair. "I know it's wrong to feel that way."

"Feelings aren't wrong. They just are."

"So what do I do?" I asked.

"You answer his questions so he can do his job and then you focus on your rehab. You make notes and follow where those memories get you. You get better, and you move forward."

She made it sound so easy, but it was way more complicated. "Did you read any of the stuff online about my accident?" I asked her. Anna had shown me a site, a blog, *Justice for Simone*. Anna hoped knowing more about the accident might have poked something free in my memory, but reading about it had been like reading about something that happened to someone else. "Other kids who were on the program with us are saying that Simone and I weren't getting along."

What the blog had posted was that everyone thought I was a stuck-up bitch. I was used to this. The truth was I was awkward around strangers, but it's somehow illegal for someone who is reasonably attractive and popular to be shy, so I got labeled a bitch. Simone was the one who could talk to anyone and in five minutes convince them she was their best friend.

"Is that possible?"

I shrugged. "We fought sometimes, but it was never anything—" My brain stuttered to a stop. "Big."

"What's the last thing you remember fighting about?"

"Simone was mad at me because I was considering going to Michigan State." I could tell she was confused. "I also got into Yale, which was my top choice. My dad went there." I wasn't sure why I felt like I had to add that, but I did it every time where I was going to college came up. "How could people think I could kill Simone when I was thinking about giving up going to the Ivy League just so we could still be near each other?"

"But Simone didn't want you to do that?" Dr. Weeks's tiny mouth pursed tighter, almost disappearing into her face.

I sighed. "No. She said even thinking about it was stupid. That if I wanted to go to law school, I needed to go to the best. It wasn't that I didn't know Yale's a better school, but we've been best friends since forever. The idea of her not being in my life seemed wrong."

"You could have stayed friends, even if you went to different schools."

I fought the urge to roll my eyes. This was exactly what my mom kept saying. "Sure, but it wouldn't be the same. I wouldn't be around. Simone would make new friends, people she could hang out with."

"And you would have made new friends too," Dr. Weeks pointed out.

"Yeah." I knew she was right. It wasn't like I thought I was going to be some loser who only had meaningful conversations with my stuffed animals. Even with me being shy, I would find someone. It was just hard to imagine I'd ever find a friend like Simone. She was special. She *had been* special. "Some guy named Brad told a reporter he thought we were fighting over a guy, but that wouldn't happen."

"Why not?"

"I'm not really interested in guys." I looked up quickly. "I don't mean I'm interested in girls, just that I'm not the kind to have huge crushes. I'm more focused on school."

"But Simone did?" Dr. Weeks played absently with one of the puzzle blocks in her hand.

"Sort of. Simone liked the game. Getting someone to be crazy for her. In ninth grade there was this exchange student from Germany, Mathias. He was really shy. I swear he looked like he would explode if anyone spoke to him. Simone didn't even like him, but Tara bet her that she couldn't get him to ask her out, so she went after him until he did. She liked the challenge. She hooked up with him once and told everyone he was a terrible kisser. Maybe it was having a front row to my parents' marriage, but I'm not a huge fan of the happy-ever-after concept," I admitted.

"These articles and their accusations really upset you."

Duh. "Did you see any of the comments?"

"People often lose their inhibitions online. They say and do things they would never do if they were face-to-face."

I gave a cynical laugh. "Trust me, I'm very familiar with Internet trolls. I used to have a website." A sick sensation rolled through my stomach, as it did every time I thought about it. When people asked me about the blog, I always shrugged like it was no big deal, but it still ate away at me. "I'm into a bunch of social justice issues. I plan to go into law. I used to write a blog about that stuff, feminism and things from a teen perspective. Trying to get other people my age interested. It started so I'd have a project to put on my college apps, but it was more than that." I glanced over to see if I could tell what she was thinking. "It's not that I actually thought some blog from a high school student would change the world, but I wanted—" The words dropped out of my head.

"But you wanted to give voice to what you found important," Dr. Weeks said.

I leaned back in the chair and wiped my eyes. She got it. So few people did. My blog had been the first thing I'd done that felt like it might matter. Getting an A in AP physics wasn't going to make the world a better place, but the stuff I cared about was important. Real issues, those mattered.

"There was someone who found my site and started trolling me like crazy. Every time I put up a post, he would go on and say all this nasty stuff. It didn't even matter what I was talking about. It got out of control, so I shut it down." I crossed my arms over my chest, defensive. "There wasn't anything else I could do."

The truth was there was a part of me that was ashamed I'd given in. I hated that I'd quit as soon as it got difficult. I should have fought back, but that's easier in theory. Someone constantly calling you a stupid slut day after day is an ugly reality.

I had the sense she was going to push me on the issue, but she must have decided to let it go. "My advice is that you stay off the computer and avoid these articles for a while. Reading them is only going to be a distraction from what you should focus on—getting better." Dr. Weeks glanced over at the clock on the wall. "That's it for today. You did good."

"I bet you say that to everyone," I said.

"Yeah, but I mean it with you."

I wheeled out of her office, passing the next person coming in. I paused to let a group of people go by. I turned the chair and looked down the hall, first one way, then the other. A flash of panic ran down my spine. I wasn't sure where I was supposed to go. My heart picked up speed. I told myself I was being stupid. It wasn't like I'd wandered into a neighborhood full of crack dens and rabid bears. I was still in the hospital. All I had to do was ask someone for help or figure it out on my own. Even with the maze of halls and different departments, the place was only so big.

I made myself roll forward. There were posters announcing everything from a movie night to times for various workshops. The entire place was painted neutral bureaucratic beige. I stopped. There was a blue plastic sign mounted on the wall announcing POOL with an arrow. Someone had made the two O's into crossed eyes by drawing in pupils with a black Sharpie.

I'd passed the pool on my way to see Dr. Weeks. I remembered the smell of chlorine wafting down the hall. I chewed on the inside of my cheek. I glanced up and down the hall to see if there might be another clue. Last year my favorite teacher, Mr. Landis, picked me to mentor the incoming freshmen on the debate club. He said I was one of the best problem solvers he'd seen since he started teaching.

I couldn't remember how to get back to my room, but other useless information kept flooding into my brain. If you're lost in the woods, you can follow drainage or a stream downhill. Keep the sun over your right shoulder so you can be sure you're walking in a straightish direction. Moss tends to grow on the north side of a tree. I'd never even been camping, and yet all this knowledge flew into my head unbidden. Now if there were only a few streams or trees, I'd be all set. That's when I noticed the lines.

Down the center of the floor, there were painted stripes. They reminded me of the mazes I'd just talked about with Dr. Weeks. Buried deep in my brain, something reached out. The lines were there to help people find their way around.

Follow the yellow brick road.

I pumped my fist in the air. I remembered Anna telling me about the color-coding. The yellow line would lead me back to the patient wards. I wanted to announce at the top of my lungs that I'd figured it out, but I was pretty sure no one else was going to be impressed. I'd tell Anna later; maybe I'd start calling her my own personal Glinda the Good Witch. I pulled out my phone and clicked on the recorder. "The yellow line leads to the wards. I'm in room 511." I switched it back off. Done. Now if that detail disappeared from my brain, I'd have a way to recall it.

The thrill of victory passed quickly. If I could barely find my way around the hospital, how was I going to figure out what happened with Simone in Italy? I rolled into the elevator and punched the number for my floor.

I closed my eyes. I needed a nap. Between taking the tests and talking about everything, I was worn out. The doctors had warned me that fatigue was normal with a brain injury, but there was being tired and then there was this. I was so exhausted my bones ached. There was a ping as we passed another floor on the way up. Suddenly my mind flashed and I saw Simone. Her mouth was open in a howl, and her eyes were wide. I reached for her and realized I was screaming. There was a sickening crunch of metal.

"You coming out?"

My eyes flew open. I was still in the elevator. There were two people standing in front of the now-open doors staring at me. I blinked.

"Are you okay?" a girl asked.

I nodded and rolled forward. The group moved past me, already talking about something else, and the doors drifted shut with a soft thunk.

I closed my eyes to see if the image would come back, but it was just black.

Chapter Nine

Let's Travel! **Guidebook**

Rome: The city spans centuries and—from the ancient Roman Forum, to the sprawling halls of the Vatican, to the upscale shopping near the Spanish Steps—has something for every traveler. Be sure to toss a coin in the Trevi Fountain so you can wish to return, because it will take more than one trip to see all that this beautiful city has to offer!

***

Excerpt from Police Interview Abigail Johnson, Fellow Student in the Adventures Abroad Program

Date: 4 May
Time: 10:30
Present: Abigail Johnson, Christopher Johnson (Abigail's father), Detective Leon Smith
Transcript to be provided to Italian police

Abigail: Everyone met for the first time in February. The

program had a meeting for our parents and us so we could go over all the rules, the paperwork we needed to have filled out, and the itinerary. That's when I met Jill. She seemed okay, kinda quiet. I remember she talked about how she really wanted to see the statue of David in Florence. We laughed about it because David is hot. You know, for a stone statue. She made a big deal about how excited she was to travel on her own. It seemed like it was important to her. That's why it was weird to me that Simone ended up coming too.

Simone wasn't at the meeting in February—she applied late. I thought that was sorta bullshit, because the rest of us applied forever ago, and you had to do all this stuff like write an essay and get letters of recommendation from your teachers and stuff, and I don't know how she would have gotten that together so late, but whatever.

I didn't meet Simone until the whole group gathered at the airport in Detroit for our flight. Simone was laughing and joking around like it was a party instead of a departure gate. I could tell she was one of those people who always ended up the center of attention and it made Jill mad that she sorta disappeared when Simone was around.

Detective Smith: Was this anger something that Jill expressed to you, or was it just your feeling?

Abigail: I could just tell.

Detective Smith: If you could, try to keep focused on things that you saw or heard.

Abigail: Fine. Jill and Simone were the only two people who were friends before we left. The rest of us all came from different schools. It was weird that they were already best friends; it made the rest of us feel sorta left out. I mean, we all made friends eventually. The two of them seemed happy together at the start. They buddied up right away to sit together on the flight and everything. I was crying because I had to say goodbye to my boyfriend, Trevor. He and I have gone out forever, like, since September. I caught the two of them looking at each other, and I could tell they thought it was stupid that I was crying, but maybe that's because neither of them had a boyfriend, so they didn't get it. Saying goodbye to someone you love sucks.

***

Excerpt from Police Statement given by Liz Ochoa, Program Director for Adventures Abroad

Transcript to be provided to Italian police

I've been doing this for eleven years, and I've never had anything remotely this awful happen. I hadn't even imagined it in my worst nightmares, and trust me, I can have some real doozies. I've had a kid fall down a stairwell and break an arm. Every year I lose at least one of them for an hour or two. Food poisoning, homesickness, fights. One kid tried to steal one of those cheap carnival masks from a store. You name it, I've pretty much seen it happen. But this . . . I just don't even know what to say.

This year we had a group of twenty. We've done smaller groups, but we've found they don't work as well. Twenty is large enough to have some interesting energy from different perspectives. More than twenty becomes a logistical problem. Keeping track of a group of teens is like herding cats. If they see something that catches their eye, they wander off before you know it. The program has two leaders on the trip, myself and Tim Wright. We travel with the group and provide supervision. We hire a university student in the home country to act as a guide. These are typically majors in the history or art departments. They get school credit, and we get a local expert of sorts.

For this trip we brought on Niccolo Landini. He's a college student at Sapienza—Università di Roma, where he's studying Italian history. I suspected when I saw him we might have trouble. Of course you shouldn't discriminate against people because they're good-looking, but teens are already basically a big bag of walking hormones, so having him around felt like chumming shark-infested water. The day he was introduced, you could see almost every girl in the program get that dreamy, someday-my-prince-will-come look. And you could tell he loved the attention, soaked it up like a sponge and just oozed back out the charm. I thought he and one of the girls might end up together. What can you do? At that age romance is practically a biological need and they're all predisposed to expecting some kind of magical experience on their trip abroad. I blame all those teen romance novels.

I have to admit, I'd never have suspected Nico would be attracted to Jill. Don't get me wrong, she's quite pretty.

Not in the way kids today seem to want to be, all skinny and hard-looking. Jill reminds me of a starlet from Hollywood's golden era, a brainy young Sophia Loren or Elizabeth Taylor. I didn't see her as his type. She was quiet and clearly very focused. One of those few people who doesn't talk if she has nothing to say. My mother used to call them old souls. Jill felt older to me than her actual age in some ways, and in others, she seemed a little naïve. I had the sense she was going to be one of those people who really blossomed in college. You know, Jill actually emailed me as soon as she got her acceptance and asked for suggested reading for the trip. And she read them too.

At first I don't think Jill knew what to do with Nico's attention. My guess is that she wasn't super experienced with boys. Her friend Simone egged her on, for sure. Simone would make a big show of suddenly wanting to change seats on the bus so that Nico and Jill sat together—that kind of thing.

I didn't think much of it, to be honest. The kids in the program are all seniors in high school. They're old enough to run their own love lives without me poking my nose in. I had no idea things would go so badly. At least, not at first.

Chapter Ten

I looked up to try to gauge how far we were from the hospital entrance. Less than a hundred feet. It might as well have been in Kathmandu. I was too exhausted to make it.

"You can do it," Sam said. He was trailing behind me with my chair while I tried to lurch along on my crutches.

Physiotherapy should be declared torture. Screw waterboarding. If you want terrorists to confess, lock them up in a physio gym. They'd be begging for mercy in less than an hour. When I met Sam, my therapist, I wasn't sure why Anna had made him sound so scary. He was a slight Indian guy who looked like he still bought his Dockers in the kids' department of Sears. His front right tooth was crooked and overlapped the left tooth. He bounced as he walked across the gym to introduce himself. He had the perkiness of an elementary school teacher.

Sam was a sadist.

My arms were shaking. In addition to his other abuse, Sam got me up on crutches. He said I'd spent enough time in the wheelchair. It seemed like a good idea until my shoulders and arms began screaming for me to sit back down. My leg, in an effort to not be left out, was a pulsing dance music remix of agony. Even my skull felt too tight, like someone was cranking a vice around my brain. I would have cried, except it would have taken more energy than I had left. The only good thing about the day was that I was too tired to think about Simone. The pain had blunted the nonstop loop of *why?* that normally ran through my head.

"Make it to the door, and I'll buy you some ice cream in the cafeteria," Sam offered.

I hated this guy. "The ice cream is free," I pointed out.

Sam laughed like I was starring in a one-woman show on the Comedy Network. "This is true—you got me," he said.

"I'm too tired," I insisted. It had sounded fun to go outside, but now I was sweating like I'd run a marathon, and all I wanted was to go back to my room.

"You can do this. Take ten more steps."

I gritted my teeth and swung the crutches, counting each step.

"Good," Sam said. "Now ten more."

Was he kidding? I turned to face him. "You said I could quit after ten."

Sam shook his head. "No I didn't. I just suggested you start with ten. You know what they say, a journey of a thousand miles starts with a single step." He raised his finger up in the air like he was a politician making a point. "Same thing with getting to the front door."

"Screw you," I said.

Sam didn't seem remotely angry or upset to be cursed at. I suspected it happened to him a lot. A person got out of the car parked right next to us on the sidewalk.

"Jill Charron?"

I flushed. I was embarrassed to be caught acting like a snot. I wanted to be the kind of patient who was noble and kind, like

85

the Kate Middleton of rehab, but my mood sometimes spilled out hot and nasty. The person whipped out a camera, its huge lens almost hitting me in the chin before he began snapping pictures. I swung my hand up to cover my face.

"Do you have anything to say about the death of Simone McIvory?"

I wanted to run, but I couldn't. Adrenaline flooded my system like molten silver in my veins, and I took a few more steps with my crutches, but I was unsteady.

"Did you kill her because of Nico?" The camera continued to click. "Was it a broken heart that led you to do it?"

Sam shoved the wheelchair into the back of my good leg and tugged the tail of my shirt so that I fell into the seat. "Hang on," he said in my ear, and began bolting for the door. The stranger kept pace. I bent in half, trying to bury my face in my lap. We bounced along the cracked sidewalk. Each bump sent a hot jab of pain down my leg.

"Did your family pay off the Italian authorities to sneak you out of the country?"

A security guard from the hospital must have seen what was going on and was jogging out the front door toward us. Someone else was holding the door open. My wheelchair hit the edge of the doorjamb, and I nearly flew out of the seat. I had to grab the armrests to keep from being tossed onto the lobby floor.

The security guard had his hand on the chest of the photographer and was pushing him back. I couldn't make out his last screamed question. Once we were away from the door, Sam leaned down so he was even with my face.

"Are you okay?" He looked rattled.

I felt like I was going to throw up. Everything hurt, and I was shaking. "What—" I couldn't finish the sentence.

"I am so sorry," Sam said. "I had no idea there would be reporters here."

I thought of the stories I'd seen online. I cringed. I could already imagine how I would look in the photos: sweaty, blotchy, my baggy sweatpants likely making me look like a fat lump. As soon as I had the thought, I was embarrassed. How I looked in a picture didn't matter. Simone was dead.

"It was a mistake to go outside," Sam said. He touched my shoulder, hand, and leg cast over and over, as if he wanted to assure himself that I was still in one piece. It bothered me that he seemed flustered. It was his job to be in control, to make me feel better. I shouldn't have to reassure him. "I just thought the weather was so nice—"

"I want to go back to my room," I said, cutting him off.

"Sure," Sam said. He pushed my chair past the group of people who were standing in the lobby staring at me. Once we were in the room, he helped me into bed. "I'll send an email to the rest of your team and let them know what happened. We'll talk to security and make sure you're not bothered like that again."

I nodded and willed him to leave.

"Do you want me to see if Dr. Weeks can squeeze you in this afternoon?" Sam offered. "Maybe talk it over?"

I wanted to scream for him to get out and let me be alone, but if I lost it, he would be even more likely to stick around. Hovering. "No. I'm fine. Just tired."

Sam stood in the door, hesitating. "I really am sorry," he said.

"It's fine," I said, my tone implying it was anything but okay. "I'll rest for a bit." I glanced over at the window and imagined the guy outside with a zoom lens. "Can you close the—" I concentrated, but it was still blank. "The window coverings?"

Sam leapt into action as if he'd been waiting to be assigned a task. He crossed the room and pulled them shut with a yank.

I made myself count to sixty after he left, just in case he came back in, but he was gone. I spun the combination on the locked drawer next to my bed and pulled out my MacBook Air.

The door flew open, and I almost dropped the laptop onto the floor. Anna rolled in. "Holy shit—I heard the paparazzi attacked you."

"It was one guy; it wasn't exactly a pack."

"Stalked by the media. You're like Kim Kardashian, only without the ass." She held up a hand. "I mean that as a compliment," she clarified.

"It was scary," I admitted. I could feel my lower lip shaking.

Anna's face turned serious. "Sorry. I didn't mean to act like a spaz. You okay?"

"I thought the story wouldn't be a big deal anymore," I admitted. "But if they sent someone to take a picture of me, that's pretty serious, isn't it?" Anna didn't answer. "The reporter made a comment about my dad buying people off to get me out of Italy."

"Did he?"

I shrugged. "I don't think so, not like in a come-here-and-take-this-envelope-of-cash kind of way, but would he throw

88

some money around and make a lot of noise? Probably. It wasn't like my dad was trying to keep me out of trouble. He just wanted me home."

Anna glanced at my laptop. "You planning to look up what they're saying about you?"

I hesitated. Dr. Weeks had told me not to, that it was a distraction, and I'd managed to avoid the Internet for the past couple of days. "Is it a mistake?"

"Probably," Anna said. "Smart thing would be to work on getting better. You know they're not saying anything good. There's nothing to be gained from torturing yourself by reading it."

"Yeah," I said.

Anna rolled over to my bed. "Don't let me stop you. It's not like I ever did the smart thing." She nudged me over and pulled herself up onto the bed using the metal rail.

I flipped the lid open, and the laptop lit up. I paused for a second before typing my own name into the Google bar. Even though I'd been expecting it, I was still surprised to see the list of stories appear. There were way more than there had been last time I'd looked. They kept scrolling down the page. It made me feel lightheaded.

"Click on that one." Anna's finger, tipped with chipped black polish, picked out the *Justice for Simone* blog.

When the link opened, it took me a minute to recognize myself. There was a large photo of Simone and me. It was from last Halloween. Simone had picked out our costumes. I'd been a slutty nurse. By the time the photo was taken, I'd already ditched most of the costume and was only wearing the tight white dress, not much longer than a shirt. I was holding a fake knife at Simone's throat, and she was making a goofy expression. There had been a party at Sophie's house. You could see a stack of empty beer cans behind us. I hadn't even wanted to go to the party; it had been Simone's idea. I wanted to go back in time and throw a blanket over myself. How had she talked me into wearing that out?

CHILLY JILLY WITH SIMONE IN HAPPIER TIMES

I speed-read through the article. There was no mention of the fact that the picture was taken at Halloween. They'd let the reader think I was the kind of person who dressed like a whore and carried a knife that I brandished at friends. They made it sound like I drank all the time and slept around, and they hinted that I might have been into drugs too. When I finished the article, I wanted to chuck the computer.

"Chilly Jilly?" Anna asked. The article made a big deal out of the nickname, implying that I was called that because I was frigid and cold-hearted.

"It caught on in middle school," I explained. "Simone was always the drama queen and I was always super calm, so people called me that. That's all it meant. It's not that I don't freak out too—I just like to do it in private." I wondered who had even mentioned the nickname to the blog. I didn't like the idea of people I knew talking about me.

"So who is the guy they mention? The one you were crazy for in theory?"

I skimmed the article again, but there wasn't any real information. "I don't know. The reporter outside mentioned a name, but I forgot it."

Anna pulled the computer back onto her lap and clicked around. "Found him. Damn, he's hot." She tilted the screen so I could see it better.

Niccolo Landini. The large photo of him looked like a shot from an Italian *Vogue* magazine—slicked-back hair, smoldering eyes. The smaller shot showed him being led inside a police station, his arm up trying to block some of the cameras.

I stared at the photo, waiting to see if the sight of it would bring something back, but there was nothing. It was a picture of a stranger, as far as I could tell. I closed my eyes, and there was a flash, the feeling of someone's hot mouth pressing down on mine. His rough whiskers scratching my skin, marking me. I could feel myself straining toward him as if I wanted to crawl inside him, be a part of his flesh. My eyes flew open. I felt flustered like I'd been caught doing something. Was it a memory or just wishful thinking? I couldn't imagine recording that in my phone to hash over with Dr. Weeks.

He didn't look like anyone I would go out with. He looked like the kind of guy who wouldn't even notice me. I'd only had one boyfriend before, and calling Josh a boyfriend was generous, as it was only a few kisses behind the canoe storage cabin at camp the summer of my junior year. The article said that Simone and I had fought over Nico, that people in the program said we'd had a screaming match about how I was ditching her to be with him.

They always talk about how teens are supposed to be slaves to our sex drives, that we're walking hormones, but I've never been like that. When everyone was falling in and out of love with some random guy they sat next to in history, I never felt swoony or envious. It seemed a waste. Guys, or at least the ones I'd met, didn't seem worth the bother. There were so many other things that interested me more. I wondered at one point if I might be gay, but I didn't feel some huge wave of longing when I thought about girls either. I found guys attractive, but I just couldn't bring myself to care that much.

I'd cried a few times when Josh and I broke up after camp, but it felt more like what I was supposed to do than actual despair. If I was honest, I felt almost relieved. I wouldn't have to keep that charade going. First love. Check. Dumped. Check. Moving on. Check. The entire situation with Josh felt like something that I had to get out of the way. At least now I wasn't the person who'd never had a boyfriend. Since then, there hadn't been anyone I'd even had a crush on. Post-Josh I went back to my role, which was listening to Simone talk about her love life. I was the observer. I didn't bother with messy relationships. I preferred crushes on unattainable people—actors, musicians, or characters in a book. Fictional boyfriends were way more satisfying, in my experience. They almost always said the right thing, and when you got bored with them, you just put them back on the shelf.

This Italian guy even had a stupid name. How could I be in love with someone named Nico?

Anna was still clicking around on different stories. I caught a few lines here or there, but I didn't have the stomach to read further. They all implied the same thing. I was a slutty, rich bitch who killed my best friend over a guy, then got my parents to rescue me. There was an interview with a psychologist on the *Justice for Simone* site. She talked about how people described me as aloof and cold. She made it sound like evidence that I could be a psychopath, devoid of any empathy. She also made a big deal of a quote that I had on Facebook from the book *The Talented Mr. Ripley*, implying that "people like me" often have a fascination with those who killed. She didn't mention that the book was on our extended suggested reading list for English. She acted like I had posters of John Wayne Gacy, Charles Manson, and Ted Bundy hanging in my bedroom, all adorned with lipstick kisses.

"You should have talked to the reporter outside," Anna said.

"Why?"

"He's going to tell a story, you might as well give him one that is favorable to you. If not, he's just going to fill the space with other stuff." Anna clicked from story to story.

I pulled my sleeves over my hands and thought it over. "It's not worth the risk. They're just as likely to twist my words around, make me sound worse."

Anna cocked her head. "I'm not sure they can make you sound worse."

I shook my head. "I'm not good at that stuff."

"What stuff?"

"Making people like me," I said. Simone was the charmer. She was the one people picked to be team captain, voted for on the prom court, the one people sought out to come to their parties. I was the added bonus. If you wanted Simone, you also got me. Like the tiny bottle of conditioner that came free when you bought a nice bottle of shampoo. I tended to say the wrong thing—something I meant as a joke would come out wrong or I'd make a reference that no one else would get and then I'd feel awkward and end up just being quiet. But I didn't care, because Simone got me. We were a team. I didn't need to be popular with a wide group of people.

But I didn't like being *this* unpopular. I shut the lid of the laptop to keep Anna from pulling up any more stories. "It doesn't matter. None of this is true. Once they prove that, it won't matter what people are saying."

Anna looked at me as if I were delusional. "It doesn't matter what's true—what matters is what people believe."

I shrugged, pretending I didn't care.

Anna swung herself back into her chair. "Your funeral."

Chapter Eleven

Let's Travel! Guidebook

Venice: A city made for lovers. As you walk the narrow alleys with not a single car in sight and only the sound of lapping canal water under the bridges, you'll feel transported back in time. Be sure to wander out of the tourist sections of the city to see the real Venice. Settled by the Veneti people as long as ten thousand years ago, and shaped by the doges who, starting in the 700s, oversaw its development and growth, this magical city built on the water remains home to many—there is no place like it in the world.

***

Forensic Psychology Consult Report, Dr. Jerome Kerr

Date: 3 May
Client: Detective Alban, Florence Police Department
Original report in Italian, translated to English by Stoker and Mills Translation Services, New York, New York

I am a psychologist with over twenty-two years' experience. At my client's request, I have reviewed the documents provided to me and agreed to render my professional opinion as to possible psychological motivations and complications in this case. The documents reviewed are listed in Appendix A of this report. I have not met with any of the individuals discussed in this report, and my opinion is based solely on the information reviewed and my professional experience.

A summary of facts and assumptions in this case, as well as details of the crime, may be found in Appendix B of this report.

Relationship between Jill Charron and Simone McIvory

The documents reviewed indicate that this was a long-lasting friendship. I note they were listed as friends from either fourth or second grade, depending on the source. They appear to have an enmeshed social structure, with the two attending the same high school, sharing a peer group, enjoying many social activities (such as drama and dance), and spending significant amounts of recreational time together.

There are no indications of abuse in either family or histories of mental illness. I note Ms. McIvory's mother has been treated for depression in the past, but this appears to be related to family stressors versus meeting the clinical diagnosis of chronic depression. While both girls appear to have experimented with alcohol and perhaps marijuana, there is no documentation or health records that indicate any past or current substance abuse or addiction issues, and the events were likely typical teen exploration.

The available school records indicate that Ms. Charron was a strong student with a focus on coursework that would lead to university study. Ms. McIvory's grades were average and her academic progress mediocre. However, I note on standardized testing, Ms. McIvory's scores would indicate that she was capable of greater academic success than was demonstrated in her grades.

Indications of Possible Conflict
Although Ms. Charron and Ms. McIvory were involved in a long-standing friendship, there were indications of areas of possible conflict. These include, but would not be limited to:

1. Limited Friendship: Although the two girls had other social connections, most notably Tara Ingells, their friendship was primarily a dyad. As they relied upon each other for social support, any change in the relationship could have been seen as a threat by the other.

2. Financial Difference: Ms. Charron's family is best described as wealthy, while Ms. McIvory's is lower middle class. This likely created friction in terms of available resources (one girl could do things, purchase things, etc., that the other could not).

3. Popularity/Status: While both girls would be considered "popular" by their peers, the documentation indicates that Ms. McIvory was

better liked overall. If Ms. Charron was tired of playing "second fiddle," this could have led to conflict.

4. Family Moral Values: Ms. McIvory's family is strongly religious and, on a disciplinary spectrum, would be seen as more strict and rigid in terms of expectations. It does not appear that Ms. McIvory had a strong personal relationship with either parent; she likely preferred to keep personal confidences within her social circle. Ms. Charron's parents are divorced and appear to be agnostic in terms of religion. She likely has a strong desire for her father's approval, but a dislike of his new wife and children. Ms. Charron seems close to her mother, but likely will have difficulty in this relationship as she seeks more independence in the coming years.

5. Future Plans: Ms. Charron was university bound, while Ms. McIvory had no firm academic plans following her high school graduation. This transition from high school to adulthood can be fraught with high emotion, as long-standing relationships grow and change when individuals take different paths. In my opinion, it is unlikely that Ms. Charron and Ms. McIvory would have maintained as close a relationship in the future, as they likely would pursue different areas and, as a result, make new friends with whom they had more in common.

Without meeting either girl, it is difficult to say if friction existed or if the reported difficulties they had on the trip were related to the stress of travel. However, there was clearly a range of issues that could have led to high emotion and the resulting action.

***

Television Transcript for *Crime Watch with Nina Grimes*
(*Theme music.*)

Nina: Good evening and welcome to *Crime Watch*, with your host, Nina Grimes. We'll have an update on our story from last week about the sick pervert Anthony Hutchins's case in South Florida and how his defense team is trying to use a technicality to weasel out of the jury's decision. However, first up tonight, we've got an exclusive on Murder Abroad, the tragic death of Simone McIvory and the suspicion that her best friend, *her best friend*, Jill Charron, is to blame.

(*School picture of Jill Charron staring straight out at the camera.*)

Nina: Her nickname is Chilly Jilly. We've had our researchers talking to her fellow students at Jefferson High School, and they paint a picture of a girl who kept to herself, a loner, with a possessive claim over her best friend. Here I have a quote from a member of the Jefferson High cheer squad, who spoke to me but requested to remain anonymous. I asked her what she knew of Jill. Her full quote is:

(*Quote appears typed on screen.*) "Simone was awesome. Everyone loved her, but a bunch of us never knew why she hung with Jill. Jill was always lurking around, wanting Simone's attention. I could tell that Simone sometimes got tired of how needy she was. Jill was like a parasite living off Simone. Sucking her dry."

Nina: A parasite. I think that's very telling. I heard a lot from Jill's fellow students about how she was standoffish and was very cold toward the opposite sex. Yet it's come out in the past twenty-four hours that Chilly Jilly had fallen hard for a college-aged Romeo on this school trip. He'd found a way to thaw that stone heart of hers. Now, it's been some time, longer than I'd like to admit (*chuckles*) since I was a young girl, but I can tell you when a young lady is in the throes of passion, she can have a lot of high emotion. Is that what happened here? Was this beautiful, innocent girl—

(*Picture of Simone cuddling a kitten on screen.*)

Nina, continued: —cut down in the prime of life, snatched from the bosom of her family, over a boy? We've got Brad Thompson on the line with us. Brad was one of the students on the trip with Jill and Simone and is talking to us exclusively tonight about this Nico character to give us some insight into what happened in Italy. He's coming to us from his home in Rochester, Michigan. Brad, can you hear me?

100

Brad (*voiceover*): I can hear you, Nina. Thanks for having me on your show.

Nina: Can you tell us a bit about this Italian tour guide, Nico?

Brad: He was a bit of a douchebag, if you ask me. He was always doing the humble brag.

Nina: Humble brag?

Brad: Yeah, you know. Like he'd say (*takes on an Italian accent*), "Oh, excuso me, my English is not so good, I speak five languages, and know everything about Italian history, so I hope you can un'stand my sometimes mistakes." I mean, who needs to speak five languages? If you ask me, he only made mistakes with English so all the girls would be all (*talks in high falsetto voice*), "Oh, Nico, let me help you with figuring out which word you want."

Nina: So you think he was flirting with the young girls in the program?

Brad: Totally. He was talking them right out of their panties with that accent.

Nina: Was Jill Charron one of the girls who fell for him?

Brad: Not right away. I think that's why he liked her. She was the only one who wasn't panting after him. I think he saw her as a challenge. He was always trying to sit with her on the bus and acting like everything that came out of her mouth was genius. He was clearly into her. He didn't act on it, though. Simone figured he needed a push.

Nina: Simone wanted to help her friend? How was she going to do this?

Brad: Simone asked me to act like I liked Jill so Nico would be jealous and finally make his move.

Nina: And did he?

Brad: At first it seemed like it didn't work, but then they definitely hooked up when we were in Venice. I think Jill and Nico thought the two of them were keeping things all top secret, but pretty much everyone knew they were together.

Nina: How did people feel about it?

Brad: I think a few of the other girls on the trip were jealous, but mostly people didn't care that much. Everybody was doing their own thing. The trip kept us pretty busy, we were changing cities every couple of days, and there were readings and lectures and stuff.

Nina: But eventually something happened, isn't that correct?

Brad: Oh, yeah, all hell broke loose between Simone and Jill.

Nina: We'll want to hear more about that after the break!

(*Commercial.*)

***

Excerpt from Police Interview with Niccolo Landini

Date: 9 May
Time: 09:30
Florence Police Department
Present: Niccolo Landini, Detective Alban, and Detective Marco
Original transcript in Italian, translated to English by Stoker
and Mills Translation Services, New York, New York

Detective Marco: Please detail your relationship with Jill Charron.

Niccolo: Jill and I were in a romantic relationship. Unlike so many girls, she was not all giggles and games. She was very smart and beautiful. She had a love for history, like me. A sense that we are all connected and that to understand the past is to know the future. There is now a lot of discussion that I took advantage of her, but we are not so different in age. She is eighteen; she is not a child. I am twenty-two. I cared for her, and she for me. Age did not make a difference.

Detective Marco: When did the relationship start?

Niccolo: I took the group to Caffè Florian in St. Mark's Square. Some of the most prestigious people have sat in those very same seats—Charlie Chaplin, Hemingway, Dickens, even Casanova. Most of the students had no sense of the importance of the place; they just wanted a Coke and to sit down. I knew this was something Jill would like. She would notice the art on the wall, the details, she would feel the history in the space. There was a boy hanging about her, crowing about being her boyfriend. I told her that she was sending mixed signals. If she didn't want my attention, I would leave her alone, but she told me it was a mistake, that she had no interest in high school boys. I kissed her that day.

I did not take advantage of Jill. She wanted this too. I never led her to believe this was love. We are both young, and she was on a four-week school trip. I was not playing with her, but I do not think either of us saw it as a serious relationship. It was summer love. Nothing more. You must believe me.

Chapter Twelve

My mom was late. When she came into the room, I could tell she was flustered. Her blouse was pulled out from her skirt waistband, and there were beads of sweat perched on her upper lip. She dropped into a seat, not looking at my dad. The hospital meeting room was too small. I was already hot. My fingers kept running over the table. Someone had carved the word *anarchy* into the laminate tabletop, but had spelled it wrong. I couldn't decide if that was tragic or ironic.

"Traffic," Mom explained. She reached across and squeezed my hand.

"This is why the rest of us leave early, so we're on time." Dad looked at Evan as if he expected to be given a gold star sticker.

The vein in Mom's forehead pulsed.

"It seems we're all here now," Dr. Weeks said, patching over the tension.

Evan Stanley opened the file in front of him and looked down at the papers inside. It seemed too full to me. That he shouldn't have accumulated so much already. "Today's meeting is about getting a foundation for our case and determining what steps we want to take next. Can you tell me anything more about the accident?" He took a fountain pen from his jacket pocket and pulled a brand-new Moleskine notebook close to him. The top of his pen had a white enamel star in the cap. I recognized it, but I'd forgotten the brand. It was expensive.

"I don't remember anything," I said.

"Nothing? Even something small could be helpful."

"I don't remember anything until I woke up at the hospital."

"Huh." Evan riffled through the pages. "You sure about that?"

"Yes."

"Absolutely sure?" He spun the pen through his fingers as though this was a casual conversation, but his eyes never left my face. It felt like he was trying to crawl behind my eyes and read my mind.

"She told you she doesn't recall," my mom said.

Evan rubbed his chin. His five-o'clock shadow was already coming in, and the rasp of his whiskers when he touched his face could be heard in the small room. It reminded me of insects scuttling inside a wall.

He sighed. "There's a note in your medical file made by a Dr. Ruckman, saying that you told him right after you woke up that you *did* remember the accident."

My throat squeezed shut.

"It's important to understand that Jill didn't 'wake up.' Regaining consciousness after a head injury isn't like a light switch. Off or on," Dr. Weeks said. "She would have had periods when she would have seemed awake, eyes open, possibly even speaking, but would not have been oriented to time or place. She wouldn't have any—or at least very limited—recall of that time."

"Ruckman says that on Sunday morning, May 1, she was lucid," Evan insisted.

Dr. Weeks leaned forward. "I've read her file too. What he says is that Sunday morning was the first time she was able to respond to commands. However, you need to understand that doesn't mean she wouldn't still have been experiencing confusion."

"So you were confused when you said you remembered the accident." Evan stressed the word *confused*.

I nodded, a bit overly eager.

"Were you able to figure out anything from the car?" my mom asked.

"Early indications are that the car was in perfect working order. No engine or brake trouble." He shrugged. "They're not our mechanics, but we've got no reason to doubt the report."

"I don't know what you want me to say. Maybe there was a deer on the road, and I swerved to—" My brain scrambled. "To not hit it," I said. I didn't even know if there were deer in Italy. Maybe they had some other kind of wild animal, a boar perhaps.

Evan tapped his pen on the table. "Could be. However, the witness didn't report seeing anything." He flipped through the file and pulled out a paper, his eyes skimming over it. "The witness stated that the car was driving erratically and too quickly for the road." He looked around the table. "This is easy for us to tackle. She's not an expert; she can't testify to speed if it comes to a trial. The comment from Dr. Ruckman might be tricky. Not everyone is going to understand this awake-not-really-awake thing."

The blood rushed out of my head. Trial?

"The witness says the car hit the stone wall at what she describes as full speed. The car hesitated for a second—most likely the undercarriage caught—and then it went over and down the hillside." Evan spun a photograph across the table. It showed a low cream-colored stone wall, a hole torn into the side, loose stones littering the roadway. Beyond the hole, the ground dropped away. I tried to look through the picture and see myself there, but nothing looked familiar.

"Do you recognize anything?" Evan asked.

I refused to say that I didn't remember again. Briefly, I imagined what it must have been like in the car. Teetering back and forth, weightless for a split second before plunging down. I blinked slowly and forced the image out of my head. It wasn't real.

"How did you and Simone get along?" Evan asked.

I blinked at the sudden conversation change. "G-g-g—" My throat seemed to want to hold on to the words. Zap them into oblivion. "We got along really well. She's my best friend."

He nodded. His pen still tapping on the table. I wanted to reach over and smack it down. "How long have you known each other?"

"Fourth grade."

"Long time."

Dr. Weeks's forehead was creased. She didn't know where he was going with this either. That made me feel better. Talking with Evan reminded me of playing chess with my dad, in the sense that he was at least five moves ahead of me at any point.

"I suppose you two had some big fights over the years," he said with an almost chuckle.

"Not really," I said. "I mean, sometimes, but nothing big." Despite what everyone said, I knew there had to be a reasonable explanation for the accident. Something with the car that had been overlooked. I would never have done this on purpose. Yes, we fought sometimes, and sure she could annoy me, but never like what he was hinting at.

"What about recently?"

I sighed. "I don't remember."

He nodded. "Oh, right, of course." He paged through his file again. "Retrograde amnesia." He said it lightly, like it was a joke.

My headache was coming back. A pounding drum right behind my eyes. It felt as if my eyelids must have been pulsing out from the pain. "Yes."

"How would you respond if I told you that a few of the people on the trip said you two had been fighting?"

A prickle of unease made the hair on the back of my neck stand up. It would be easier to answer his question if I could remember anyone on the trip. I'd seen their names, but they meant nothing to me. Just a list of strangers. I'd met them back in February for an hour, but I hadn't bothered to connect with them then. I figured I'd get to know them on the trip. If I'd known it was important, I would have figured out who I could trust.

"I don't know why they would say that. Simone and I were fine. Maybe one of us had been cranky about something one day and someone made it into a big deal. I know there are a lot of reporters on this story. Some of the people on the program might have said something so they could feel important."

Evan was staring at me like he wanted to pin me in place with his gaze. "Sounded a bit more than cranky. We have a witness who says you slapped Simone. Hard. She reports that she saw the whole thing and a red mark across Simone's face."

He had to be lying. Or the witness was. I would never hit Simone. I had never hit anyone. I closed my eyes and tried to picture it. The meaty wet sound of a slap echoed in my head, and I felt the flesh in the palm of my hand sting. *No!* My eyes flew open. I squeezed my hands between my knees. I had to keep my imagination from running away.

"Maybe she was flirting with someone you liked? Kissed this guy you had a thing for?" Evan Stanley asked, fishing around. "This Nico fellow."

"No," I said, my voice firm.

"I thought you said you couldn't remember."

"I don't," I said, "but I know Simone. She wouldn't kiss someone I liked. I wouldn't do that to her." I couldn't even remember if there was someone Simone was dating.

"I'm sorry, can you tell me how this is helping?" Mom interrupted. "Jill and Simone have been friends for years. If, and that's *if*, Jill and Simone had a fight, it wasn't a big deal. They're teen girls. Do you have a daughter this age?"

"No," Evan Stanley replied.

"Well, I can tell you they have a flair for the dramatic. They have a fight and then it blows over. It doesn't mean anything. They're enemies one minute and friends forever the next."

"Sorry, but it didn't sound like this was some simple argument. We have multiple sources saying there was something between the girls," Evan said.

"Simone's my best friend," I said. I wasn't sure if I was trying to convince him or myself. "Even if we had a fight over something, it never would have ended like this." I stabbed the picture in the middle of the table with my finger. On this I was confident. Maybe we'd had a fight and I'd been crying. Maybe the car had slipped off the road—but it wasn't intentional. I knew it.

"I brought pictures," my mom said. She reached into her Fendi bag and pulled out an envelope. "I thought they might help Jill jog her memory."

I picked up the envelope and spilled the glossy photos out onto the table. It was surreal. I was in many of them. Posing in front of some ancient pillar, an arm wrapped around Simone. Me at the Roman Forum with my arms spread wide. There was a shot of a group of students squashed around a small table, a glass of wine in front of each of us. Pictures of thin-crust, black-blister-edged pizza and piles of pasta with a range of sauces. A few shots of various streets and old buildings, market stalls piled high with vegetables, fish, or wheels of cheese. None of it seemed connected to me. It was like a slide show of someone else's vacation. I pulled one of the pictures toward me. A guy stared out from the photo, his eyes a glacial blue-green. His lips were thick and full, like he'd had some kind of mouth enhancement.

"Nico," I said.

The adults around the table all exchanged glances. "Honey, do you remember him?" She turned to Dr. Weeks. "That would be good, right, if she was remembering?"

"No. I don't remember him at all. I read about him online. They had pictures." I looked down at the picture, willing myself to recall something, but my mind was blank.

111

Mom leaned back, disappointed.

"Is there some way we can go after this fellow? What kind of deviant is chasing after high school girls?" my dad asked.

Evan shrugged. "He's only a few years older than your daughter. The age of consent in Italy is fourteen. It goes up to sixteen if the other person is in a position of influence like a teacher, but Jill was eighteen when all of this happened. There's no cause on that end. We might be able to go after the program; it's based in the U.S. Should they have practiced greater care in choosing the mentors, that kind of thing." Evan's hand waved in the air. He clearly saw that as a waste of time.

"What about hypnosis as a way to bring back memories?" Dad suggested.

"I think we need to be very cautious," Dr. Weeks said. "Jill's very vulnerable at this point to false memories. She could easily hear a suggestion and incorporate it, thinking it's a real memory. Something like hypnosis would be irresponsible, given her condition. I know everyone would like an easier solution, but in my experience, there aren't any shortcuts. The best course for Jill is to continue to participate in rehabilitation. Her memories may return."

"But they might not," Evan said dryly.

Dr. Weeks took a calming breath. "They might not."

"Which means we're left standing around with our bare asses in the wind, waiting for someone to take a shot at us. We respond and have no idea how that answer might get knocked out from under us," Evan said. He leaned forward over the table so he was in my face. I could smell a hint of peppermint on his breath and, beneath that, garlic. "If you remember, you

112

need to tell me. I know this might be scary, or maybe you don't know how things got so far out of control, but you must be one hundred percent honest with me. I can't help you if you're not. I will back you all the way—that's my job—but I need to know what we're doing. This isn't the time to play games."

Did he actually think this was a game to me? I was angry, but instead of letting out a cutting comment or icy cool detachment, I started silently crying, the tears tracking down my face. He sighed and leaned back.

"If she says she doesn't remember, she doesn't remember," my mom insisted.

"Now isn't the time to coddle her," my dad said.

"It's also not a time to harass her," Mom fired back.

"Look, I'm not trying to upset Jill, or anyone else," Evan said. "I'm trying to impress upon everyone how serious this is. The Italian government is applying a lot of pressure for Jill to return to Italy to answer questions."

"They can't force her to come back," my mom said.

"Yes they can. They can have her extradited. The U.S. government isn't going to stop them. The Italians aren't looking at this as an accident. They're looking to file murder charges."

The word *murder* seemed to bounce around the small room, striking each of us, leaving the space smeared and foul. I wanted to crawl under the table to escape.

"The Italians want answers," Evan continued. "If you think you're seeing a lot about this case here, you can multiply it times ten to get what's in their papers. It's got everything a story needs to have legs—two girls, one with money one without, friendship turned dark, sex, and a chance for a bunch of Europeans to hate Americans who seem to get away with everything. The police over there have had lots of problems with charges of incompetence, so now that they've gone out on a limb, implying they think something happened, their pride isn't going to let them back down easy. They aren't going to want to admit they might have made a mistake. The Italians will drag her back if they go forward with charges, and I'm not going to be able to stop that. No lawyer can."

"How can they make her return? She's a high school student," my mom said. "She's a *child*."

Evan shut the file in front of him "She's eighteen. That makes her an adult."

I forced myself to take deep breaths. It was one thing for a bunch of blogs and reporters to imply I'd done something, but did the police actually think I was guilty? I couldn't go to jail. I was going to Yale, for crying out loud. How could anyone think I was guilty of murder? Panic was building in my stomach, like a water balloon expanding out of control. I stared at Evan, trying to figure out if he was serious or simply hoping to scare me into having some kind of memory. Maybe he wanted to paint an ugly picture so, when everything turned out fine, he'd look like a hero.

"Surely, things aren't that dire," my mom said.

"What did I tell you?" my dad said to Evan. "Head in the sand."

Mom looked like she wanted to peel the skin off my dad's face.

Evan raised his hands in surrender. "I'm not saying they're going to be successful in going forward with charges, but it's important to understand what we're facing. This girl is dead. There was nothing wrong with the car, and a witness says it looked purposeful. We've got kids on the trip saying the two girls weren't getting along and people who saw the disagreements come to some kind of violence, even if that was just a slap. There's some Italian Romeo who admits he was messing around with your daughter and reports that the girls had at least one screaming match about him. Now, on the positive side, you've got me." Evan smiled. It looked to me like he bleached his teeth. They were reflective in the fluorescent light of the conference room.

"Well, I guess we can rest easy now," my mom said dryly.

"You can at least rest a little easier. The Italian police have a very circumstantial case. What we want to do is avoid being blindsided by some piece of evidence that we didn't see coming. If there's something that's going to look bad, like this report of Jill slapping Simone, we want to get out in front of it. Then we can put the right spin on it. Keep it from looking worse than it is."

"What else do you recommend?" my dad asked.

"We need to dig up some dirt on our own, muddy the waters a bit. Imply that Simone isn't the angel that the media is painting her to be. She slept around, she drank, she was envious of Jill and her advantages. Jill had no reason to hurt Simone—she had everything going for her. We want to imply the police screwed up the investigation, that kind of thing. It's not hard; you can count on any police department making at least a few stupid mistakes. It's not like the best and brightest always go into law enforcement. Then we add in the fact that no one really trusts foreign cops. We distract people and come up with some alternate theories. What we want are plausible options for people to believe."

A thought tickled my brain. "There is someone who hates me."

Everyone looked at me surprised, as if they'd forgotten I was even in the room.

"I had a blog year ago," I said.

Dad chuckled. "Ah, yes, the Feminist Manifesto from my favorite liberal."

I ground down a layer of enamel on my back teeth. "That's not what it was called. It was the *Feminist Caller.*"

"How could I have forgotten," Dad deadpanned.

"Keith," my mom said, her voice a warning.

I forced myself to not rise to his argument. My dad had never been a big fan of my views. He used to send me links to Rush Limbaugh's website to make me mad. "My point is that I shut down the blog because there was someone trolling me. He said a bunch of really nasty things," I said. "It was . . ." The word zapped out of my head. I hated how all of them stared at me waiting. It made the word even harder to push out.

"Hurtful?" Mom offered.

"Upsetting?" Evan chimed in.

"Personal," I spat out finally. "What he said was personal. It wasn't just that he disagreed. He didn't like me."

"Who was it?" Evan asked.

"I don't know. I never figured it out." Evan dropped his pen on the pad of paper, and I could tell he was losing interest. "Maybe we could look into it now—" I suggested.

"Not worth it," Evan said, cutting me off.

I was annoyed. "It might be. You said you were looking for a possible other th-th-th-theory." I forced myself to take a deep breath. My speech pathologist had warned me the aphasia would be worse when I was stressed or trying to push through it. She talked about having to talk with the current instead of swimming against it. After another deep breath, my chest loosened. "This was a guy who talked a lot about how much he hated me. Maybe he's out to get me now and making up all these . . ." Breathe. "Stories."

"With Evan charging us three hundred and fifty dollars an hour, I think if he says it's not worth the time, then we should be listening," Dad said.

Evan smiled at me. "I appreciate your idea, but we need viable options. I'm not saying that this troll was a nice guy, but it strains believability that he harassed you online, then, when you shut down your blog, stalked you for a year, followed you to Italy, and killed Simone while framing you. We'd be better off trying to blame aliens."

It sounded stupid when it came out of his mouth, and I was embarrassed that I'd brought it up at all.

Evan pinched the bridge of his nose as if he was trying to marshal his thoughts. "I know this isn't easy. I'm not trying to upset you."

I wanted to yell out *bullshit*. He didn't care if I was upset. I could tell whatever I wanted to say would stay trapped in my throat, so I kept my mouth shut.

"What do we do?" my mom asked.

Evan tapped his folder on the desk, organizing the papers. "We'll have Jill focus on her rehab. If the Italians push the idea

117

of having her return, we want to be able to point out that she's fully engaged here and that it would be against medical advice for her to leave." He looked across the table at Dr. Weeks. "That's fair, isn't it? I may need you to write up something if it comes to that." He didn't wait for her to respond. "In the meantime, I'll be working with another one of our firm's partners who has some solid international law experience. With your okay, I'd like to hire a lawyer in Italy."

"Is that necessary?" my mom asked.

"I'd feel better if we had someone on the ground there, someone who speaks the language and is going to be on top of the Italian system. This is no time for us to be on a learning curve."

"Are they going to send me to jail?" I asked.

"Not if I can do anything about it," Evan said with a confident smile.

I noticed that he didn't say it was impossible.

***

Anna balanced on the back two wheels of her chair. It always made me nervous when she did that. I could picture her leaning too far, tipping over, her head smacking hard onto the tile floor.

"So what are you going to do?" Anna asked.

I shrugged. "What can I do? I can't make myself remember. Dr. Weeks talked to me after the meeting and stressed that I needed to be careful I didn't set myself up with false memories. She said it's likely I wouldn't know a real memory from a fake, that if someone tells me a story, it would be super easy for my brain to convert it from something someone just told me to what I believe is the truth."

Anna's face screwed up. "That seems weird. How can someone convince you to believe something that's not true?"

I snuck my pinkie finger down into my cast and tried to scratch my leg. It itched all the time now. "She says it happens a lot, especially with brain injury, but also to anyone. She was really clear that I can't try to trick myself into remembering, that I have to let the memories"—I scrambled to think of the term she'd used—"organically return."

"Organic, huh?" Anna sniffed. "Like your brain is Whole Foods." She leaned forward. "I get what she's saying, but it seems to me you have to do something. Trust me, you don't want to go to jail."

"I know," I said. I could hear the tone in my voice turning snippy.

"I spent some time in juvie for shoplifting," Anna said. She smiled when she saw my expression. "Don't tell your dad. I'm pretty sure he already hates me."

"He's—" The word was gone, but I couldn't tell if it was due to my aphasia or because there was no word to describe my dad. Instead I just waved my hand around as if that explained everything.

"Anyway it sucked, and I'm guessing it would be like Disney compared to some Italian jail."

Talking to Anna wasn't making me feel any better. I knew she wanted to help me, but I also couldn't escape the feeling that she also found what was happening to me really exciting. Like she had her own in-room entertainment center. If I did

119

go to jail, she'd be able to sell her story for sure. When I closed my eyes, I pictured a dank dark room with bars on the windows and hard-eyed women looking to mess me up. My only experience with jail was a show on Netflix, and I was willing to bet my cellmates wouldn't have such a great senses of humor.

"Tell me more about this troll," Anna said.

I flopped down on my bed. "It's stupid. My lawyer all but called me paranoid or delusional, maybe both."

"But this troll guy hated you, right?" Anna nudged my foot. "In my experience, if someone hates you, there's no telling what they might do."

I sighed. "I don't even know if the guy knew me at all. For all I know, he just spends all his time on the Internet trying to get a rise out of people. It felt personal at the time, but now I'm not sure." I remembered when the guy was leaving all the nasty comments for me online, it felt like the worst thing that could ever happen to me. I wished I could go back in time and tell that me to grow a pair and stand up to him. Online harassment sucked, but not nearly as bad as my life now.

Anna rolled over to her side of the room and grabbed a notebook and pen. "Just because your lawyer blows you off doesn't mean it isn't worth checking out."

"It's probably a big waste of time," I said.

She raised one eyebrow, the stud in her nose winking in the sunlight from the window. "You've got some other big project you're working on?" When my shoulders slumped in resignation, she clicked her ballpoint pen and opened it to a blank page. "Okay, so what did the guy bug you about?"

"All sorts of stuff. He'd go on and on about rich bitches who should keep their mouths shut and their legs open. How *feminist* is just another word for 'fat and ugly.' It wasn't like he was a great orator or anything, he just had this way of getting under my skin. He would make fun of anything that I wrote about, the stuff that was important to me." I looked over at her. "At first I started the blog because I wanted to have something to put on my college applications, but the more I learned about that stuff, the more it mattered to me. I know it was stupid to think I was going to change the world just by writing about it, but I really wanted to."

"I don't think caring about something is stupid."

It felt like I'd tried to swallow rocks, and I had to stare up at the ceiling to give myself a chance to get control before I started crying.

"Do you remember his screen name?" Anna asked.

How would I ever forget? I used to feel nauseous every time I saw it pop up on my screen. He was my own personal bogeyman. "VoxDude."

"Do you still have anything from when you had the site? Anything you saved?"

I glanced over. She was scribbling notes on the page, her hair falling forward hiding her face. "Why?"

"I know a guy who's good with computers. He might be able to trace the messages somehow."

I sat up. "Really?"

Anna snorted. "No, I'm making it up. I just like to mess around with the head-injured. Yes, really. He may not be able to find anything, but he might. Even if we can figure out if the troll wrote to you from your school computer, that would tell you it's likely someone you know, versus if the messages came from Brazil."

A flutter of fear ran through my chest. *What if it was someone I knew?* I pushed down the thought. "I can get you some stuff," I said. I'd kept a lot of it because, since I'd mentioned it on my college apps, I wanted to have proof it existed if they ever asked, and also because I'd been proud of some of the writing. I glanced over at Anna again. Would she sell the contents of the blog? I knew my dad thought she couldn't be trusted, and with the amount of attention my case was getting, I couldn't fool myself. Someone would offer her money.

Anna clicked the stud buried in her tongue on her front teeth as she made notes. We couldn't have been more different. Near as I could tell, we had nothing in common, and at the same time, in my gut I trusted her. I wanted to believe she was on my side. I needed to believe it. I wasn't going to survive if I second-guessed everything and everyone around me.

I said a quick prayer that I wouldn't regret this decision.

Chapter Thirteen

***Let's Travel!* Guidebook**

Venice: Don't miss out on the city nightlife. Be sure to visit the small cafés for *cicchetti*, meaning "small bites," or appetizer-size nibbles. Our favorite is Cantina Do Mori, continuously in business since 1462. That's right—this place was a wine bar before Columbus even dreamed of finding America.

***

***Justice for Simone* Blog**

We are Anonymous, but:
We will not hide from the truth.
We will not allow justice to be bought and sold.
We will not be silent.

Reader Post: Kate Murphy
I don't care what people are saying about how Simone and Jill were supposedly best friends. Maybe they were at one time, but I know they weren't getting along on this trip. First

it was small things, like Simone wanted to go get a coffee and Jill wanted to spend more time in an art gallery. Once I heard Simone making fun of Jill for always having her head in a book and Jill stormed off, but it was just usual stuff. But our last night in Venice I saw Jill hit Simone. I swear to God.

I ran into Simone in the hall around midnight. She'd gone to get a bottle of water from the lobby. She told me she was super worried. Jill had snuck out to have some hot date with our tour guide Nico and hadn't come back yet. She didn't know if she should tell Ms. Ochoa or what. She didn't want her to get in trouble, but what if something was really wrong? Simone said Jill was totally focused on this guy and she was really upset because they were supposed to be on this trip together—sorta like a big blowout before graduation and everything. I could tell that she was upset that her best friend was basically ignoring her and only interested in this guy. I've been there. My best friend my freshman year blew me off as soon as she got a boyfriend. She only had time for me when he was busy. It sucks to be dumped like that—especially by someone who is supposed to be your friend. I told Simone I knew where she was coming from.

We went back to Simone and Jill's room to decide what to do and that's when Jill came climbing through the bathroom window and began telling us all about her romantic dinner. It was like she totally didn't get why Simone was upset. She was more interested in giving us the blow by blow of her big date, how Nico took her to this tiny café that was right on one of the canals and how people around them were staring because everyone could tell how much in love they were.

She made it sound like a romance novel—how one of the gondoliers sang to them as he drifted by. Nico ordered the whole meal and did cheesy shit like asking her to close her eyes and then sliding an olive into her mouth. Like some kind of *50 Shades* crap.

So Jill finally realizes that Simone is upset and then totally makes it Simone's fault! Jill kept talking about how she used to cover for Simone sneaking out when they were back home and how the only reason Simone was mad now was because Nico liked *her.* I could tell that really hurt Simone's feelings. Simone told Jill that it was rude to make her stay up late worrying, but Jill just laughed her off, saying she was jealous. Then Simone said there was no reason to be jealous of a cheap vacation fuck and then Jill lost it. You should have seen her—she looked totally crazed. She just hauled off and hit Simone. Really hard. Then she ran down into the lobby. It took me forever to calm Simone down. I mean, maybe Simone shouldn't have said that, but that was no reason for Jill to hit her. When I told the cops about it they were REALLY interested. They say they might need me to testify if it goes to court.

Comments:

Pixydust9: Sounds like they were both bitches.

Kgrenolds: I hate when girls forget how important friendships really are!

Lindy989: You are so full of shit. The last night in Venice you were in my room all night. Simone told us both about the fight in the morning. You didn't see squat. You're only writing this up because you want to be on TV like Brad. Get a life. The cops never asked you anything.

* * *

To: hcharron@winstonubc.com
From: jillycharron@gmail.com
Subject: Venice is AMAZING
19 April 20:48

Hey Mom!

Yes, I got your zillion other messages, but there's almost no time to write. We took the train from Rome to Venice two days ago, and now I can't decide if this is my fav city or Rome. Walking around here feels like you've stepped back in time, there are all these alleys and skinny walkways. It is super easy to get lost, but don't worry—it's an island. I can't go too far! Ha!

There's this weird mix of super-tacky stuff (you have never seen so much tourist crap in your whole life) and then this amazing stunning art. I thought about buying you this glass vase (they make it here—look it up—it's famous) but I worry that it will get broken on the way home. I did buy Grandma a lace table runner thingy that I know she will like.

Simone and I are getting along great. I know I was worried she wouldn't want to do some of the stuff I wanted to, but

126

it hasn't been a problem at all. I just know when we are old ladies together we'll still talk about this trip.

Love you

Jill

***

Taken from Italian Police Files

Incomplete note to Simone found in Jill's school notebook. It was torn in two and stuffed in the back. It is not clear if Simone ever saw the contents of this message.

Si—

Every time I talk to you it just ends up in a fight. I never should have slapped you last night, but you never should have said that stuff about Nico either. Don't you get that I really like him? I'm not stupid—it's not that I think he and I are going to run away together or something, but I really, really like him. Can't you be happy for me? You acted like you wanted us to get together, but once we did, it's like you can't stand it. I know Nico isn't likely a forever thing—but I thought you were.

We always talked about how someday after college we'd move to New York together and how we'd be in each other's weddings and work it out so we could have kids at the same time and they could grow up as besties too. And I get that, now that we're closer to graduation, it starts feeling like this is all just a stupid daydream or something, that we might not even live in the same place—but that freaks me out. I can't imagine my life without you in it.

I'm thinking we need

(*The rest of the page is blank.*)

***

Text log dated 20 April:

Simone to Jill: I h8 we r fighting.
Jill to Simone: Me 2. BFF?
Simone to Jill: Always babe

Chapter Fourteen

My eyes flew open, and I worried that I might have actually made a noise, screamed out even, but the room was quiet. I turned my head and saw the vague shape of Anna in her bed, buried under a pile of blankets, one arm thrown up over her head. I held my breath for a beat and could hear her quiet breathing in tandem with the rain that was falling.

The streetlamps outside buzzed, and their light oozed around the edges of the window and down the crack in the middle of the curtains like a crooked lightning bolt. I breathed in and out to a count of five as I did in my yoga class, trying to slow my racing heart. I tried to picture myself relaxed and loose on my blue mat, savasana, but it wasn't working.

I had smacked Simone. I remembered it now. The image of it had been enough to wake me up. I concentrated, trying to recall more, but it was like my brain was constipated. My hand streaking out in front of me, and the sharp smack of the slap against her face. The heat on my palm, and how she gasped. Simone reaching up to touch her cheek as if she couldn't believe it. The hurt in her eyes. Surprise. But something else. Triumph, like she'd *wanted* it to happen. I reached for my phone to record the memory, but then hesitated. Could my phone be used in court?

It wasn't worth the risk when I didn't even know if it was true or if I was just imagining what I saw. I hated that I couldn't even trust my own head not to fuck with me. I wasn't sure what it meant if I had hit her. There was a big leap from slapping someone to driving the both of us off a cliff.

A car went by outside, the tires making a whispering sound on the wet roads. I rolled over onto my side and pulled my knees up to my chin. My cast scratched on the sheets. It felt as if my heart was tearing in half. I'd never pictured it possible that I could hurt Simone. And if I had been able to block that memory—it made me wonder what else I was forgetting.

***

I wasn't sure what I'd expected. I hadn't thought that Dr. Weeks would gasp in horror, her eyes wide, but I hadn't expected her to yawn either. Like I was keeping her awake.

"Sorry about that," she said. "I started watching this BBC show on Netflix, and next thing you know, I'd binge-watched the whole series. I find that David Tennant so dreamy." Dr. Weeks made a face like she was biting into something super tasty.

I blinked. Maybe she hadn't heard me. "I was telling you how I remembered hitting Simone," I repeated.

She raised a finger. "Careful. What you had was an image of hitting Simone."

"Isn't that the same thing?"

She shook her head. "Nope. We've talked about this. It could be a memory. It could also be your mind conjuring up a picture to go with what your lawyer told you. Right now your brain knows there is missing information, and it's desperately trying to fill in those blanks." She opened a desk drawer and fished out a paper. "Ever see something like this?"

I looked down. At first the words looked like gibberish, and then they clicked into place.

I cnduo't bvleiee taht I culod aulaclty uesdtannrd waht I was rdnaieg. Aocdcrnig to rseecrah at Cmabrigde Uinervtisy, it dseno't mttaer in waht oderr the lterets in a wrod are, the olny irpoamtnt tihng is taht the frsit and lsat ltteer be in the rhgit pclae. The rset can be a taotl mses and you can sitll raed it whoutit a pboerlm.

I passed the sheet back to her. "I've seen something like it online."

"Amazing, isn't it?" Dr. Weeks knocked on top of the model of the brain she kept on her credenza. "The darn things still fascinate me as much as they did when I started in this field. How they can fill in what's missing—find patterns and create meaning where there was nothing. One of the most primal survival instincts the brain has is finding pattern and assigning meaning. When there is a breakdown, it will scramble to find those patterns again as quickly as possible."

I wished I could share her excitement, but it was my brain that was misfiring. "How do I know what is true versus my imagination?"

"Part of it comes down to knowing yourself. Does this piece of the puzzle fit with everything else you know about how you act, or react, to situations?"

I stared down at my hands in my lap. A crumpled piece of paper hit me in the head and I looked up, shocked.

"No pity party on my time," Dr. Weeks said with a smile. "Let's take it step by step. Had you ever hit Simone before?"

"What? No. I'd never hit anyone before."

"Even if you did, it doesn't have to mean anything. People get angry."

"But they're not accusing me of being angry," I pointed out. "They're accusing me of trying to kill the both of us, some weird murder-suicide thing." I swallowed hard. "Killing her." I repeated it again as if saying it over and over might make it seem more real.

"Were you two the kind of friends who had big fights? Screamed at each other? Vowed you'd never speak again?" She must have caught my expression. "It's not that unusual. Friends fight."

I was about to tell her that Simone and I didn't, but then paused. "Once we had a pretty big argument." She leaned back in her chair, inviting me to say more. "Freshman year. In junior high, it was always just the two of us, but when we transferred to the high school, Simone made the cheerleading squad and I didn't."

"Was that difficult for you?"

I rolled my eyes. It was stupid. I was never one of those people who even *wanted* to be a cheerleader. I could think of nothing more boring than standing around the sidelines acting like I cared about the score of a game I couldn't even be bothered to understand. I'd tried out just because Simone really wanted to and she was afraid to go on her own. We both knew I had almost no chance of getting on the squad. I could barely do a cartwheel without falling over, but still, when they'd posted the list of who made it and she was on it and I wasn't, it hurt.

I was happy for her. I squealed and hugged her. Simone bounced around the hall with the other girls who had made it, teen popcorn. And at first I didn't think it mattered that much, but then she spent more and more time with the other cheerleaders. It didn't help that they even dressed alike, as if they were some kind of dorky huge family of overly perky school-spirit sisters. The more time she spent with them, the more inside jokes, the more I could feel her pulling away from me. So I gave her the cold shoulder. What I wanted, what I expected, was that she would instantly come to my side, wanting to know what was wrong, but the truth was I didn't think she even noticed I was blowing her off.

That was when we had the fight.

It was in the classiest of places, the girls' bathroom. The biggest fight we'd ever had happened surrounded by sinks and tampon dispensers. I hadn't planned to confront her, but when she'd forgotten to meet me at lunch, choosing instead to hang with her new friends, I went to find her. We had it out, screaming at each other, but it didn't last long. It was like one of those freak flash storms. It took forever to build up, but once the storm broke, it was over fast. By the end we were hugging and crying, vowing we'd be best friends forever.

I told Dr. Weeks the whole story.

"It never came to blows," I assured her. "We didn't even push each other. We said a bunch of nasty stuff, but I didn't mean any of it."

133

"It's okay if you did." I shifted uncomfortably in the seat. Dr. Weeks leaned back. "We can still be good people, even if we don't say or do good things all of the time."

"So you think I am capable of something like this."

She smiled. "That's not what I said at all. What I'm trying to tell you is that I imagine your feelings for, and about, Simone are really confusing right now."

"I *know* she was my best friend."

"I don't doubt that. But you need to be careful that you don't recreate your relationship with her, editing out any of the negative parts because you're afraid to let yourself see the whole picture. Simone may have been a good person, but I doubt she was perfect."

I had the sense there were memories just outside of my line of vision, dancing around the boundary of what I could see. It scared me. I wasn't sure I wanted to see everything.

"Let's back up from Simone for a minute," Dr. Weeks said. "How do you deal with anger in general?"

I shrugged. "I dunno. I don't get mad that often."

"Does being angry make you uncomfortable?"

Her question made me uncomfortable. "I just don't get upset that easy."

Dr. Weeks nodded, but didn't say anything for a beat. I shifted in my chair. I wished I could get up and pace.

"It's not like every teen has anger issues," I said.

Dr. Weeks smiled. "I didn't ask you if you had anger issues; I asked you how you dealt with *getting* angry. It's one of the big emotions in life. Love, fear, hope, desire, sadness, happiness, anger." Her hand waved in the air to indicate there were even more. "It's normal for people to get angry. Maybe someone hurts us or disappoints us, and our response is to be upset. Now, there are people who take it too far. And in those cases, often what's happening is that they're confusing fear with anger. They don't want to let themselves be scared, so they lash out."

"That's why this whole situation seems so weird. I don't lash out. Yeah, sure Simone and I have times when we are ticked at each other, but it's no big deal. Stupid stuff, like that she wore my cashmere sweater in art class and got paint on it, or how she would back out of plans if something better came up and leave someone hanging. When Simone and I did have a fight or disagreement about something, I was almost always the one who did the making up, even if it wasn't my fault," I said. "I'm, like, the peacemaker."

Dr. Weeks smiled at me. "That can be a great trait, to stay calm when other people don't, but it can also be a way of avoiding emotions that make us uncomfortable." She leaned forward, and her creaky office chair gave a groan. "Sometimes we don't let ourselves be angry because we're afraid we could lose those people if they knew we were upset."

"You think that's what I do?" I didn't know why I bothered with the question. As soon as she'd said the words, they rang around the room with a peal of truth. I always backed down. Always. "But, see, that's why I couldn't have done this. Doesn't that prove it?"

"The problem with bottling up anger is that because we aren't used to expressing it in a healthy way, it can come out in a way we don't want. Like self-harm, for example."

"Or by blowing up and hurting someone," I added.

There was a loud knock on the door, and it flew open. Dr. Weeks looked surprised. There was a sign on the door indicating that we weren't supposed to be interrupted.

Evan was standing there with my dad. Dr. Weeks stood. "Can I help you gentlemen?"

"Your mom called," Dad said. "She told me about the dream you had last night. I talked about it with Evan, and we thought we'd better come right over." The two of them shuffled for space in Dr. Weeks overstuffed office.

"I called her this morning to tell her I remembered hitting—"

Evan cut me off before I could say anything else. "You *don't* remember. You had a *dream.*" He smiled at Dr. Weeks. "I think it would be best if Jill's therapy stayed away from difficult topics."

Dr. Weeks's mouth twitched. "As I'm sure you can understand, the entire point of therapy is that nothing is off-limits for discussion, including difficult topics. I would like her to reflect more on her relationship with Simone so she can move forward."

Evan straightened his paisley tie. "As you can surely understand, anything, including your notes, could be subpoenaed in a trial."

The two of them stood on opposite sides of the room, like an Old West showdown. I could picture Dr. Weeks pulling the plastic model of the brain out of a holster at her hip. Evan would have to counter with his fountain pen.

"Maybe Jill shouldn't have any counseling until this whole thing is resolved," my dad suggested. "Focus on the physical stuff for now."

"She's been through a traumatic event," Dr. Weeks said. "It's important that she get emotional support as she processes what happened."

"I'm standing right here," I said, rolling forward so I was between them. "You guys don't need to—" The word was gone, and I clenched my fists, wanting to scream. I thought my aphasia was getting better, but at times it still popped up like a nasty jack-in-the-box, sucking back my words in giant gulps. My brain fished through my memory, trying to find a replacement term. "Speak about me like I'm not even here."

Dr. Weeks smiled at me. "You're right. What do you want, Jill?"

"I like the counseling," I said. "Coming here helps." There were all these thoughts swirling around in my head, and Dr. Weeks seemed like the only person who would be able to anchor them in place.

Dad rubbed his eyes. "Look, this isn't the time to put this to a vote. This isn't a democracy. We need to do what's best for Jill."

"Why do you assume I don't know what . . ." I bit down. The word was right there. "That I don't know what . . . what's best?"

"Fine, we'll play it your way," Evan said, holding up his hands in surrender. "But I want you to picture this. You're on the witness stand, and they're asking you about every little detail you shared in here. They're reading out loud how you remember hitting Simone. They'll show that slutty photo of you that's all over the Internet, some stupid quote you put on Facebook. They'll put people on the stand who remember you two fighting and repeat any nasty thing you ever said about her—even if it was a joke at the time. That's how they build a case, block by block, until the jury believes everything that comes out of their mouth. They're putting enough together without you giving them a loaded gun."

"I didn't kill Simone," I insisted. My voice came out harsh. I held on to that fact, that certainty, as if I was trying to withstand a hurricane.

My dad looked away. "The truth doesn't matter," he said. "What matters is how the prosecution spins the facts."

"The truth matters to Jill," Dr. Weeks said quietly.

Evan interrupted her again, telling her that he wasn't trying to shut down the truth, but simply ensure that things wouldn't get twisted.

I kept looking at my dad. I could feel all the blood in my head abandoning ship and sinking down to my feet. He thought I might have done it. He believed I killed Simone, or at the very least that it was possible. I swallowed hard. I should have been happy that my dad was still trying to keep me safe, but maybe he was only doing that because he didn't want to be dragged through the mud with me.

"What does Mom think?" I asked.

Evan crouched down so he was even with my wheelchair. "Your mom agrees that it's important we circle the wagons right now. Make sure we don't make things easier for the prosecutors." He patted my arm like I was some addled old woman in a nursing home who was raving about something that happened years ago. He stood. "Perhaps there's an easy compromise. What if Jill continues with counseling, but we don't discuss Simone?" Evan smiled as if he'd figured out a particularly difficult calculus problem.

I had to swallow a rush of bile in my throat. My parents believed I killed Simone. They thought I was guilty.

There was a buzzing in my ears. I was willing to believe that Simone and I might have fought, and even that if things had been very bad, that I might have shoved her, or hit her. But driving off a cliff with her in the car? Never.

Except that the two people who should know me best in the world seemed to think it was possible.

Chapter Fifteen

Taken from Simone McIvory's Facebook Page

Date: 22 April

Status Update: Please tell me I'm not the girl who peaked in high school? That it's downhill from here? I'm going to be one of those people who works as a grocery clerk, wears fake nails, and talks about how I was prom queen back in the day like it actually matters. Graduation SUCKS!

Comments:

Robin Reynolds: This needs a dislike button!

Tara Ingells: So not true—Gurl you are awesome.

Simone McIvory: I know, I know. It just sometimes URGH. Call me a drama queen.

Jill Charron: Drama Queen.

Simone McIvory: Bitch. :)

Sandi Overbay: How can your life suck? U R in ITALY.

Simone McIvory: I know. I know.

Desi Hernandez: Apply to State we could both go—it will be one big party!

Simone McIvory: Ugh can you see me in college? Way too much work. If I'm lucky I'll do beauty school.

Desi Hernandez: Promise me you'll do my hair. I want you to touch my head. Get it? Head? Touch it baby.

Simone McIvory: Desi you are a total perv. Figures the only way you could get someone to touch your head is to pay them.

Pam Bowen: Burn!

***

Police Statement from Jenn Walsh, MA, Jefferson School Guidance Counselor

Transcript to be provided to Italian police

Just under eighty percent of our student body goes on to college, either community college or a four-year university.

This is a very high number, compared to other high schools our size. Having said that, one thing to understand is that going directly into higher education isn't the right choice for everyone. Some students need a period of time to decide what they want to do.

Everyone here was very excited when we heard that Jill got into Yale. She's not our first to get into an Ivy League, but certainly, with the cost of college these days, we see way more of our students going into state schools. Jill was always a student to watch, very well rounded. Excellent grades, participated in various extracurricular activities, impressive scores on standardized tests. She didn't have any kind of disciplinary record. Mind you, we don't have a lot of trouble here in terms of violence—things are worse across town at Lincoln—but I can assure you Jill was never a student who caused the administration concern. She was editor of the school paper and captain of the debate team. I was fairly sure she would end up going into law or public policy. She was very active in social justice issues; she ran a blog for a period of time. I can't remember the name, but she was always researching topics and really involved in activism. I remember she lobbied the school student council to change the company that had our vending machine contract because the current vendor had a discriminatory policy on gay partnerships. She won too, I think.

Simone was also a delight. She was one of those students who just lit up a classroom. I encouraged her to look at community college. She was capable of the coursework, and with her parents' income levels, she would have qualified for student loans. I believe she was reluctant to go because she didn't have a particular passion. Lots of students need more time to find their way. I also wouldn't want to imply that Simone was lazy, but it could be difficult to get her to put forward a full effort if something wasn't of interest to her. Now, if it was something she thought was important, then you better stay out of her way! I remember last year the student council put forward a motion to get rid of the idea of a prom court with a queen and king. There was concern it wasn't sensitive to the LGBT population. Well, Simone wasn't having that. She made herself into a one-woman warrior brigade to uphold school traditions. If you'd asked me, I would have said the student council was going to pass the motion, but that was before Simone got a burr up her fanny on the issue. Two weeks later, the council dropped the issue, and a month after that, Simone was wearing that crown. I had no doubt that she would have worn it this year for the senior court too.

I had full confidence that, once Simone found her focus, she would do really well. She talked about drama. She had the lead in this year's school play, but I didn't have the sense that she had that acting bug. Not enough to deal with the years of rejection that are required. Simone preferred things that came a bit easier—areas where she could shine.

I can tell you that I can't believe that Jill would have had anything to do with what happened to Simone. Those two were thick as thieves. I always saw them together in the hallways and at school events. I'm sure they had their moments—they're teen girls, after all—but I really can't imagine that it would have gone as far as . . . that. I'm certain something will come to light that will clear up this situation.

***

Statement to Brian Ferry, Reporter for the *Record Eagle*, from Gary McIvory, 10 May

It makes me sick to see all this stuff in the papers about how some people can't believe that Jill could do anything to hurt Simone. I want you to clear this up. What kind of proof do these people need? There are people who saw them fighting before all this happened. Jill was driving the car, a car the Italian police tell us was in good working order, and she drove it straight off a cliff, and as a result my baby girl is dead. Who else should we blame? Some imaginary friend? This isn't about revenge. This is about justice. "Do not take revenge, my friends, but leave room for God's wrath. For it is written—it is mine to avenge and I will repay, says the Lord." That's from Romans. My wife and I have no choice but to have faith in God that he will see us through this. But it would be a lot easier if everyone weren't worried about Jill. I don't give a damn about that girl.

I liked Jill okay before all of this. She was smart and always really polite when she was at our house, but almost too polite sometimes. I know people like that—they look fancy and like butter wouldn't melt in their mouth, but they can be trouble when no one is watching. I never really trusted her. I knew Simone liked Jill, so I tried to, but I think at some level I knew she was a bad seed. That she would get my girl into trouble.

Last year we found a bottle of vodka and a marijuana cigarette in Simone's closet. She admitted it belonged to Jill. She was one of those kids that you can just tell isn't happy with who she is. Those are the ones who end up drinking at parties—trying to swallow confidence, that's what it is. Simone didn't need liquid courage. My baby girl was a star.

***

Police Statement from Helen Charron, Jill's Mother

Transcript to be provided to Italian police

I cannot even imagine what the McIvorys are going through with the loss of a child. I feel horrible for them. I loved Simone too. The girl was in and out of my home every week since both girls were small. In some ways, I felt she was like another daughter to me. I'm crushed that she's gone, but that doesn't give her family a reason to lash out at Jill. I understand they want to find someone to blame, but sometimes awful things just happen.

They should understand that Jill didn't do anything, she couldn't. Jill doesn't have the capacity to hurt Simone. Heck, she practically worshipped her. If anything, that was a bigger worry for me, how Simone was always in charge. She was the one who sometimes—I guess you would call it peer pressure— pushed Jill into doing something. At times I sensed she was doing it just to see if she could get Jill to do what she wanted. If either of them were going to have a problem with anger, it would have been Simone, not Jill.

Chapter Sixteen

I could hear the murmuring sound of people talking inside the room, but I couldn't make out what they were saying. I rolled toward the door of the makeshift interrogation room and paused. All I wanted to do was turn around and wheel out of there as fast as possible, but I knew it wasn't an option. Eventually I was going to have to talk to them. Anna turned her chair so our wheels tapped together. The rehab version of a fist bump.

"I'll wait for you in our room," Anna said. "When it's over, come on up and we can talk."

"You didn't need to come down with me," I said. "I could have found it on my own. I hardly ever get lost anymore, thanks to you, Glinda." It was a feeble joke, but she smiled.

"I wanted to go to the café anyway." Anna shrugged like it was no big deal.

I swallowed hard, trying to convince myself that I was brave enough to do this. "'Kay, see you later," I said.

"Remember what I told you. They can kill you, but they can't eat ya." This was down-home advice that Anna's family always pulled out when things were tough. I guess it was supposed to make me feel better, but I wasn't sure I was made of the same stuff as her relatives. Anna rolled back a bit, but paused, waiting for me to go in. It felt nice, knowing she had my back.

I shouldn't have been this nervous. Evan had prepped me for this meeting for hours over the past couple of days. He'd even had a few of his co-workers come in and role-play with me so I could get a sense of how it might go, but I was still terrified. I'd never talked to cops before, unless you counted when I met with the school safety officer as the student council rep to look at how we might cut down on drinking at prom. When I came into the conference room, everyone stopped talking. My parents were sitting off to the side. My mom appeared ready to vomit. She had this strangled expression. Dad kept clenching his jaw as if he were considering throwing some punches.

The Italian detectives were exactly as I'd pictured them in my head—some casting office at a movie studio could have sent them over. They were both dressed in sleek, fitted suits that looked like they were designer labels, but only one of them had the looks to match. He was younger and had that Abercrombie & Fitch sultry guy thing going on. The other detective was older, closer to my parents' age, with short buzz-cut hair like he was in the military. He had a spray of angry looking red pimples across his forehead. I did my best not to stare at them. Making him feel self-conscious about his skin condition wasn't going to get us off on the right foot.

Evan stood and waved me in. There was a moment when it was clear my wheelchair wasn't going to fit into the tiny conference room with all the other chairs that were already around the table, and everyone got up, bustling around to make it work. I tried to look like I wasn't annoyed. It wasn't as if they hadn't all known I still used a chair. I wondered if the Italians had done it deliberately so I would be thrown off before we even started. I'd read enough murder mysteries to know it wasn't impossible.

I was finally pushed up to the table, and Evan slid over a glass of water. We'd rehearsed that I should pause and take a sip anytime I wasn't sure how to answer a question. That would be his cue to help me out. I hoped I wouldn't drink so much water that I'd have to ask for a bathroom break. I didn't want anyone to think a weak bladder was a sign of weak character in general.

The two Italian detectives stared across the table. The older guy looked angry, but the younger one was smiling. Good cop, bad cop. My life was turning into a *Law & Order* episode.

The younger cop looked around the room as if taking roll call, then held out his hand to me. "I am Detective Alban and this is my colleague, Detective Marco."

I shook Detective Alban's hand, but my hand simply hovered over the table in front of the older detective, Marco. He sat staring at me. I dropped my arm.

"Detective Marco's English is not as good as my own," Alban said. "I will talk mostly."

I thought about asking why Marco had flown all the way here to talk to me if he wasn't actually capable of speaking, but figured this would go against advice Evan had given me under the heading *Don't allow them to engage you in pointless conversation. Everything you say matters, so say as little as possible.* He'd told me it was fairly unusual that the Italian government paid for them to come over. He said normally they would request a local detective to take my statement. The fact they were here meant they were taking things seriously.

Detective Alban pulled out an iPhone and put it in the middle of the table. "I will make a recording if that is okay with all."

Evan pulled out his phone, a version newer, and placed it next to Alban's. "We'll make our own recording as well."

The two men looked at each other, and I had the sense this was the legal equivalent of "Who has the biggest dick?" After a pause, Alban gave a stiff nod in agreement. Round one to my lawyer.

Detective Alban listed the date and who was in the room for the recording. The skin on my neck prickled, and I suspected I was breaking out in blotchy hives. Detective Marco seemed to be staring at them, which made it worse. I wanted to explain that I did this anytime I was nervous. At state debate finals, I had to take antihistamines just to keep from exploding at the lectern.

"We have some questions about what happened on 28 April," Detective Alban said. "I understand you still do not remember these events?"

I nodded.

Detective Alban made a sad face. "I am so sorry. I need you to speak because of the recording." He motioned to the table where the two phones stared up at me.

My tongue felt too big for my mouth, and for a split second, I wasn't sure I'd be able to say anything, but I finally pushed it out. "I don't remember."

"No memories at all?" The detective's face was scrunched up as if he were deeply concerned for my health.

"We have provided you with a medical report from Ms. Charron's treatment team here. The impact of the brain injury on her memory is clearly documented," Evan said.

"Would it be possible for us to get her full medical records?"

Evan leaned back. "No. I'm sure you can understand that we're not going to just hand over her private medical history. You'll need to request that through the court if you want it."

"We may request that Ms. Charron see experts of our choosing for an independent medical exam."

Evan spread his hands. "That's your choice."

I wanted to interrupt and say I saw enough doctors, but I kept my mouth shut.

Detective Alban pulled a worn leather briefcase onto his lap. It had buckles and looked like it was from a World War II movie. I half expected him to pull out spy plans, but instead he slid a photograph across the table to me. It took me a while to figure out what it was supposed to show and then I realized it was a car, *the* car. I swallowed hard when I saw it. It was so dented and mangled, I didn't know how anyone had survived. I'd seen it online, but somehow in the giant glossy photo, it looked even worse.

"We had the auto inspected." Detective Alban paused, but when neither Evan nor I said anything, he continued. "We now have the full report. You may be interested to know there was nothing mechanically wrong with the car. No reason for it to go out of control. Can you explain this?"

I wanted to pump my fist in the air. This was one of the questions I'd practiced with Evan and his co-workers. I felt the confidence that comes with knowing the right answer.

"I'm not a mechanic, I can't say how the car was working or not," I said. "And I don't remember the accident." Evan had stressed to me not to offer alternative theories, no suggesting that maybe there had been a tiny kitten in the road or a blown tire.

"We've requested access to the car," Evan said. "For our own inspection."

Detective Marco sniffed. I sensed he wasn't that impressed with Evan.

"Of course," Detective Alban said. "We are also happy to give you a copy of the mechanic's report. You will see, there are no doubts the car was fine. Which means that Ms. Charron must have driven off the road on purpose."

I shook my head.

"I thought you said you do not remember this event," Detective Alban said.

"I don't," I said.

He spread his hands. "Then it is possible, no?"

"No. It's not possible. I would never—" The word was gone, and I felt a flash of panic. I'd been afraid my aphasia would pop up again. Both detectives leaned forward as if they couldn't wait to hear what I would say. "Hurt," I finally spat out. "I would never hurt Simone."

Detective Marco mumbled something in Italian to Alban. "What can you tell us about Niccolo?"

"I have no memory of my time in Italy," I said.

"But is this your first love?" Detective Alban said.

"I told you, I have no memory of Nico." I pushed away the flash of kissing someone. I shifted uneasily in my seat as if they could see the racy image in my head.

Detective Alban smiled. "But surely you remember if there have been other loves in your life, or have there been too many?"

I could hear my dad shift in his chair behind me. I sensed I wasn't the only one who picked up the message that I must be some kind of slut who couldn't keep track of all the people I'd been with.

"I don't have a boyfriend," I said.

"A pretty girl like you." Detective Alban's eyes sparkled.

"Is that a question, Detective?" Evan said.

Detective Alban fiddled with the papers in his file. He made sure I could see the copy of the photo of me from Halloween in there. Then I saw something else, a phone number next to Nico's name. My heart picked up speed. I used my finger to trace the numbers on my thigh over and over, a way to try to force them into my memory. This was not a time for one of the black holes to open up. Ten digits. I could remember that. I would make myself remember. "We have some screenshots from your Facebook page," the detective said, breaking my attention.

I nodded. I wasn't sure what he was going to show, but I kept repeating the number in my head over and over.

Detective Alban passed a sheet of paper over to me. He tapped it with his index finger. "Here you say—" He twisted the paper slightly so he could read it, "Revenge may be wicked, but it's natural."

"It's a quote from *Vanity Fair*," I said, recognizing it instantly. "I read the book in my English class."

He pursed his lips, "But why repeat it on your page? Is it, how you say, a motto?"

I felt a wave of frustration. "No, it's just a quote, something I thought sounded—cool."

"Revenge is cool," he said. His voice went up on the word *cool.*

I wanted to explain that *cool* hadn't even been the word I wanted; it was the one I could think of. I didn't say anything. It wasn't a question. If I'd known I'd be questioned on everything I ever said, I would have censored myself more. Not everything had a deep meaning.

Detective Alban pulled another sheet out. "This is from when you were in Italy." He laid it down on the table. *Love is like an arrow in the heart. To have it pulled out is to die.* "What is meant by this?"

"I don't know," I said. I didn't glance over at my parents. Evan had quizzed me for hours on every posting I had on my profile page and every comment I'd made on anyone else's status. I couldn't remember writing them. I'd thought Evan was being paranoid and that the police would never bring it up, but they had. "I don't remember Nico. It's possible I liked him, but I doubt it was that serious. I wouldn't have known him that long."

Detective Alban nodded. "Do you sleep with people when it isn't that serious?"

"What the hell—" my dad said before my mom clutched his knee. His mouth snapped shut.

I flushed red hot. "I'm a—a—I haven't slept with anyone."

Detective Alban spread his hands. "I don't mean to offend. It is just that one of the girls on the program"—he looked into his file—"Abigail, said that you asked her for condoms."

I blinked rapidly. I slept with this guy? I'd never slept with anyone. My temperature shot up several degrees. Alban made it sound like I'd lied, but I hadn't known. And now, in front of my parents and a group of strangers, I'd found out I had lost my virginity.

"Okay, let's stop here," Evan said. "We agreed to this meeting because you said you had issues you wished to discuss. But this is nothing more than a fishing expedition. Do you think we don't know you're the ones leaking these pictures and quotes to the press?" He gestured to the file on the table. "You're trying to build some kind of story because you have no case."

"But we wish to understand the story," Detective Alban insisted.

Evan leaned forward so both of his palms were on the table. "There is no story. Here are the facts. These girls were friends. They were friends for years. Ms. Charron has no history of violence or mental health issues. There was a tragic accident in which Simone McIvory was killed and my client was seriously injured."

"How you explain this?" The older detective tossed an item in a plastic bag onto the table, and it made a clanking sound as it hit. My eyes took a moment to focus on it and then I realized it was a knife. I drew back, shocked. There was something all over it. Something I was pretty sure was dried blood. The older detective said something loud in Italian. I couldn't look away from the knife. My breath came low and shallow.

"What the hell is this?" Evan said.

"It was found in the car," Alban said.

Evan threw his hands up in the air. "So what? It was a rental car. I wouldn't be surprised at anything you found in one of those."

154

"So the reason it matters is the blood on it is Simone's." The detective laced his hands together on the table. "The autopsy shows she was stabbed."

The word hit me between the eyes, as if he'd suddenly spun around and whacked me with a hammer. Stabbed? Not possible. First they were saying I caused the car to crash on purpose, and now they were saying that I'd stabbed her?

"This is bullshit. That information wasn't shared with us," Evan said.

Detective Alban shrugged. Detective Marco leaned back with a smile. For a guy with major skin issues, he seemed pretty confident. I kept glancing back at the knife; my eyes were magnetically drawn to it. Even when I looked away, I felt my gaze being pulled back. It was a regular kitchen knife. Something you'd use on a steak, to cut up meat. The word *meat* kept repeating in my head. It made me lightheaded. There were too many things happening at once. Finding out I'd slept with Nico, that Simone had been stabbed. My chronic headache, which had been getting better, returned with a vengeance. I could feel the blood pounding in my skull.

"We are sharing the information with you now." Detective Alban nudged the knife so it slid closer to me. "We have found prints on the knife."

Evan looked like he wanted to spit nails. "I need to speak to my client's father," he said, standing. His chair screeched on the tile floor. He took my dad by the elbow and marched him to the door. He spun around. "Say nothing," he barked at me.

I started to nod, but that made my head worse. I wanted to rest on the table and close my eyes.

"Are the prints going to match yours?" Detective Alban asked.

"Don't talk to him, Jill," my mom said. She was twisting the strap to her purse like she was wringing out wet laundry. I wanted to tell her I knew I had a head injury, but I hadn't forgotten Evan's instructions from two seconds ago to shut my mouth.

Detective Marco said something to Alban in Italian, and they both chuckled. Alban pulled a small box from his bag and flipped it open on the table. It was an inkpad. He tapped a stiff card on the table and placed it carefully next to the pad. The paper was cream colored and was broken into five equal-size squares outlined with thin dotted blue lines. Alban pulled out a thick metal fountain pen and wrote my name across the top of the card.

I shot a glance at my mom, but she looked as scared as I felt. We sat in silence, each second seeming to grow larger until it consumed the one that came before. It felt like hours before my dad and Evan came back into the room. My dad's entire head and neck were purple. He looked like his blood pressure must be setting new records.

"They can compel us to give them your prints," Evan said.

Detective Alban clapped his hands together as if he were a cruise activity director trying to encourage us all to do some stupid game. "Lovely." He reached for my hand, but I snatched it away and buried it in my lap.

"You have to let them," Evan said. I could see his jaw grinding down. "However, it would have been the professional, the gentlemanly thing to have given us a heads-up that this was the plan."

Detective Alban forced his face into a fake sad expression that you saw on newscasters' faces when they spouted off about some tragedy before breaking into a huge smile to announce that tomorrow's weather included sunshine. "We have no intent to be upsetting. Perhaps we do not understand how you do things."

Evan's expression broadcast what he thought of this excuse. "Take her prints and then we're done here."

"We still have some more questions for Ms. Charron—"

Evan sniffed dismissively. "Too bad. We don't have to make her available for questioning. This was a courtesy meeting." His tongue ran over his lower lip. "I think we can agree we're done with niceties."

"All we're wanting is to clear up what happened. If Ms. Charron would not hurt her friend as she says, wouldn't she want this to be resolved?"

"I told you, I didn't hurt her. I wouldn't." My voice was too loud for the small room.

Evan reached over and touched my arm. His expression made my mouth click shut. "That ham-fisted kind of manipulation might work if she were here alone, but I'm not going to let you get away with it." He pointed at the inkpad. "Let's finish this."

I took a sip of the water, trying to stall. I didn't want them to take my prints. It felt too . . . criminal.

"You have to do this," Evan said softly to me. "It will be okay."

My hand shook. Everyone in the room seemed to be staring at it as I reached across the table. Detective Alban took it and separated my index finger, pressing it onto the pad, then rolling it from left to right on one of the squares of paper. The ink was almost sticky, and in the silent room, there was a sound like peeling adhesive as my finger moved across the paper. He repeated it with each finger before handing me a Wet Wipe and motioning for me to give him my other hand. The other detective whipped out a fresh card for the prints.

I didn't say anything, because if I did, I would start crying. I couldn't believe this was happening. When they were done, the cards were tucked back into the briefcase. Detective Alban made a big show of collecting his things, tapping the papers on the tabletop to make them straight and square before putting them back in the file.

"We'll let you know the results as soon as we have them."

Evan nodded curtly.

"We'll be staying in town a bit longer." Detective Alban turned to my parents. "I also have a daughter. I know this must be difficult. Perhaps you should think other than Mr. Stanley. Have your daughter talk to us. We can clear this up."

"We'll take our lawyer's advice over some greasy foreigner's," my dad said.

Detective Alban looked pleased, as if he were flattered by the idea of being called greasy.

"You got what you came for," Evan said. "You can return to Italy."

Detective Marco leaned forward. "We come for justice for the girl. We no have that."

***

158

I'd told Anna I needed to be alone. I knew she wanted to know what had happened in the meeting, but I wasn't ready to talk about it. As soon as she was gone, I went into the bathroom and washed my hands over and over, trying to get the ink stains off my fingers. I couldn't get rid of all of it; there was still a faded gray tint on my skin. Great, now I was Lady Macbeth. *Out, damned spot.* I sat on my hands so I couldn't see them. I stared at the clock and tried to do the math for the time change, but I couldn't figure it out. Screw it.

I dialed the number I'd memorized. It rang forever before a sleepy voice picked up.

"Pronto."

"Nico?" I asked. He was silent. "Um, I'm trying to reach a Nico Landini, is this him?"

"Jill? Is this you?" Nico sounded awake now.

I nodded and realized he couldn't see me. "Yes," I whispered. His voice warm and thick, like poured honey. It seemed to echo in my chest, but I couldn't tell if I found it familiar or if I only wanted something to be.

"Are you still in the hospital, *bella*?"

"I'm in the rehab center. I was in a car accident," I whispered. Nico was silent for a beat. "Yes, I know."

"I met with the Italian police today. They say Simone was stabbed," I said. My fingers dug into the blanket as if I could pull each of the fibers apart.

"Are you all right?" Nico asked. "Should we be talking?"

"I have to ask you something. They're implying we slept together. Did we?" I held my breath. He was quiet, and I wished I could see his expression. I didn't want to ask if he was still there.

159

"You don't remember?"

"If I remembered, do you think I'd be asking?" I snapped.

"Yes, *bella*, we were lovers," Nico said softly.

Black dots appeared in the corner of my vision. What the detective had said was true. I'd lost my virginity and I hadn't even known.

"Oh," I said in a small voice.

Nico sighed. "Oh, *bella*. I had heard you did not remember, but I didn't know you had forgotten all. I wish I could see your lovely face. To hold you. To make this better."

I ignored this and barreled on. "I need you to fill me in on what happened. If we were together, if we had this big passionate affair, then you owe me that," I said. Maybe if he kept talking, it would shake something free. "I need you to tell me if I talked to you about Simone." The list of questions I had for him started to pile up in my throat. A traffic jam of words.

Nico's voice hardened. "I have had to speak to the police. They are wanting to know my role in all of this. I have had to get a lawyer. I must take care of myself. I think it is not good for either of us to speak."

I'd wanted to feel some rush of affection for this guy, but I felt nothing. He was a coward. He wouldn't even try to help me; he was too busy covering his own ass. "I *need* you to help me," I said. "They're trying to blame me for Simone's—" The word was gone. "For her dying. If you and I were together, I must have talked to you, maybe said something."

"I am sorry. I cannot help, *bella*." Nico paused.

"But if we were sleeping together, we must have cared for each other. You owe me that."

"I do care for you. But there's nothing I can do. I wish you the best."

I thought he was pausing, figuring out what to say next, but then I realized he'd already hung up. I tossed the phone onto the bed in disgust. I really could pick them.

I hoped I hadn't killed Simone over this guy, because he clearly wasn't worth it.

* * *

Dr. Weeks leaned back in her chair, putting her feet up on her desk. The socks that peeked from the bottom of her pants had tiny blue robots on them. "Are you more upset that you slept with this Nico or that you don't remember him?"

"Can I be equally upset over both things?"

She nodded. "Of course. But you do realize that while I'm not advocating premarital or teen sex, it's not exactly unheard of either. It sounds like you liked this young man; you asked for condoms, so you were practicing safe sex. I think you need to make sure you don't confuse being upset that you found this out in front of everyone with being upset that you did it at all. Even if it was your first time."

"My dad is disappointed in me." I picked at a loose thread on my jeans.

"I doubt that. Your dad was young once too."

"He told me he was disappointed in me. He said"—I paused, letting his words replay in my head for the one-millionth time since the meeting—"that he thought I was a better person than someone who slept with a man she'd just met."

Dr. Weeks sighed. "We all say things we don't mean. Parents, dads in particular, can be a bit sensitive where their daughter's sex lives are concerned. It's natural for him to be upset, just like it was natural for you to want to sleep with an attractive man you had strong feelings for."

"I can't believe I fell for him. He's a jerk."

"You won't be the first young woman who discovers that someone she dated failed to live up to her internal fantasy of who she wished that person to be." Dr. Weeks tossed me a Hershey's Kiss.

I peeled off the foil and considered what she'd said. If I had been able to imagine that Nico was a better person than he was, was it possible I was also doing that for myself? Maybe I only wanted to believe I was the kind of person who would never do something to Simone. Maybe I didn't want to believe what I might be capable of doing.

Chapter Seventeen

Siena: History and culture abound in this Tuscan gem of a city, founded by the Etruscans as early as 900 B.C. If you're there in the summer, consider taking in the Palio horse race, held twice a year in the Piazza del Campo. The race is a tradition that dates from the 1600s.

***

Police Statement from Ms. Ochoa, Program Director for Adventures Abroad

Transcript to be provided to Italian police

I didn't know for certain that Jill and Nico were romantically involved. I suspected it, but I wasn't sure. We were visiting the Siena Cathedral. Have you ever been? I like it almost better than the cathedral in Florence. Granted, it's no Brunelleschi's Dome, but it's still very impressive. The marble mosaics are worth the trip alone. I heard Simone describe it to another student as like being in a giant Sephora—and she was right. They have these black and white marble striped columns that seem to reach right up to the sky. Even the kids who were growing tired of all the churches still found this one impressive. I was talking about the artist Donatello—he did a bust of the Madonna and child just inside the Porta del Perdona, the Door of Forgiveness—when I realized that Nico and Jill weren't with the rest of the group. One of the girls mentioned they'd gone into the library to see the manuscripts, but there was something about the way she said it that made me want to check into it for myself. When you've been teaching as long as I have, you've got a sixth sense when things are a bit off.

I left the group to find Nico and Jill. The library is just about halfway down the nave. I wasn't trying to sneak up on the two of them, but when I entered the room, they sprang apart like a fuse had been lit under their butts. Nico was smooth, talking about how he'd wanted to show Jill the psalters—those are the illustrated choir and psalm books. I might have believed him, except for Jill's expression. That girl was a horrible liar. She was bright red and couldn't look me in the eye. She might as well have been holding a giant neon sign over her head declaring they'd been kissing. I told Jill to go out and join the rest of the group.

Once Jill was gone, I asked Nico directly what was going on between the two of them. He denied any inappropriate behavior. When I pushed him on it, he admitted that he knew Jill had a bit of a crush on him and that he enjoyed the attention, but that it was nothing more than some harmless flirtation. I thought that would be the end of it.

Justice for Simone Blog

Reader Forum: Feel free to post a question of your own for discussion.

JaneGerman: So were Nico and Jill sexually active or what? Because if she was in love that explains A LOT.

Comments:

Betty4just: Duh. Have you seen pictures of Jill? If she wasn't sleeping with everyone I'd be surprised. She dressed like a slut.

KyleJohnsson: I went to school with Jill. I never even knew her to date anybody.

Dreamgurl: Why are women always slut shamed? Who cares if she was sleeping with him or anyone else? Last time I checked it wasn't the 1950s.

AbigailJstar: I was on the trip and Jill ASKED me for a condom, so either she was sleeping with Nico or she was interested in teaching a class on sex ed. Ha! I don't really care if she slept with him or not, but I know it bugged Simone that she was always sneaking off to be with him. She hung out with us the night we were in Siena. We had the night off from the program, there was some optional concert thing at the music school, but I don't think that many people actually went. A bunch of us had dinner at some place that was built into the city wall like a million years ago or something. Simone told us that Jill and Nico weren't going out that night, they were going to have a private dinner in his room. You don't have to be a genius to figure out what that means.

**

Jill Charron's Facebook Page

Date: 22 April

"Maturity is a bitter disappointment for which no remedy exists, unless laughter could be said to remedy anything."
Kurt Vonnegut

**

Adventures Abroad Homework Assignment, Dated April 23

Jill Charron

Please write up to 300 words about one of the pieces of art in the Siena Duomo and its impact on you.

With the impressive frescos by the Renaissance painter Pinturicchio in the library, it is almost possible to overlook the statue called *The Three Graces*, but this would be a mistake.

It was my favorite piece in the whole church. The statue is a Roman copy of the Greek original. The Graces stand for charm, beauty, and creativity. It is three women who are holding hands and dancing in a circle.

I think I liked it best because it was so understated and it made me think about how rare it is to see those three things together. You might meet someone who is charming, or handsome, or smart and creative, but you rarely get all of it together. The problem is that we want to. Sometimes we want the missing grace to be there so badly that we almost imagine that it is—our brain creates it and refuses to let us see that it's not. Then something happens, and we realize that all we've fallen for is the idea of something, not the reality.

I think it is okay to be disappointed by things. It doesn't matter if things don't work out exactly as we want. The important thing is that we keep trying and keep shooting for that ideal. That's why this statue was my favorite. It is the perfect reminder that sometimes everything does work out just the way it is supposed to.

**

Excerpt from Police Interview with Niccolo Landini

Date: 11 May
Time: 10:00
Florence Police Department
Present: Niccolo Landini, Roberto Gallento (lawyer for Mr. Landini), Detective Alban

Original transcript in Italian, translated to English by Stoker and Mills Translation Services, New York, New York

I didn't know she was a virgin. Jill didn't say anything until . . . well, until it became clear. I told her that I appreciated she would give me such a beautiful gift. I felt . . . I guess, proud, that I was able to give her such a wonderful first time. I am not trying to brag, but to be honest, I have been told I am a giving lover.

***

Police Statement from Samantha Yu, Fellow Student in the Adventures Abroad Program

Transcript to be provided to Italian police

I don't think Jill ever really slept with Nico—it was just a story. When we were in Venice, I was telling her about my boyfriend and how we hadn't done, you know, it, and that I wanted to wait until I was at least a sophomore in college. She said that she hated feeling like she was the last American virgin on the planet and how she was hoping to "get it over with" by sleeping with Nico. Then later, everyone was talking about how she'd borrowed a condom from Abigail, and I mean, honestly, Abigail brought a whole jumbo Costco-sized box on the trip. She said her mom gave it to her—how gross is that? Anyway, Jill was really vague about what happened, but I asked her directly, and she said something that made me think that in the end she'd backed out and hadn't gone through with it. Something like the whole thing was such a let-down and wasn't even worth talking about. She was figuring out that he was actually sort of a knob.

If Nico is saying he slept with her, I bet it's just because he wants everyone to think he's some kind of Casanova. He wouldn't want it to get around that some high school girl actually shot him down. I think the rumor that they were sleeping together was just a lie.

Chapter Eighteen

I couldn't believe they'd bought cake. It was nothing fancy—a grocery store sheet cake, the kind where the frosting tastes like Crisco mixed with a pound of sugar—but it was the thought that counted. Someone had piped *Congrajulations* across the top. It seemed petty to point out the misspelling. I still felt absurdly touched.

"I'm afraid there's no ice cream," Dr. Weeks said. She scraped the *j* off the top with a sigh. She began cutting it up and placing the slices on paper plates.

Sam, my physical therapist, took two pieces. "Looking good on those crutches," he said.

I'd officially retired the wheelchair. I'd still be in the cast for several more weeks, but I'd graduated to a walking boot, and my arms no longer felt like they were going to rip free from my shoulders after using the crutches for longer than twenty minutes.

Dr. Weeks tapped her coffee cup with her fork. "Everyone have some? Okay, before we let this party get out of control, let's cover business. This is our last official team meeting for Jill. She'll be headed home next week."

There was a brief round of applause before they started to go around the room and make their reports. Each of my clinicians went through what I could expect in my outpatient program. My occupational therapist, Linda, gave me a long list of equipment she suggested I have when I got home. I could see my mom mentally ticking off the cost of everything. I looked at the items and figured we could skip at least half of it. I didn't need a raised toilet seat. I wasn't eighty. The group took a break for more coffee once everyone had spoken.

Mom squeezed my hand. "Be sure to thank each of them," she whispered in my ear. My mom was a walking talking copy of Miss Manners. The idea of someone not sending a written thank you note made her break out into a nervous sweat.

"I will," I said. I did appreciate what everyone had done, even Sam the torture artist. "It'll be good to get home and sleep in my own bed."

Mom shifted uncomfortably in her seat.

"You didn't sell my bed and replace it with a hospital one, did you?" I asked it half jokingly, but she had a look that broadcast bad news was coming.

"I've rented an apartment for us," she said.

My stomach sank. "Did you lose your job?" I knew she'd spent too much time with me at the hospital. What kind of dick was her boss to let her go when she had me—the brain-injured kid—to deal with?

She jolted slightly, startled. "What? No. It's nothing like that."

"Then why aren't we going home?"

Mom sighed. "There have been problems with the press."

I stared at her, trying to make sense of what she was saying.

"Your story is fairly big news. Lots of TV trucks and reporters wanting a story hanging around." Mom shrugged.

"They've caused some trouble, and the homeowner association complained."

"They can keep me from going home?" Like it wasn't enough power for the homeowner association to control what color we painted the house, the plants we were allowed in the yard, and the type of curtains in our windows—but it seemed now they could decide who to evict. "Can they do that?"

"There's a clause in the bylaws about causing a disturbance," Mom explained.

"But I'm not the one causing the trouble," I said. I knew it didn't make a difference. It wasn't a battle we were going to win; the association was willing to go to war over the shade of red people had for their tulips. Then I had an idea. "I could stay with Dad, just until things die down." My dad and his new family lived in a gated neighborhood. There was even a security guard. Granted, he was roughly 110 years old, but I was still willing to bet he could keep the media out of my hair. I wasn't keen on having to put up with my stepmonster and her two spawn, but at least it would have been better than staying in some rent-to-own apartment.

Mom's eyes slid away from mine. Then I knew. My dad, or more likely my stepmonster, didn't want me at his house. They must have already talked about that option. She saw the realization in my eyes. "He worries that the press attention could be bad for the kids," she said.

I snorted to indicate what I thought of that excuse. Wasn't I his kid too?

"They're younger than you," Mom said.

"Oh," I said. There was no point in arguing about it with my mom. It wasn't her fault.

"Now, don't look so glum. It will be fun." Mom squeezed my arm. "I got an apartment in that complex near the mall. We can pretend to be college roomies." She squeezed my arm. "Plus, there are no stairs to deal with, so it will be easier for you to get around. There's even a pool. Sam said swimming would be good for you."

Her voice was full of false cheer, so I made myself smile and nod as if the idea sounded like a riot to me. "How am I going to get to school if we're across town?"

Mom swallowed. "Well, that's some good news. Since there's just a couple of weeks left, your teachers are going to let you wrap up things as a homeschool student. Then you won't have to worry about exams, or getting around to classes on your crutches."

The school didn't want me there either. No one wanted me around. Being discharged didn't feel as exciting as it had an hour ago.

***

Anna looked over her shoulder and motioned for me to be quiet.

"You're the one who keeps laughing," I said in a whisper, and she snickered again. We were down in the treatment wing after hours. The overhead lights were off, but the emergency lights in the corners made the hall bright enough to see where we were going. "What are we doing here, anyway?" I asked.

173

Anna rolled to a stop and held up a key she'd pulled from a pocket. "Behold!"

"How did you get that?" I hissed.

She slid the key into the door for the OT gym, and the lock gave way. "Don't ask and then I won't have to tell," Anna said. "A girl has to have some secrets." She rolled inside, and I crutched after her, checking over my shoulder to make sure no one was watching us.

"What are we doing?" I asked.

Anna motioned to the switch. "Don't turn on the light, in case the security guard comes around," she said. She rolled to the far side of the room and parted the curtains so the light from outside came in. She pulled the pack from the back of her chair. She held up a finger to make sure she had my attention and took out two cans of Diet Coke and a bag of Chips Ahoy cookies.

"Can I get a drumroll?" she asked.

I made a sound with my mouth that I hoped would work as a drum sound, and with a flourish, Anna pulled out a bottle of Captain Morgan Spiced Rum. "How did you get booze?" I looked over my shoulder, half expecting to see someone bearing down on us.

Anna laughed. "You realize we're in here alone, right? You don't have to whisper." She rolled over to the stack of mats. There was a transfer bar above, so she swung herself out of her chair and patted the mat. "Join me. We're having a party. We're celebrating you getting sprung from here and the fact you were the best roommate I've ever had."

"I don't leave until next Wednesday," I pointed out.

"True, but tonight's Friday, and that means neither of us has to get up at seven tomorrow to be chased around by an OT or get stuck in group therapy listening to someone else whine about how much harder it is to be them," Anna said. "I am consumed with envy that you won't have to go to group anymore." She popped the two cans of Diet Coke and took a sip from each before filling the cans up with rum. Before the accident, it would have grossed me out to have someone drink from my can. I was totally past caring about germs from Anna. She'd seen me naked in the shower, with my leg cast in a giant plastic garbage bag to avoid getting it wet, while a nurse washed me down. She'd seen me cry after physiotherapy and listened to me snore. Swapping a bit of spit was nothing.

I joined her on the mat and dropped my crutches to the side. I took a long drink, and as soon as I finished, Anna topped it up with more rum.

"I'm going to miss you," I said. My friendship with her was completely different than what I'd had with Simone. That had been built on years spent together, endless sleepovers and shared experiences. Things between Anna and me were more intense. We'd seen each other at our worst, and instead of hating that anyone had seen me that way, it made me like her more. I wondered if this was what soldiers who survived combat felt like.

Anna tapped her can with mine. "I'm going to miss you too." She looked over at me. "I wasn't sure about you at first, but you're pretty tough for a pretty, rich girl."

I swallowed hard, suddenly certain I was about to start crying. "You're pretty tough too," I managed to squeeze out past the huge lump in my throat.

Anna rolled her eyes. "Don't go getting all overemotional on me. Besides, I'm supposed to be tough. You're the soft, squishy one with all the feelings." She dragged out the word *feelings* so it sounded almost dirty.

"We're totally going to keep in touch," I said.

Anna smiled, but didn't say anything.

I sensed that Anna didn't think we would. We were too different. All we had in common was rehab.

"I'm going to call if I ever figure out the whole troll thing," she said. "I'm still working on it."

I sighed. I'd half forgotten she'd offered to try to track it down. "Don't bother," I told her. "It doesn't matter."

She turned to face me. "You're not giving up, are you?"

I shrugged. "No, but as much as I wish there was someone to blame for all of this, there isn't. I've seen the pictures. My lawyer brought me the accident report. I was driving the car. What I don't know is why the accident happened, but I'm sure someone who used to bug me by calling me a feminazi didn't cause it."

We sat silently drinking. "It will all work out," Anna said after a beat. "They don't have any proof. The only reason the cops are still causing trouble is because it makes for a good story."

I hoped she was right. "I don't think I'll make it if I have to go to jail," I said softly. I hadn't admitted this to anyone else. My parents were too busy perfecting their state of denial, and Evan and I didn't exactly have the kind of relationship that encouraged sharing my innermost thoughts.

"It's not going to come to that," Anna insisted. "Worst-case scenario, you get some kind of minor charge and aren't allowed to go back to Italy."

I noticed Anna hadn't argued that I'd be fine if I ended up having to do time. I knew she was trying to make me feel better, but the idea that I might never be allowed to go to Italy hit me like a pang. What made it worse was that I couldn't even remember going the first time.

"I can't stand how long all of this takes," I said. "Evan said that it's possible this whole process could drag on for a couple of years."

Anna tipped back the can and drank. "Wheels of justice suck."

We sat in silence in the dim light. I could only imagine how much Evan was costing my parents. I hoped my dad wasn't making my mom split the cost evenly. She couldn't afford it. I'd tried to bring it up with her, but she'd changed the subject. Were they spending the money that had been earmarked for college? Was I going to have to give up on Yale and go to State instead? I felt sorry for myself having to give up my Ivy League dreams and then remembered there was a chance I'd be doing college online from an Italian jail. The light in the room changed as cars drove past, their headlights sliding across the walls.

"Is it weird if I don't want to leave?" I asked eventually. "I thought there would be nothing I wanted more than to get out of here, but now that it's actually happening, I'm not so sure. It's not like I even actually get to go home. Until the reporters find someone else to hound, we have to stay in this stupid rental." I rubbed my eyes. "I know I don't really have a reason to complain. I'm lucky we have anywhere to go, but I still can't act like I don't care."

Anna shrugged. "I don't want to leave in a few weeks either."

I looked up surprised. "Really?"

177

"Yeah." She poked me in the side. "Don't get me wrong, it's not the food, but I get it here, you know. I understand how things work. I know the hot water never really gets hot, and I know the tuna casserole is actually pretty good despite the fact that it looks like cat vomit. I know where things are, and I know exactly what's expected of me. Where I'm supposed to be and when. I know how people are going to react."

I nodded.

"I fit in," Anna said. "Nothing weird about a wheelchair in here. Hell, I'm functional compared to at least half the people on our ward, but out there, it's going to be different. There's going to be all this pity. I'm going to be the crippled kid." Anna chewed on her thumbnail. "I hate when people feel sorry for me. The thing is, no one here feels sorry for you. You're not special because there's been this horrible accident."

"People here don't think it's weird that I don't remember anything. I can tell everyone on the outside thinks I'm lying. Covering up. The kids at my school think I did it," I said. "I looked online. There are all these comments about how they always thought I was weird."

Anna laughed. "You are a bit odd."

I shoved her shoulder. "You know what I mean."

"They're only saying that stuff because they want to feel like they're in the know and that someone gives a shit about their opinion. Drama is like honey—it draws all the flies," Anna said, spouting off another Lopez family nugget of wisdom.

"They're twisting everything, though. One girl said I laughed during a presentation on the Holocaust. Simone had whispered something to me about this guy in our class, and that was what I was laughing about. I got in trouble for talking to my friend. It wasn't like I was yucking it up over the death camps or something." I shook my head. "Then the person who wrote the article referenced one of my old blogs where I supported the idea of a Palestinian state and decided that, along with my laughing during that lecture, it means I hate Jewish people. Which is absurd," I pointed out. "My friend Tara is Jewish, assuming she still is my friend, since I'm not allowed to talk to her."

Anna shrugged. "I don't even have a clue what a Palestinian state is, other than I'm pretty sure it's not part of the fifty we've got, but if it makes you feel better, I'm positive you don't hate anyone."

I flopped back on the mat. "It sucks."

Anna flopped next to me. "Yep. But you know what the people here would tell you."

"Everyone has some suck in their life," I said, quoting Sam.

Anna giggled. "Is it just me, or does it seem weird coming from him? He's the perkiest person I ever met."

I started laughing too. Sam telling you to toughen up was a bit like a toddler telling you to quit your fucking whining. I took another sip. "Tell me it's going to be okay."

Anna tapped my can again. "I've got no idea if it will be okay, but I know you're going to be okay."

Chapter Nineteen

Police Statement from Helen Charron, Jill's Mother

Transcript to be provided to Italian police

Jill called me to tell me her plans from a café in Florence, some place that was in the main square, I can't remember its name. She called to describe the hot chocolate—she said it's like liquid molten pudding. She and I are both chocoholics, so she couldn't wait to tell me all about it, but I think the truth was that she missed me and wanted to share what she was experiencing.

Jill and I are very close. We have the kind of mother-daughter relationship that I dreamed of having as soon as I heard I was having a daughter. Once her dad left, we became even closer—just us girls. I never spoke badly about her father in front of her, but she's a smart girl. It wasn't difficult to see that her father pretty much abandoned both of us. I tried to tell him that if he wanted to play house with someone almost half his age, that was one thing, but it didn't make it okay for him to walk away from his daughter too.

It was in that call that Jill mentioned that she was considering going to college overseas, but I never took it as a serious plan, more that she was simply in love with the entire experience of her trip. With Italy in general. Jill had gotten into Yale. She wasn't going to give up that opportunity to run away to Europe! She was caught up in the moment. Who doesn't think about what it would be like to move to wherever you are when you're on vacation?

Jill's always been a planner. Even as a little girl, she was always serious and mature for her age. If you don't believe me, you should talk to her teachers. They were so impressed with her schoolwork, but also how she behaved. The idea that she was going to throw away her future over some boy that she'd known for a few weeks is absurd. Yes, she liked the idea of living in Italy—who wouldn't? Jill was made for Europe; she's always been fascinated by art and history. She talked about how great it would be to go to school there and learn another language, but it was just talk. Jill's been looking forward to Yale for years. My dad, her grandfather, went there, and so did her dad. She has a sweatshirt with the bulldog mascot on it that she wore almost every day after she did a school visit a year ago. All the talk that she was moving to Italy to chase after this boy is ridiculous. If there is anything that Jill knows after seeing my marriage, it's that she needs to make sure she is always able to take care of herself. I dropped out of college to marry her father, and look at how well that worked out.

Jill is a very smart young woman. Yes, she was enjoying her trip and daydreaming about how she could stay, but that's all it was, a daydream.

***

Police Statement from Lydia Charron, Jill's Stepmother

Transcript to be provided to Italian police

I didn't speak to Jill about this half-baked plan to move to Italy, but she talked to her dad, and he and I discussed it. Jill called to tell him that she'd gotten the idea in her head that she wanted to go to college there. This after something like two weeks in the country. She didn't even speak Italian, for crying out loud. There's some international school in Perugia, especially set up for foreigners. She'd already looked up the application requirements, costs, you name it. She was raring to go.

Her dad was sick over the whole thing. He wasn't happy that she was thinking that, after all the planning and investment, she could change her mind on a whim. We didn't know about Nico, but we both suspected something had happened over there to get her so gung-ho. She's a quiet girl, never really dated, so I'm not surprised that when she finally did meet up with someone, she confused any kind of attention with love. The girl was desperate for a relationship.

Jill had no real plan on how she would pay for all of this. The tuition, apartment rental, language lessons, travel back and forth to the U.S. Jill seemed to think that it was her dad's responsibility to give her everything she wanted. She'd applied to a bunch of Ivy League schools, and she knew her mom wasn't going to pay for that, but she made it seem as if her dad owed her this.

Yes, of course she's his daughter, he should help pay for her college, but she was convinced that it had to be the best, most expensive school out there. Did she give any thought to the fact that her dad was already paying her mom child support and then still having to cover our mortgage, and that our two boys would need to go to college at some point too? No. It was all about Jill and what she wanted. She wanted Ivy League—fine, Keith agreed to pay for Yale, but Italy? That wasn't going to happen.

I don't mean to sound harsh. I know it was difficult for Jill when her father and I got together. Her mother poisoned her against me before we even met. I never stood a chance. Making it out like I was some kind of homewrecker. The truth is, if their marriage had been fine, then nothing would have happened between the two of us. They weren't divorced, but their marriage had been over for a long time by the time I was in the picture. Helen and Jill resent that Keith and I have built a life and family together. Jill is welcome to be a part of our family, but she's resisted, kicking and screaming, every time we've tried. I always hoped that she and I would eventually find a way where we could be, if not friends, at least friendly, but it's not up to me.

**

Justice for Simone Blog

Money really does buy freedom—Jill Charron's dad used his money and a family friend's private plane to whisk Jill out of the country immediately following the accident. The family's official story is that they *"wanted the best care that could be provided, and we felt such care was best offered in the United States, where Jill could also be surrounded by her family and friends.*" Yeah. Sure. It wasn't that they were worried that their baby girl was going to end up in jail.

Fact: Jill had been flown to the hospital in Florence, which is listed as a world-class health-care facility. We've contacted five neurologists, and all indicated that it is EXTREMELY unusual to transfer a patient immediately after such a serious accident, when she supposedly hadn't even regained consciousness yet. If they were so concerned about Jill's health, why move her, unless they had something to hide?

Fact: The Italian police were never allowed to interview Jill until after she returned to the U.S. and had a lawyer. If she had nothing to hide, why not talk to the police as soon as she was awake, the way they requested?

Fact: Jill Charron never went to Simone's funeral. Best friends for years, and yet she couldn't be bothered to go to the service for even an hour? We know for a fact that she was already out of surgery at this point and was about to be transferred to the rehab hospital. We checked; people at the rehab facility frequently attend outside events including weddings, birthday parties, family dinners, or even picnics. In fact, the front desk of the rehab hospital indicates that they ENCOURAGE people to connect—but not Jill. She'd like us to believe she was too sick to attend.

184

Fact: A little digging shows that Jill Charron's dad had sales last year that would have netted him commissions in just under the two-million-dollar range. Two million. Not bad for a year's work. Plus, public records show he owns an apartment complex and an office building in addition to his own home. Homes in his neighborhood start at $1.5 mil and go up from there. Way up. Jill's got access to all this cash. Her dad has already hired Evan Stanley from Murphy, Stanley, Biggens, one of the top law firms in Michigan. Check out the photos below of Jill's dad's palace as well as Simone's house—ask yourself where you would rather live!

Our sources tell us that the Italian government has made a formal request for Jill to return to answer some questions. Who wants to bet that she and her family find a way to put this off? Someone better grab her passport or, with her daddy's money, she's going to take a "vacation" someplace that doesn't have an extradition treaty.

Add your name to the petition below, where we request that police officials confiscate her passport. JUSTICE FOR SIMONE!

[21,678 supporters/128,322 needed to reach 150,000]

Chapter Twenty

"Thank you for meeting with us again," Detective Alban said. Detective Marco didn't even look up from the file in his lap.

I didn't bother responding. I hadn't been given a choice. Evan and my parents had shown up at the hospital last night to tell me the news. The U.S. government wasn't going to protect me. The Italians were going to make me return to face charges.

"We'll be filing an appeal," Evan said. He removed his jacket and rolled up his sleeves like he intended to have a street brawl right then and there over the issue.

Detective Alban shrugged as if to say we were free to do whatever we wanted. "We have agreed to wait on making the arrest until Wednesday to allow Ms. Charron to finish her program here."

My heart went into free fall. I couldn't believe this was actually happening. Evan had warned me that they would try to intimidate me, but he'd said I shouldn't worry. He insisted there were still a lot of things we could argue before I would have to go to Italy.

My gaze slid over to Evan. He was wearing a suit that likely cost as much as my first year in college was going to run my parents. The creases in his pants were so sharp you could have used them to shave cheese. He was the kind of lawyer designed to make his clients feel confident. What bad thing could happen if this guy was on your side? What made me nervous was that the two Italian detectives didn't look even the tiniest bit worried. If anything, they looked smug.

A thought crept across my consciousness like an oil stain. What if Evan wasn't really confident? He might have been telling me what I wanted to hear so that I wouldn't make a run for it. There was likely some kind of bail or fee. If I ran, my dad would be on the hook, and while Evan might say he was my lawyer, there was no doubt in my mind that his allegiance belonged first to my dad.

"We require your passport," Detective Alban said.

My mom pulled it out of her purse and passed it over. Evan had told us this would happen. He'd made it sound like this was standard procedure, but I'd seen the truth online. They thought I was a flight risk.

The blog had a picture of my dad's house, along with inside shots, including one of the posh garden and the lavish master bathroom that had been on the real estate site when my dad and Lydia bought the place. The high ceilings, fancy crown moldings, granite countertops, and six-burner Viking stove, not to mention the picture of the huge wine cellar, stood in sharp contrast next to the photo of Simone's house. Maybe it was the lighting in the picture, but it looked even more run-down than I remembered it.

They had another picture of me too. Someone must have taken it during rehearsals for the play. I was wearing my costume, and I had on bright red lipstick. The photo had caught me midlaugh so my mouth was open wide. It looked like I was cackling. I looked like "that person." The kind of person who talks during a movie, who cheats at Monopoly, who drops food on the pages of a library book and just turns it in, the person who uses the last of the toilet paper and lets the next person air dry. The kind of person you hate.

They'd used one of Simone's senior pictures. It had diffuse lighting, so she appeared vaguely angelic and soulful. She could have been the poster child for world peace.

"We're partnering with a legal firm in Florence," Evan said. He slid a paper across the desk. "This is their contact information."

Detective Alban passed it directly to Detective Marco without even looking at it. He wasn't impressed. "We are hoping to book flights for Thursday," he said.

My heart sped up. My mom put her hand on my shoulder as if she planned to hold me in place to keep them from taking me.

"I'm afraid that won't be possible," Evan said.

"If you wish to file an appeal, your team in Italy can do that," Detective Alban said. "The U.S. government has cleared Ms. Charron for extradition."

"No. What the courts said is that Ms. Charron is cleared once she has finished rehabilitation." Evan placed a letter in front of the detectives. "Ms. Charron's treatment team feels that she requires further support."

The only sign that the detective wasn't happy was a twitch above his eyebrow. Detective Marco burst into the conversation. "The doctors have released her. She is leaving the hospital on Wednesday." He slammed his hand on the table and we all jumped.

"No," Evan said strongly. "Her treatment team had *hoped* she'd be released this Wednesday, but they now feel she requires

188

further medical care." Evan gestured to the paper he'd already put down. "This is a letter from her physician, Dr. Weeks, outlining what care she will be receiving in the coming weeks."

I stared down at the table. I felt guilty that Dr. Weeks had had to lie for me, even though I'd never asked her to. Evan had done that. Of course he hadn't been that blunt. He more implied that if I were to stay hospitalized for a while, it would keep me out of jail while he argued the appeal against sending me to Italy. It hadn't exactly left a lot of options for her. I was supposed to do outpatient therapy, but they'd shifted it to inpatient.

"This is a delay tactic," Detective Alban said angrily.

I winced. I half expected him to stand, whirl me around, cuff me, and drag me out of there, but instead he and Evan were staring each other down across the table.

"We will take this to the court," Detective Marco said.

"Of course," Evan said.

"Give us a moment." Detective Alban leaned closer to Detective Marco, and the two of them began to talk in low, hushed voices. I didn't know why they bothered to whisper; none of us spoke enough Italian to know what they were saying.

"If there is nothing else—" Evan said, starting to stand.

Detective Alban motioned for him to wait. "We have a question for Ms. Charron."

Evan looked at me as if to make sure I was okay and then agreed with a short nod. "Go ahead."

"You remember this from our last meeting?" Detective Alban put the knife on the table.

Of course I remembered. I had a head injury, but I wasn't likely going to forget the accusation that I'd stabbed my best friend. I opened my mouth to agree, but I was suddenly sure the word wouldn't be there, so I nodded instead.

"And you say you've never seen it," Detective Alban said.

"Not that I remember." It looked like we were going to play the game where he asked question after question, as if he expected my memory to suddenly drop into place.

"Then can you explain why, in addition to Simone's blood, your DNA and fingerprints are on it?"

I heard my dad suck in a breath. I stared at the detective. I wanted to pause reality, rewind it and play it again, as if I might hear better the second time.

"What?" I whispered. It had to be a lie to trick me into admitting something. It wasn't possible. They were trying to frame me.

"Tell us why your fingerprints are on the knife that was used to kill Simone."

"You remember slaughter of your friend?" Detective Marco barked. "Surely you remember that?"

I swallowed hard against the wave of bile that was creeping up my throat. I stabbed Simone? The image of every slasher horror movie I'd ever seen flashed through my mind. The arch of a knife above someone, the sick wet meaty sound as it slammed into a body.

I pushed back. I had to get out of there. I had to get away from the knife, from all these staring, accusing eyes. For a split second, I forgot I was still in a cast, and I went to run out of the room. I took a half step and then collapsed on the floor. A bolt of white-hot pain shot down my leg, and I screamed. My mom and dad were at my side in an instant, trying to lift me back into the chair, but it was as if there were no bones in my

190

body. I slumped forward, crying. Not ladylike tears either, but deep sobbing gasps, with snot running down my face.

"Step outside," Evan yelled at the two detectives.

"What the hell are you trying to do?" my dad snapped at Detective Marco.

My parents helped me back into my chair. I still wanted to leave. I needed to get out. I flailed around to get back up. When my mom stepped in front of the chair, my arm whipped around and smacked her in the face. I heard her grunt in pain before she stumbled back.

"Someone get a doctor," Evan called out.

My dad was now the one holding me in place. I knew he was trying to keep me from hurting myself, but I couldn't stop struggling. It was as if I couldn't get a decent breath and they were smothering me. I was trying to scream, but the sound coming out of my mouth was this weird grunting.

An instant later, there was a nurse in the room who instantly took charge, calling out "Code White," into the hall. With me under control, Evan grabbed the elbow of Detective Marco and shoved him toward the door.

The knife was still on the table. Through the thick plastic bag I could see the dried blood on the blade. Black dots filled my vision, starting at the edges and rushing toward the middle. The last thing I saw was Detective Alban smiling as he walked past me.

**

My mom rubbed my back in small circles, the way she used to when I was little and sick. One of the nurses came in and placed a glass of water on the table for me. I overheard my mom whisper something to my dad, then the door shut, leaving us alone. I could tell he was freaked out by my reaction. Our family wasn't supposed to be the kind that got hysterical. As soon as I'd come to, I realized he was disappointed. Once again, I wasn't the kid he really wanted. He must hope that his new boys would be the do-over. Evan wasn't happy either. He didn't like that the detectives had gotten to me. He wanted a more stoic client. I'd let everyone down, but I'd never expected that news. My fingerprints were on the knife.

Mom and I sat in silence, the only sound the loud ticking of the clock on the wall.

"How are you doing?" my mom finally asked.

I shrugged. "What will happen if I have to go to Italy?" They'd managed to delay everything, but I could see the writing on the wall, the knife on the table so to speak. This wasn't going to go away. It wasn't going to magically get better just because I wanted it to. My daddy wasn't going to buy me out of this problem.

She leaned back in her chair. "Your dad and I have talked about it. I'll take a leave from my job and travel there. The lawyer there said there are short-term apartment rentals. That way I can support you and keep your dad up to date with what's happening."

I nodded, grateful. It would be good to have a regular visitor. I was going to have to toughen up. I couldn't keep talking about how I wouldn't make it if I went to jail. I wasn't going to have a choice. If rehab had taught me anything, it was that people were a lot tougher than they thought they were. Whining about it didn't help. You either lay down and died or kept going. Those were your options.

"Your dad would want to be there too, but with his job, it's more complicated. In exchange for me going over, he'll cover my costs." I could tell she was trying to put a positive spin on everything and it was exhausting her.

I started sniffing. I wanted to put my head down on the table and cry. I could already imagine what would happen if this process was dragged out for years. She wouldn't be able to stay forever. I'd be alone.

"It's going to be okay," Mom said. "You heard what Evan said. Those detectives are making it sound worse than it is. Your fingerprints could have gotten on that knife a whole bunch of ways." She waved her hand in the air like she didn't even have the time to list them all. "You could have struggled with Simone and taken it from her, or if the knife is from the kitchenette where you were staying, you could have used it to make a snack. There's no way to date when you touched the knife. And who knows why it was in the car. Heck, maybe Simone wasn't stabbed. Maybe she fell on the knife."

I couldn't even look at her. Even she had to understand how absurd her theory sounded.

"Evan was telling your dad and me that the Italian police have a history of incompetence. He's got some questions about how evidence was collected at the scene. There were emergency people in and out of the car, so who knows how that might have screwed things up." Mom tucked her hair behind her ear.

"I didn't do this," I said.

"Of course you didn't," Mom said. She patted my hand. "The police aren't going to be able to prove a thing."

That's when I knew beyond any doubt she believed I'd done it.

Chapter Twenty-one

Uffizi Gallery Staff Incident Report
Location: Outside Hall 10/14 Botticelli
Staff Member: Maria Spadonni
Date: 25 April

There were a number of school visits in the museum on this day. I was aware that several of the groups were doing the organized "art scavenger hunt" activity that the museum sponsors. The purpose of this activity is to have students visit the major works and collect information about the artists. All security staff had been informed that this was happening and to be watchful for any students running in the halls or galleries. We were instructed to remind them of the rules about this and tell them that if they did not slow down, they would be disqualified from the potential to win the activity.

At approximately 14:55, I heard someone yelling in English in the south stairwell. I instructed my colleague Roberto Ganci to watch the hall, and I left my post to attend to the commotion. When I entered the stairwell, I saw three visitors on the lower landing. A male and female were against the wall, and a second female was yelling at them. Later these would be identified as Niccolo Landini, Simone McIvory, and Jill Charron. Based on what was being said, my impression was that Ms. Charron had entered the stairwell and spotted Mr. Landini and Ms. McIvory in an embrace. I noted that Mr. Landini and Ms. McIvory were standing very close and that Ms. McIvory's lipstick was smeared.

Ms. Charron was yelling and cursing at Ms. McIvory. She lunged forward and pushed Ms. McIvory. Ms. McIvory fell backwards and cracked her right elbow on the stone baluster. Mr. Landini assisted Ms. McIvory in regaining her feet. I restrained Ms. Charron to ensure the situation didn't escalate, and she began to cry. I asked them all for their names and school group. Mr. Landini requested that I not call the incident in and said that he would take responsibility for the two girls, as he was one of the program heads. Given that he was involved in the altercation, I declined his offer and used my radio to contact the main desk. Security then located the school coordinator, Ms. Ochoa, and she met us in the stairwell.

Health and Safety attended the scene. They indicated that Ms. McIvory had a small scrape on her right elbow, and she was provided with a Band-Aid. It was their impression that the arm was not broken, but they suggested that she could obtain further medical attention and X-rays at the hospital. Ms. McIvory declined this option. She was given a disposable ice pack. Ms. Ochoa was informed that the disturbance would be noted in museum records and that her organization would be on notice that disturbances such as this are frowned upon by the museum.

This represents my full understanding of this event.

Maria Spadonni

***

Text Log dated 25 April:

Simone to Nico: Meet me south stairwell.
Nico to Simone: More with the teasing?
Simone to Nico: Come and find out.

***

Excerpt from Second Police Interview with Niccolo Landini

Date: 17 May
Time: 11:00
Florence Police Department
Present: Niccolo Landini, Detective Salette
Original transcript in Italian, translated to English by Stoker and Mills Translation Services, New York, New York

Detective Salette: Why did you fail to mention your involvement with Ms. McIvory in our initial meeting?

Niccolo: There was no real *involvement*. It was a single encounter. This is why I didn't mention it. I knew something would be made of it that wasn't true. You are twisting the situation.

Detective Salette: But you were romantically involved with her, isn't that correct?

Niccolo: If you consider a single kiss romantically involved, then yes. It was unfortunate, and I am ashamed. I did care for Jill, very much, but I am also human. Her friend Simone was very . . . persistent.

Detective Salette: So you're saying that Simone was the instigator of the relationship?

Niccolo: Again, there was no relationship, but yes, Simone was the one who chased me. It started with smiles, brushing up against me when we passed. She would lean over, make sure that I saw she wasn't wearing a bra. Then she started saying things, letting me know that she was interested. It was silly and childish. I could tell she didn't like that my attention was on Jill. She wanted to see if she could move my focus to her. We kissed, but it was only the one time at the museum. A mistake. I will admit that.

Detective Salette: And how did Jill respond when she caught you?

Niccolo: Jill was upset of course, but the situation has been blown out of proportion. There was no screaming or yelling. I hear the papers say there was a fight between the girls, but that isn't true.

Detective Salette: The museum security guard reported that Jill shoved Simone.

Niccolo: No, no, no. This didn't happen. She poked at Simone with a finger, and Simone stepped back and stumbled into the wall. Jill was angry, but had we had a chance, we would have made up.

Detective Salette: Did Jill tell you that she had forgiven you? Or Simone?

Niccolo: Sadly, we never had a chance to discuss it. I never saw either girl again. The teacher, Ms. Ochoa, overreacted. Americans are very uptight about sex. This is what passion is—strong feelings—but they run from it. They are scared of emotion. If we had had a chance to talk, then everything would have been fine, but I was denied this option.

***

Police Statement from Ms. Ochoa, Program Director for Adventures Abroad

Transcript to be provided to Italian police

I met with both Simone and Jill that evening. I can't express how disappointed I was in them for causing an incident at the museum. I'd made it clear to all of the students at the start of the trip that they are ambassadors for this program and for their country. This was clearly not the kind of behavior I expected or would tolerate.

I informed the girls that I had fired Nico and that I would be in touch with his academic advisor. It was obvious to me that he was involved with both girls and that this duplicity had blown up in all of their faces. He was in a mentorship role with our organization, and he abused that trust.

Jill attempted to stand up for Nico, indicating that she wanted to be in a relationship with him. This seemed to upset Simone, who insisted that Nico wasn't worth it. She stated that she had been with Nico to prove to Jill that he was no good. Needless to say, Jill felt strongly that there would have been better ways for Simone to express her unhappiness with her relationship.

I informed the girls that I would be sharing what had transpired with their parents. Both requested that I not do this. Jill was concerned that her parents might try to make her leave the program early, and Simone indicated that her parents were very strict. As I mentioned in my previous statement, both girls were eighteen. I typically do not involve parents unless it is an issue of safety or health, as I think it is important in this time of helicopter parenting to let the girls stand on their own. I admit I decided not to email either set of parents. I felt it would be best to wait a few days to see if the situation could be resolved.

I informed both Jill and Simone that what disappointed me the most was that I was aware that the two of them had been friends for a very long time. It seemed a shame to me that a long-term friendship would be ended over an ill-advised romantic entanglement. One thing that Jill said stuck with me. She agreed with me that Nico wasn't worth it, but Jill had thought she should have been worth it to Simone. That it didn't matter that Simone had kissed Nico; what mattered was that Simone had stabbed her in the back.

Jill indicated that she wanted to change her room assignment and that she didn't believe she could share with Simone any longer. I told the girls that I wasn't going to change the room assignments because it would be disruptive to the entire group. I hoped that if they were forced to interact, they would work things out. Obviously, I regret this decision in hindsight, but I honestly believed that with the long-term history between the girls, as well as how it seemed clear to me that they really cared about each other, even if there were some issues in their friendship, they would resolve things.

***

CNN Breaking News Report

Italian authorities have confirmed that the rental car driven by Jill Charron in the accident that killed Simone McIvory had been rented for Niccolo Landini.

Inside sources have reported that the police were suspicious when they realized the rental car had been rented to a student in the same university program as Mr. Landini. Initially, the individual maintained that he had rented the car for himself, but under intense questioning, admitted that it was for Mr. Landini's use. Once the accident occurred, Mr. Landini reportedly did not want to be connected to it and asked his friend to conceal his involvement.

Police also noted that in an earlier statement, the individual stated the keys had been left in the car while he was loading it, and that was how Ms. Charron got access to the vehicle. Now, knowing that the car was Mr. Landini's, the authorities are left wondering if he provided the car for her use.

Mr. Landini had his employment terminated by the Adventures Abroad program as a result of his relationships with Ms. Charron and Ms. McIvory. It raises the question why he had followed the group to the small Tuscan hillside instead of returning to his university program. Mr. Landini has denied having any contact with either girl after leaving the program, but police will certainly want to check his story and determine if anything may have occurred that would have contributed to the tragic events that unfolded.

***

Justice for Simone Blog
KILLER TOLD SIMONE HER DASTARDLY PLAN

Sources close to the investigation shared a note written by Chilly Jilly to Simone just a day before the so-called "accident." A copy of the note is below, but in case you can't read Chilly Jilly's handwriting, here's what it says:

Don't even bother trying to make it up to me. YOU ended the friendship. Someone who can be so disloyal is dead to me!

The note shows what other witnesses have confirmed. Chilly Jilly was furious at Simone for her supposed disloyalty and threatened to kill her. However, it's clear to us at JUSTICE FOR SIMONE that Jilly was blaming the wrong person. Our research dug up that Nico was a player with a long history. Sources tell us that Nico was the one pursuing Simone! Simone's parents describe her as a pretty girl who didn't have a lot of experience. When Simone didn't respond to his overtures, he started messing around with Chilly Jilly, hoping to make Simone jealous. Clearly Jilly couldn't handle the fact that her low-rent Romeo preferred her best friend. That's when her rage exploded and Simone was viciously butchered.

Comments:

Ari45: No wonder Nico chose Simone over Jilly. Jilly's a dog. RIP Simone.

Murderfan22: Jilly probably paid Nico to screw her. I hope he charged her double. Sluts like her can't stand when guys choose the good girl.

Swinter: Is she still saying she can't remember anything? How can the police buy that bullshit?

Anton: Someone should teach Chilly Jilly a lesson by peeling her alive. See how she likes knives then.

Mtape: What do you expect from Jilly? Her dad is married to some teen whore and her mom is a dog face too.

Ebaby36: I bet Nico did it. When Jilly and Simone found out about each other he was afraid he'd get in trouble so he sabotaged the car. BOOM took out two problems at once.

Murderfan22: Don't be stupid Ebaby36—Simone was STABBED, then there was the accident.

Ebaby36: Don't call me stupid.

Comments continue on next page

Chapter Twenty-two

I saw Anna looking around the physio gym from the doorway. I was in the back on a plinth. Sam had hooked me up to a TENS machine. It was supposed to help with the pain. I wanted to get completely off the pain medication. I figured I should have a goal as long as I was going to be sticking around the hospital. Dr. Weeks said there was no reason to believe that the low levels of drugs I was on would have any impact on my memory, but I wasn't sure. When the nurse delivered the tiny beige pills just before bed, I loved the warm fuzzy feeling they gave me. It was like being under a fleece blanket with a mug of hot chocolate. It smoothed out all the edges, made things feel soft. But that softening came at a price. Maybe my mind wouldn't let me remember if it was too easy. Without the pills, my life was sharp and jagged. Maybe I needed those edges to snag, to rip a memory free. I had to remember so I could prove I hadn't done it. I was running out of time.

Anna spotted me and wove her chair through the gym. She was keeping an eye out for Sam. He didn't like people to have their sessions interrupted. She rolled up next to me.

"When are you out of here?" Anna asked.

I glanced at the clock over the door. "Another twenty minutes."

"Meet me up on the roof deck. I've got some stuff to show you." She wheeled off without saying anything else.

Whatever she'd found couldn't be good news. She hadn't hunted me down to tell me my hair was looking great or that some hot actor or athlete was stopping by the rehab center to visit with patients and take pictures. I checked the clock again. Not even a full minute had gone by. If I tried to wait nineteen more, I'd explode. I peeled off the electrodes. I'd tell Sam I had a headache. He'd give me the face, but then he'd let me go. Technically I should be discharged anyway. The only reason I was still in the program was as a way to hide me from the Italian authorities. I could tell everyone on the treatment team felt awkward about the situation. I was taking up a bed that could have been used by someone else.

***

The rehab hospital had tried to make the rooftop deck a pleasant place, but that plan had failed. There were planters built by volunteers. I knew this because there was an engraved sign: PLANTERS A GENEROUS GIFT FROM COMMUNITY VOLUNTEERS. They likely had the sign made so people wouldn't think blind individuals who'd had some kind of seizure disorder had created them. They looked ready to fall apart at any moment. The plants inside, limp and slumped over, weren't doing much better.

The roof was covered with a layer of slate-colored pea gravel, but swathes of black tarpaper showed underneath where the stones had worn away. There were clusters of chairs sprinkled around up there, but today it was empty. The cold gray clouds that pressed down from the sky seemed to have scared everyone off.

There were a few dozen wet discarded cigarette butts rotting just below a sign that declared THIS DECK IS A NONSMOKING AREA. THANKS FOR YOUR SUPPORT.

Anna had wheeled over to one of the clusters of patio furniture and had her face tipped up to the sky. "You left early," she said without even opening her eyes. She had a laptop balanced on her knees.

"What did you find?" I asked.

"The Internet exploded. So that guy, Nico? Not only was he hooking up with both you and Simone, but he also followed you guys to that small town, for some reason. He lied to the cops."

My stomach felt sour, like I'd drunk a Big Gulp of red wine vinegar. I wasn't sure what that meant. Had he followed me or Simone? And did I even care?

Anna's nose wrinkled. "Your best friend hooked up with your boyfriend. That shit's messed up."

I shrugged. "I'd be mad, but I don't even remember dating him, let alone finding out he cheated on me with my best friend." I looked out over the staff parking lot. Simone prided herself on her ability to get any guy's attention. It was like her superpower. When we were younger and went to the ice rink, we'd see if she could get some random guy there to buy her hot chocolate or one of the cookie ice cream sandwiches they sold at the concession stand, and she did, every single time. It was one of those unwritten understood things in our friendship. She was the hot one. I was the smart one. We used to joke that if we could combine into one person, we'd be unstoppable. I could get that Nico would be attracted to Simone, but what still confused me was why she did it. Maybe Dr. Weeks was right that Simone did it because she was hurt, but what if she did it just because she could? Simone wasn't someone who let people's feelings get in the way of what she wanted, but I wasn't just some person—I was her best friend. I knew she could be cold with people, but I'd never thought she would be that way with me.

"Was Nico the one who told people? Because maybe it's not even true. Maybe he wanted Simone to like him, but she shot him down."

"That's not how it sounds," Anna said.

I blew out a frustrated sigh. "But that's the whole point. People are spinning all of these stories, half of which aren't even true. Maybe he wants people to think he's irresistible. Or reporters want to have a fresh scandal, so they're creating a new twist."

Anna shrugged. "I doubt it. If he was the one who broke the news hoping it would make him look good, that was a bust. He comes across like a loser. Some reporter dug up dirt that he's done this before. It looks like bagging naïve schoolgirls is his thing. They've found four other girls from different programs who have come forward, saying he slept with them too." She glanced at me. "No disrespect on the naïve thing."

I couldn't really be annoyed. It was obvious that for my first serious relationship I had chosen poorly. "I bet it was the cops who told the reporters. They're pissed that they can't make me return to Italy, so they want me to look bad. Why not tell the world that my first real boyfriend was also making out with my best friend?" I paused. "And apparently everyone else." I picked at the skin near my thumbnail, tearing off a thin sliver of flesh.

"They leaked some other stuff too," Anna said. She opened the laptop and passed it over, showing me the latest on the *Justice for Simone* blog.

"Dastardly Plan?" I asked, pointing at the headline. "Who the hell talks like that?"

"I think you're focusing on the wrong part, but I'll give you that it's sort of a shit word choice."

I scrolled down so I could see the copy of the actual note the blog had posted. There was no denying it; I'd seen it in front of me in a thousand notebooks, in cards, on to-do lists. It was my handwriting. It was hard to tell with the copy, but it seemed like the exclamation point had almost torn through the paper. I must have been really pissed when I wrote it. My finger touched the laptop screen, trying to connect with the amount of emotion behind the words. I imagined when the police found it, they must have danced around in glee. It didn't prove anything, but it was another brick in the case they were building against me.

The blog also had a picture of Nico. He was jogging toward a small car; his hand was thrown up to cover his face. The caption was "Student Sex Fiend Flees Reporters."

"Don't read the comments," Anna advised.

I instantly scrolled down to see what people were saying. I kept hoping someone would stick up for me, but the comments just kept going—page after page after page. Commenters arguing with each other, but in agreement on one thing—I sucked. I passed the laptop back to Anna.

"If one of my girls messed with my man, I would fuck her up," Anna said, looking down at the screen. She glanced up. "Not saying you did, just that I would."

Irritation made my stomach cramp up. "Why do we always blame the friend and not the guy? He's the real loser."

Anna tossed her hair over her shoulder. "Because we expect guys to be dogs. We expect more from our friends."

I rubbed my thigh just above where the walking cast cut into my leg. "That's sexist."

"Whatever."

I motioned to the laptop. "What are the other sites saying?"

Anna clicked around. "Pretty much everyone has a version of the same thing. Basically that if you found out Simone was with Nico, it gives you a motive and that maybe he was involved in the accident in some way. The thing with the car is weird."

Anyone who says "sticks and stones might break some bones, but words will never hurt you" has never been in my shoes. I'd prefer being beaten with rocks—it would hurt, but it would be nothing compared to the razor cuts of a million nasty words. People hated me. Not just a little, a lot. People who didn't even know me. They'd never spoken a word to me, never seen me in the flesh, but based on a few pictures and a story, they'd made me into some kind of monster. They talked about how torture was too good for me. They wrote in detail what kinds of things should happen to my family. I rubbed my temples. Another headache was building.

"Maybe I shouldn't have shown you," Anna said.

"No, it's better for me to know." I knew neither my parents nor Evan would show me. There had been hushed discussions about how I was "holding up" and the importance of "keeping up my spirits." I think after my last breakdown, they were all worried that I was going to snap.

"I wanted to show you because I wanted to ask you something," Anna said. She fidgeted in her chair. "Your dad has a lot of money, right?"

My eyes narrowed. "Why?"

"I think maybe you should leave."

"If I leave the rehab hospital, they're going to make me go to Italy," I said. "That's the whole point—I can't go."

Anna looked around as if she half expected someone to pop out from behind one of the planters. "No, I'm saying I think you should just leave. Get some money from your dad and disappear."

I stared at her. Was she actually suggesting that I run? I was pretty sure I wasn't fugitive material.

"Where would I go?"

Anna shrugged. "I don't know. Someplace that doesn't send people to Italy. Brazil, maybe."

My mind was blank, trying to come up with an image of Brazil. The only thing that I could think of was bananas and soccer. And I wasn't even sure that bananas actually grew there. "I can't go to Brazil. What would I do—hide out forever?"

"At least until no one cares about this anymore," Anna said. "Let it blow over. People have short attention spans. If you're not around, eventually people will get bored—focus on something else."

She was serious. This wasn't "hey, let's imagine the wildest plan we can come up with" or a daydream. Anna actually thought I should run away.

"They took my passport," I said. The knowledge of this fact sat like a rock in my gut.

Anna slumped in her chair. "Shit." That seemed to sum up my situation. "Is there a way to get another one?"

I had an image of meeting a guy in an alley behind a Starbucks and peeling off some crisp fifty-dollar bills, then him pulling a passport out of a trench coat pocket. The whole process would take place by dim light and smell vaguely of garbage from the nearby Dumpster. My picture would be inside the passport, but with a different name. An alias. All very *Bourne Identity*. I let out a slow breath.

"I wouldn't know how to do it," I admitted.

"Do you want me to ask around? I know a guy who does driver's licenses. Mostly so kids can buy or get into the clubs, but he might know who to talk to," Anna said.

"I don't want to run away. What I want is to prove that I didn't do this." I reached for her arm. "You believe me, right? I know it looks like I did and that all of this"—I gestured to the laptop—"makes it seem like I had a good reason, but I *know* I didn't. I wouldn't. I'm not that kind of person."

"I think anyone is that kind of person if the situation is right," Anna said.

I drew back surprised. "How can you say that?"

"Because it's true. People don't want to be that kind of person, but push anyone far enough, and they'll fight back."

I stood and stormed toward the door. I hated what she said, because I was pretty sure she was right, and it made me mad that she was dangling it in my face. The funny thing was that it was exactly something Simone would have said. She always

211

believed the ends justified the means, that a person did what a person had to do. But I didn't believe that. Or at the very least, I didn't want to believe it. I wanted to believe that the world was a better place than that. That there were people who did the right thing for no other reason than it was right.

I stopped short near the door. "Well, that's just great. Now no one believes me," I said. "You all think I'm just a killer."

"I didn't say that. I said I think anyone could." Anna shook her head. "And spare me all the drama. I'm trying to help you."

"By telling me to go into hiding. That's how you suggest people deal with their problems?"

"When the problem is that their ass could land in jail for twenty years, then yes. You think everything will turn out because shit has always turned out for you, but life isn't like that. Trust me, it may not matter if you did it or not. What matters is what people think, and people think you are guilty as hell."

I drew back as if she'd punched me in the gut.

Anna rubbed her face. "Look, I'm sorry. I'm not trying to upset you, but I'm trying to give you a dose of real life."

"I know it's real," I said. "You're forgetting that this is my life that we're talking about."

Anna shook her head. "You don't have a clue. You've always had it easy. There's always been food in your fridge and heat on in your house. When you see a cop, you figure that of course he's there to be helpful. You think the world turns okay as long as you try your very hardest—but it's not like that. I'm trying to wake you up before it's too late."

I drew myself up, hating that I probably looked prim and stuck-up like a spinster schoolteacher from the 1800s. "I am very aware that the world is not a fair place. I don't need you to tell me that."

The expression on Anna's face screamed that she thought I was in denial. "Fine. Whatever."

I tapped my foot on the gravel. "Fine." I wanted her to say something else, but I had no idea what.

"You better run along to your next appointment," Anna said. "You wouldn't want them to discharge you."

Chapter Twenty-three

Let's Travel! Guidebook

Montepulciano: A day in Montepulciano, one of the small fortified towns in Tuscany, will convince you that there is only one direction—up. Tiny alleys and stairwells cut between the buildings and lead ever and ever higher, encouraging the intrepid traveler to explore. The sun-kissed buildings are carved from the same warm stone that makes up the hillsides. Be sure to see the wine-aging cellars of Cantina Fattoria della Talosa and the Piazza Grande before having lunch or dinner at Le Logge del Vignola—and if you are there in truffle season, be sure to order the risotto.

***

Police Statement from Samantha Yu, Student on Adventures Abroad Program

Transcript to be provided to Italian police

Our first day in Montepulciano, we were given free time in

the morning to spend any way we wanted. You could go on a walking tour, but most people were sort of walking-toured out. Plus, we knew we were headed to some church or cathedral in the afternoon. A lot of people slept in or did laundry. A few of the guys were playing some weird magic card game in the lobby, and some others were just sitting around.

I saw Jill go off on her own. Everyone knew what had happened between her and Simone. I mean, it wasn't a secret or anything that Nico had been fired. A bunch of people were choosing sides—sort of Team Jill, Team Simone kinda thing. There was no doubt Simone had really been a bitch, but people liked her more than Jill, so it was weird. Anyway—my former best friend made out with my boyfriend last year at prom, so I was totally Team Jill.

I followed her into the city, and she was just sitting alone in the main square. She was trying to pet one of the stray cats. There are strays everywhere in Italy, but it's not like home. Someone must feed them, because they all look pretty fat and happy. Maybe they're not strays, maybe it's just a thing where the whole town adopts them. Jill finally got to pet the cat, but then something spooked it, and it ran away. She looked like it broke her heart.

I asked her if she was okay, and she said she was. I told her that if she didn't want to hang out with Simone, she was totally welcome to hang with me and my friend Keenisha. She said it would be okay and she was pretty sure she and Simone would make up. I was surprised, but she said they'd been friends forever and there was no point being mad at Simone for being Simone.

Forensic Psychology Consult Report Addendum, Dr. Jerome Kerr

Date: 20 May

Client: Detective Alban, Florence Police Department
Original report in Italian, translated to English by Stoker and Mills Translation Services, New York, New York

I was asked to review new information to determine if it changed any of the opinions in my earlier report, dated 3 May.

I was asked to assume the following facts:

1. That Ms. Charron was in a romantic/sexual relationship with Niccolo Landini

2. That Mr. Landini was also having a relationship with Ms. McIvory

3. That Ms. Charron became aware of this dual relationship and confronted Ms. McIvory

As was stated in my earlier report, the two girls had a long-standing relationship. While it is certainly possible that this situation could have led to a violent incident, it is

216

important to note that two days passed between when the affair was discovered and when the accident occurred. To me, this indicates that either a) Ms. Charron took time to plan the crime, perhaps with the assistance of Mr. Landini, given that we now know he was in the area, or b) a further incident occurred that ignited the passions of the two girls.

The crime was what profilers typically describe as disorganized. The types of injuries sustained by Ms. McIvory from the knife were nonlethal. Her death was a result of the injuries sustained in the automobile accident. In my opinion, based on the nature of the injuries, as well as the method (driving off a cliff), the crime does not appear to have been planned and more likely occurred spontaneously. As a result there would have been some type of inciting incident. While I am aware that there is a working theory that Ms. Charron killed Ms. McIvory over the relationship with Mr. Landini, it is important to note that Ms. Charron did not demonstrate a highly romantic personality. While I have no doubt she was interested in Mr. Landini, I have not seen any documentation that she had fallen in love or believed that this was a long-lasting relationship. In my opinion, if the actions on 28 April were not an accident, then something else must have enraged Ms. Charron.

With the information provided, I am unable to comment on whether Mr. Landini would have been involved. I would be happy to review this possible impact on the crime should further information become available.

***

Justice for Simone Blog

Have you seen the latest? Someone leaked photos of Chilly Jilly in rehab. I think we're supposed to well up in tears to see her working so hard. Poor thing, having to use a wheelchair. But save your pity. She'll walk again. A broken leg heals. Being dead doesn't. Seems to us Simone got the shit end of that deal. Chilly Jilly is keeping up her story that she can't remember—but her memory is awfully convenient.

Chapter Twenty-four

I was so angry, my hands were shaking. I pushed open the door to our room and just watched her. Anna had her headphones on, and her eyes were closed. Her head and arms swayed to the music. Dr. Weeks said I wasn't sure how to deal with the emotion of anger, and she might have been right that I tended to ignore it, but I wasn't going to anymore.

Anna opened her mouth and belted out, "All I've ever needed was yooooou!" She jolted in her seat when she opened her eyes and saw me. She clicked off her music. "Jesus, you scared me."

I didn't say anything.

"I thought you had art therapy," Anna said.

"Oh, sorry, did you miss your chance to get a photo?" I bit out. My dad had tried to warn me, and I hadn't listened.

Anna's eyebrows crunched in confusion. "What are you talking about?"

"I'm talking about the photos of me that are all over the Internet. Shots of me in physio, sitting in the lounge, even the one of the two of us together in the cafeteria. Nice that you included one of yourself. I guess you wanted a chance to have your shot for some fame too." I enjoyed how the sharp words flew out of my mouth at her.

Anna's lips pressed into a tight line. "I didn't share any photos. It's a big hospital. Did it occur to you that anyone could have taken those shots? Someone on staff, or another patient—"

"Don't lie. Those were *my* photos. Ones my mom or I took. They were on my laptop." I tapped the side of my head like I was thinking. "Who could have possibly had time alone in my room with my computer? Let me think."

Our door pushed open, and my mom swept in. "I brought pizza! Extra cheese. I thought we could all watch *Bachelorette* together." She stopped two steps in, no doubt frozen in place by the icy tension stretched between Anna and me. "Girls, is everything okay?"

"I've used your laptop to search around the Internet and watch a couple of movies. I never copied any of your pictures," Anna said.

"I hope you at least got a decent amount of cash to sell me out." I fixed her with a stare. "I trusted you."

Anna tossed her headphones onto her bed. "This is bullshit. I don't need to listen to this. I am good to the people in my life."

I barked out a bitter laugh. "I'm supposed to take advice on healthy relationships from someone whose boyfriend pushed her down the stairs?"

Anna pulled back as if I'd struck her. It was a low blow, but so was what she'd done to me. Maybe she thought it wasn't a big deal, the photos weren't nasty. She could have shared bigger secrets, but having those pictures of me out there made me vulnerable. I was sick of everyone sticking his or her nose in every part of my life. She'd taken advantage of me. Even if the photos weren't bad, they were mine.

"Jill, sweetheart," my mom said.

"I'm outta here." Anna pushed past me with her chair.

"Anna, please don't go," my mom said. She stood there with the pizza box as if she were considering trying to block her.

"Just leave," I said. I'd been looking forward to confronting her once I saw the photos, but instead of feeling vindicated, I was just tired. Anna left the room without looking back.

"Jill, you need to apologize," my mom said.

I threw my bag down on my bed. "No I don't. There are worse things than being rude to someone." My mom's constant need to be polite to avoid ruffling feathers was grating on me. I was sick of doing things her way. Where had putting other people first gotten her? "She sold pictures of me. Pictures of me *here*," I explained. "They're all over the Internet." I started to grab some of my things that had migrated to Anna's side of the room. "Dad was right. I shouldn't have roomed with anyone."

Mom put the pizza box down on the bedside table and stepped in front of me, holding my shoulders so I couldn't turn away. "Stop what you're doing and listen to me." Her voice was firm and cold. Her tone surprised me into silence. She took a deep breath. "Your dad and Evan were the ones who leaked the photos."

I heard the words, but they rolled around inside my head, not making much sense. "What?"

"Your dad and Evan thought it would be good if there were some photos of you here, recovering. That if people could see you really were injured, that you were working so hard to get well, it would give you some sympathy."

I stared at her. "Why didn't anyone ask me? They're my pictures."

Mom's features grew pinched and tight. There were bright spots of color in her cheeks. "I told your dad we should tell you."

"But you didn't," I pointed out.

"Your dad and Evan thought it was more important that you not be involved. Then if anyone asked you about them, you could legitimately deny knowing anything about it." She looked almost frightened, as if she didn't know what I would do.

I slouched in my chair. "Anna is never going to forgive me."

"It never occurred to me that you'd think it was her. I didn't . . . I just thought you'd assume it was someone in the hospital . . ." Her hands fluttered nervously by her side. "I knew you two were close. I didn't think you'd suspect her."

The smell of the greasy pizza made me feel nauseous. You'd think my mom would know by now that I didn't respond well when I thought a friend had double-crossed me. She was probably glad she'd gotten to the room before I stabbed Anna and stuffed her into the garbage chute. "So you were okay with me wondering who sold me out. Having to second-guess everything," I said.

Mom crouched down so she could look me in the eyes. "I honestly didn't think it would bother you this much. They're flattering photos. I made sure your dad didn't choose anything you wouldn't want public."

I wanted to pull the covers over my head. She didn't get it. I didn't care if the photo made me look like I had a double chin or if I had a stupid expression on my face. What mattered was that people had seen me here in this place I'd thought was safe. I couldn't leave the hospital because there might be reporters. Every time I went online, there were pictures of my Facebook pages, people dissecting everything I'd ever said. Copies of reports I'd written in English class had been offered up as proof of various theories. I'd thought this was the one place where I wasn't being constantly inspected. Checked over. And when I saw those pictures, it felt like I'd been stripped naked and told to stand at the front of the room so everyone could get a good look. It was as if I could feel those millions of eyes crawling over every inch.

"Talk to Anna," Mom said. "She'll understand."

I wasn't so sure. Loyalty was a huge thing for her. An ugly thought came into my head. Like a corpse suddenly erupting from the surface of the water. "Dad knew I would blame Anna. That's what he wanted."

Mom sucked in a breath. "Oh, honey, I don't think so."

I swallowed hard. I was certain of it. He didn't trust Anna, and he hadn't wanted me to either. I plopped into my wheelchair and dragged the pizza box onto my lap. I couldn't use my crutches and carry it. "I'm going to go find Anna."

"Do you want me to come? Try to explain?"

"No, I'm the one who fucked things up. I'm the only one who can make it better."

"Okay."

Things must've been bad—she didn't even tell me not to use the f-word.

***

223

I checked the lounge on the way, but I was pretty sure I knew where I'd find Anna. I pushed the door to the rooftop lounge open, and she was there, her chair at the very far corner as if she wanted to launch herself off into space.

I wheeled up next to her. "I suppose you want to shove me off."

She shrugged. "Not sure you're worth the effort."

The pizza box was soggy from the steam. I handed it over to her. "I know sorry isn't going to cut it."

"Then why are you here?" Anna didn't look at me. She kept her gaze on the horizon.

"Because even though it isn't going work, I still need to say it."

"I get it, you know. Why you're so pissed. What happens here shouldn't be seen by anyone. It's private. Do you think I want anyone to see me like this?" She gestured to her limp legs. "Everyone thinks getting through rehab is some kind of noble thing. *Oh, look at the cripple being so brave.* But it's not brave, because what else are you going to do but keep moving forward? Die? Too late—you already survived. Rehab is like taking a shit. It's ugly, and it stinks, and you don't want anyone to see you do it, but it's unavoidable."

I flinched at her words. "I should have asked you, not accused you."

"Fine, but you still thought I would do that. Me." She shook her head. "I thought we were friends."

"We are," I insisted.

Anna looked up and away. "Whatever. You should spend your time figuring out who really screwed you, because it wasn't me."

224

"It was my dad," I said in a soft voice. "He's the one who leaked the photos. He thought they might get me some sympathy."

She let her breath out in a slow whistle. "No. He did it because he's a dick."

"I know it doesn't make it okay, but I'm really sorry." I rubbed my temples. "All of this isn't who I am."

"It seems like you're not sure who you are. That's your problem." She raised a hand before I could respond. "Don't you get it? Who we are is what comes out when shit goes bad. You can't tell anything about a person when things are great. If you want to really know someone, be there when everything goes to hell."

"Maybe I'm not better than this—but I want to be," I said.

She tossed her hair back. "Fine. Look, let's not make a huge drama out of it. We're stuck together until you check out." Anna gestured to the pizza. "I'll take this as a peace offering, and we'll call it good. Just forget it ever happened."

I wanted to believe what she said, but I could tell by her expression that she wouldn't.

Chapter Twenty-five

Television Transcript for *Crime Watch with Nina Grimes*
(*Theme music.*)

Nina: Good evening and welcome to *Crime Watch* with your host, Nina Grimes. We've got a guest in the studio with us tonight. Dr. Sharon Rubio, a psychologist, is here to discuss the possible motivations of Niccolo Landini, the young Lothario at the heart of the Simone McIvory murder scandal. With the news that the rental car belonged to Nico and that he was in Montepulciano at the time of the crime, it's raised people's interest in him and what his role might have been. Welcome, Dr. Rubio, and thanks for being with us.

Dr. Rubio: Thanks for having me, Nina. Always a pleasure.

Nina: What can you tell us about this Niccolo Landini character? What kind of guy is he?

Dr. Rubio: Well, first off, I should say that I haven't had the opportunity to meet with, or do any psychological testing with, Mr. Landini, so my thoughts are more general.

Nina: And let me be sure to tell our viewers that your inability to meet with Mr. Landini is certainly not your fault. Our producers reached out to him and his lawyers, and offered him several opportunities to come on the show and tell us his perspective, but he declined. Wouldn't even send us a prepared statement. For a guy who prides himself on being a sweet-talker—he's sure keeping mum now. Our show also offered to provide him with the chance to take a lie detector test to clear his name—with one of the best examiners in the business, I might add—and he declined that as well.

Dr. Rubio: As with many crimes, it seems the core of this one is passion. I thought it would be useful to first talk about attraction. Most people seek out romantic partners based on finding someone they are attracted to who is around the same status level as themselves. For example, wealthy people tend to date other wealthy people, attractive people tend to be drawn to the same level of attractiveness, and educated people tend to choose others who have similar amounts of schooling. We say that opposites attract, but the truth is we're much more likely to seek out someone similar to ourselves.

Nina: Then how do you explain the beautiful young woman who wants to marry an old man? The rooster with the spring chicken, as my grandma used to say.

Dr. Rubio: That's easy—I bet your grandma knew the answer. People are also attracted to someone who offers them something that they are either missing or seeking. What I'm

227

saying is that a young woman may choose to date a much older man because she is seeking financial security, and the older man may be seeking youth and vitality. I can't speak about Mr. Landini directly, but I can say that choosing romantic partners who are both younger and less savvy than you can show a lack of confidence. That is, the person selects individuals based on the comfort of being relatively certain that the individual will respond to their overtures. They don't know their own worth, so they set their targets lower.

Nina: So you choose someone who will think you're a big deal because they don't know any better?

Dr. Rubio: (*Laughter*) That might be simplifying things, but generally it's right. However, there is another reason someone might seek out a relationship with someone who is of lower status. The person may be seeking out someone who is vulnerable, someone they believe they can control.

Nina: Hmm—now, that doesn't sound good. What kind of person might do that?

Dr. Rubio: There are a couple of options. One is someone who might have narcissistic personality disorder. Now, this term can get thrown around—"oh, that guy is a real narcissist"—but it is an actual psychological condition.

Nina: Tell us a bit more.

Dr. Rubio: Narcissistic personality disorder is characterized by a long-standing pattern of grandiosity, an overwhelming need for admiration, and often a complete lack of empathy toward others. People with this disorder often believe they are, for lack of a better term, the center of the world.

People with this condition often display snobby, disdainful, or patronizing attitudes. They're the kind of person who might make fun of someone who makes an error, and can be rude to people who are in service roles like cashiers or waiters, or they hijack a discussion at a dinner party to show off how smart they are.

Nina: That's interesting. A few of the students who were on the Adventures Abroad Program talked about how this Nico fellow was always lecturing them on history and art. Granted, that was his job, but they describe him as really overbearing, a know-it-all. He tended to talk down to them as if they weren't capable of understanding the things he knew.

Dr. Rubio: That would certainly fit with the disorder. Now, there is another kind of person who might seek out a vulnerable partner, and that's a psychopath.

Nina: Whoa.

Dr. Rubio: Yes, that's a diagnosis that certainly is alarming. These are individuals who might seem quite ordinary on the outside—and in fact are often described as quite charming—but are missing some key component of empathy. They tend to have rather shallow emotions, a sense of overconfidence; they tend to blame others for things that are their fault, and they're often selfish and have a predisposition to violence. Not that everyone who is a sociopath or psychopath will be violent. It's important to note that.

Nina: But they can be.

Dr. Rubio: Yes.

Nina: So let's take a look at Nico. He puts himself in a role where he gets to be the all-knowing guide, where he can show off what he knows to a bunch of impressionable young students. When we had one of the students on here, Brad, he talked about how charming Nico was. Then we know for a fact that this Nico pursued not only Jill, but also her friend Simone, without any remorse about what this might do to their friendship. Then when he was caught and lost his job, he blamed the girls and the program head, Ms. Ochoa, for being too puritanical. Then, for reasons that we still don't know, he rented a car to follow these girls and when that car ended up in an accident, he got his friend to lie about it and lied to the police about where he was when the crime happened. Who knows if this case might have broken open sooner if he'd been honest from the get-go?

Dr. Rubio: It's certainly a troubling pattern of behaviors.

Nina: Is it possible that he rented this car to follow the girls and get them to change their story so that he wouldn't be in trouble with the university? I mean, if he were angry and saw the girls as the ones to blame for his trouble . . .

Dr. Rubio: As I said, I haven't had the chance to meet with Mr. Landini, so I couldn't really speak about his motivations.

Nina: But someone who has these conditions that you described, they would be capable of something like taking a violent action to protect themselves, wouldn't they?

Dr. Rubio: Certainly.

Nina: Well, that does give us a lot to think about. Now if only Mr. Landini would be willing to speak openly, we might be able to clear all of this up. We'll be back after this commercial break to talk about how to keep your loved ones safe on vacations.

***

Excerpt from Third Police Interview with Niccolo Landini

Date: 24 May
Time: 13:30
Florence Police Department
Present: Niccolo Landini, Detective Salette
Original transcript in Italian, translated to English by Stoker and Mills Translation Services New York, New York

Detective Salette: So when you said in our last meeting that you never saw the girls again, that was a lie, wasn't it? You rented the car to go to Montepulciano. Were you going to see Jill or Simone?

Niccolo: It wasn't a lie. I didn't see them. Yes, I rented the car to go to the town, but I never met up with them. I went to apologize. When I got to the town, I realized I didn't know what to say, so I took a walk to clear my head. I left the car parked outside their hotel. I was so scattered that I left the keys in the car.

Detective Salette: A walk. Did anyone see you?

Niccolo: If I had known what would happen, then I would have made certain to have an alibi, but alas, I did not. When I heard of the accident and that it involved my car, I left. I didn't want to be involved. And I wasn't. I didn't see either of them.

Detective Salette: Your friend indicated that you didn't want to see them to apologize, but rather because you were upset about losing your job, and you wanted them to speak to the program head so that she would take back her decision.

Niccolo: Do you know how it will look on my school record that I was fired from this job for being "sexually inappropriate"? I want to go into teaching. No one will hire me.

Detective Salette: So you were angry.

Niccolo: Of course I was angry. This is my career. And it is over because of some stupid kiss with a girl who wanted to make her friend jealous? Two little girls who play games with each other over who is better than whom? It's bullshit. (*Pause*) I don't think I should answer any more questions without my lawyer.

Interview terminated.

Chapter Twenty-six

Evan bounded into the conference room like a kid on a bouncy castle. He clapped his hands together. "We've got some good news," he declared.

"Thank God," Mom said. "It's about time."

"So the news about Nico being with both girls and his lies about the car has changed the focus of the coverage. If there's anything the media hates, it's some perv who abuses kids."

"We're only a couple of years apart," I pointed out.

Evan shook his finger in my face. "No. He's an adult in a position of power and authority who manipulated young girls for sexual purposes. The media company we hired—"

I sat up. "What you do mean, media company?"

My parents exchanged a glance. "We thought it would be best to bring someone on to represent your interests," Dad said. "Someone who could make sure your perspective is out there too, spin things, so to speak."

"If it's my interests, how come I wasn't even told?" I asked. "You keep treating me like a child. This situation involves me. You can't keep shutting me out when it's information you don't want to share. First there were the pictures, now this."

Dad's nostrils flared. "You want to be an adult? Well then,

we're trying to change the story that you're a selfish, insecure slut who murdered your best friend over some guy." Dad's voice bounced around the small room. "The whole world basically thinks you did it, and if we don't figure out a way to fix this, then your butt is going to be in jail for a long time. So maybe you could appreciate how we're trying to help you instead of back-seat-driving this."

I was shocked. He'd never spoken to me like that before. Dad ran his hand over the top of his head. Everyone else in the room was silent, suddenly fascinated by the tabletop, unable to meet my eyes.

"I know you guys have done a lot," I said, my voice coming out tight and small. I wanted to explain that he was misunderstanding what I had said. It wasn't that I didn't appreciate everything, but I needed to be a part of the decisions being made. They'd stepped in and were managing every aspect of my life, but it was *my* life. I was the one who was going to have to live with whatever happened, so they couldn't shut me out with the excuse that they didn't think I could handle it.

"Do you?" Dad said. "Your mom lost her job. She's had to move to an apartment to get away from the media. Your stepmom and I had to open a line of credit against our home to cover these costs. Your mom coordinates everything, including trying to make sure that you have just the right kind of juice because you don't like the kind they serve here."

I winced. I hadn't asked my mom to buy me Tropicana, that we always had at home, I'd simply said that I couldn't stand the stuff in the cafeteria. It had pulp in it. I hated how the threads of pulp would stick in my throat. Thick strands of fruit hair. When I'd mentioned it, she'd brought in a carton of Tropicana and put it in the patient fridge on the ward with my name written in Sharpie on the side. Then I realized I'd missed the important thing.

"Wait, you lost your job?"

Mom glared at my dad. "I didn't *lose* my job. The company felt that it might be better for everyone if I took a leave. Just until things with you are settled. It's worked out perfectly; it's given me more time to be here." Mom smiled as if she were glad about how things had fallen into place, but I could tell the truth behind her fake smile. Her boss didn't want the mom of a murderer working there. That's the kind of thing that can be bad for business.

My throat tightened, and a tear ran down my face. "I'm sorry," I said, pushing the words out.

"Hey, now, this meeting got serious, and I brought us together because I had good news," Evan said.

Dad pinched the bridge of his nose. "Sorry. Everyone's a bit on edge."

Evan patted my dad's arm. "No worries. Understandable. Situations like this are hard. But the good news is things are turning around."

"You mentioned the media company," Mom said.

"Yes," Evan turned to me. "We hired Levy, Robar, and Ullman. They're one of the best in the business. They handle everything from media releases to making sure an alternate view of the story is spun out to the public. You've seen how these things happen online; they turn into a feeding frenzy. It's like there's blood in the water. Often the only thing it takes is one or two comments on a site giving an alternate view, a more tempered, humane view, and people wake up and realize they're being animals. It dials down the rhetoric."

"You said earlier that the public is focusing on Nico?" Dad asked.

Evan nodded. "Yep. It's hard to get people to like someone they've decided they dislike. The best way to get people away from thinking of you as the bad guy is to give them another bad guy." Evan spread his hands. "Nico makes for a great villain."

I felt a momentary wave of pity for Nico, but it passed quickly. I owed him no allegiance. "But the police aren't going to care, are they? They don't think Nico was involved," I said.

"No, but the fact he lied about the car makes them uncomfortable. Plus, they didn't find it out right away, so they look stupid for missing it. Besides, they've got bigger problems. Check this out." Evan pulled out his MacBook from his bag and opened it, spinning it to face my parents and me. "This video was released on Italian TV yesterday." He paused. "It shows the accident scene. Are you okay with that?"

I nodded. I didn't want to be left out. I stared at the screen, hoping I looked calm.

At first the camera shot was out of focus and jumpy, someone's camera phone—it was a road, winding down the side of a hill. There was someone talking, but it was in Italian, and I couldn't make out what they were saying. The voice sounded like a mix between anxious and excited. The person stopped running and pointed the camera down, past the edge of the wall that ran alongside the road, and you could see the car.

It was the same car I'd seen in the earlier photo. Some kind of red hatchback. It must have landed almost nose down, as the front half was accordioned in and one side was dented and scratched where it must have dragged along the wall before busting through. A tree branch had impaled the car, going in one side and coming out the back window, like it had grown there.

There were rescue people all over. One guy was almost completely in the car, his back legs sticking out of the passenger-side window. People screaming and pointing. It didn't seem to me like anyone was in charge.

A group of paramedics suddenly stood to the side of the car, a stretcher between them, and scrambled up the side of the hill toward the person holding the camera. The police waved the camera off, but they kept filming. I couldn't make out much, but I could tell from the hair that it was me they had on the stretcher.

My mom covered her mouth and looked away. I felt like I should too, but it was sickly fascinating. The stretcher with me strapped on it was shoved into an ambulance, which took off. The camera focused back on the hill. The urgency seemed to have gone down. People were still surrounding the car, but they were just standing there. Some peering into the car from the busted out windows. The person holding the camera drew closer to the accident, panning the side of the car. I realized I could make out that there was someone slumped forward in the front passenger seat.

Not someone. Simone.

There were a few police officers there. One handed the other something, sliding it into a bag. I leaned forward as if I could make the camera go closer, but that was when Evan

238

leaned forward and stopped the video. He crossed his arms and looked proud of himself. I didn't get it. This was the great news? I glanced at my parents. From their expressions, I could tell they didn't get it either.

"Did you see that?" Evan backed up the video by a few seconds and let it play again.

"Is that the knife?" my dad asked.

Evan nodded. "Yep, but that's not what's important. Here, watch it again."

"I'm not really sure what it is we're supposed to be seeing." My dad's voice was tight, and I could tell he was quickly getting tired of this game. He wasn't interested in guessing.

"The police officer isn't wearing gloves," Evan said. He played it one more time so we could see for ourselves. "He just reaches in and pulls it out. The other officer isn't wearing gloves either. That's Cop 101. My best guess is that they don't see a lot of crime way out there, and when they first arrive at the scene, they're thinking it's just an accident. By the time they start thinking there's been a crime, they've already screwed it up. See that? The knife isn't tagged or secured. It's just sitting in a bag on the ground while they collect other evidence, and look at all these people." Evan motions to the frozen image on the screen. "They've had paramedics in and out, and that's one thing, but then you can see there are a couple of locals who must have shown up immediately after the car went over to help. They're all over the place."

"That was nice of them," Mom said, ever one to be polite.

"Nice, sure, but in the official record, the police never cataloged any of their names. We have no idea who those

239

people were. What if one of them was connected to Nico? What exactly did they touch? And they didn't secure the scene after. The person taking this video gets right up to the car."

"What does all of this mean?" I ask.

"It means the cops screwed up. They've got mishandling of evidence, failure to secure a scene. On cross-examination, we're going to be able to hit them over and over with these details. It's one thing if I'd brought it up—I'd suspected as much from their report of the scene—but this video is a gold mine. Seeing is believing. By the time we're done, they're not going to be able to keep the knife in evidence. It's too compromised. There's no way to say for sure how many people might have touched it, how it might have been cross-contaminated. Sure it's got Jill's fingerprints on it, but there are also a bunch of unidentified partials. Even Simone's prints are on there."

"That's really good, isn't it?" My mom was leaning forward in her seat, like she wanted to be excited, but wasn't sure she should give herself permission.

"This is great news. The knife is a significant portion of their case that goes toward intent. There's no doubt there was an accident and that Jill was driving, but their ability to prove that this was intentional has been built on a house of cards. It always was, but any dent we put in their wall of circumstantial evidence makes the whole thing likely to fall down."

"But won't they still look at the accident?" Dad said.

Evan tapped my dad in the center of the chest. "*Accident* is the key word. I'm not saying the girls didn't have a fight. They might have—there was certainly a lot going on for them—and of course there was a car accident, but if there's no clear proof that Jill stabbed Simone, then why assume it's anything more than a tragedy?"

"But Simone was stabbed, wasn't she?" I asked. "I mean, she had a stab wound."

"We'll see if their medical expert can stand by that once we start cross-examination. Simone's body was really badly damaged in the accident. Pinning particular injuries to being caused by the knife versus glass or metal in the car will be challenging—hell, the gearshift tore through part of the palm of her hand."

Evan stopped suddenly as if he'd just realized sounding gleeful over how messed up Simone had been was in poor taste. "Even their theory of motivation, that this was driven by rage over the situation with Nico, is pretty flimsy," Evan continued. "What's to say this was anything more than a girl spat? We can line up miles of witnesses who will testify to how close you two were. The onus is on them to prove that you'd throw away a decade plus of friendship out the window for a guy you'd known a bit more than a week. They're hinging everything on meeting the legal term of having done something with malice aforethought. That you wanted to do something badly, and you planned it. They've got nothing to back that up. Nothing."

Hope bloomed in my chest, like a high-speed video of a flower expanding and growing.

Chapter Twenty-seven

Police Statement from Kate Murphy, Fellow Student in the Adventures Abroad Program

Transcript to be provided to Italian police

The last time any of us saw either of them was that morning. Ms. Ochoa had a lecture first thing on how the area had been impacted by the war and the Italian resistance. We were all going to see a movie that night, something with Cher and that lady from *Downton Abbey*. The title was *Tea with . . .* somebody. She gave us the rest of the morning off. We had a drive in the afternoon to go see something, I can't remember because after everything that happened, we never ended up going.

Ms. Ochoa sent Jill and Simone on an errand to pick up stuff to make sandwiches for a picnic lunch we could take with us. They still weren't really talking to each other yet. I think Ms. Ochoa thought that if she gave them a project to do together, then they'd have to talk and they'd work stuff out.

Neither of them seemed upset to be sent on the errand. I mean, they didn't look thrilled, but it wasn't like they were

super mad about it either. I never thought anything bad
would happen.

***

**Police Statement from Abigail Johnson, Fellow Student in
the Adventures Abroad Program**

Transcript to be provided to Italian police

Simone was pissed that she was going to get stuck making
sandwiches for the trip. First because of what the program
cost—why did we have to make our own? Second, because Jill
was still giving her the cold shoulder. Simone told me that she
knew Jill was waiting for her to apologize, but that if she would
only get her head out of her ass, Jill would realize that Simone
had only kissed Nico to make her see what a douche-canoe
he really was. Simone had tried to tell her a bunch of times
before, but Jill wouldn't listen. She was talking about how
she was going to move to Italy and defer college for a year,
and Simone was pissed. She said Jill was too smart to be that
stupid, but Jill wouldn't listen, so Simone did something Jill
couldn't ignore.

I thought it was pretty harsh, but Simone kept saying the
ends justified the means and that she did what she had to do
and wasn't going to be sorry. She kept saying, "A girl's gotta
do what a girl has to do."

So then Ms. Ochoa came up with the brilliant plan for
them to make the sandwiches. I never understand why adults

act like they know what's best all the time. If I don't want to hang out with someone, then don't make me. Why did she have to force it? They were already stuck rooming together. Why make them spend more time together? It was stupid. I saw Jill's face when Ms. Ochoa told them, and she looked really angry. I knew something bad was going to go down. You could just tell.

***

Media Interview with Antonio Conti, Local Resident, Montepulciano, Italy

English subtitles prepared by Euro-news Services

I own with my wife a small wine bar, Carmelo, in Montepulciano. We have several local wines for tasting, and we make small snacks, bruschettas, marinated olives, breads, meats for platters. We get some tourists, but we are a bit tucked away, so most of our business is locals. The hotel had called me to say some students would be down to pick up items for a picnic lunch. The charges were to go to the hotel.

The girls came in. Both so *bellissime*. (*Kisses the tips of his fingers.*) One tall and blond, the other dark and curvy. Like beautiful bookends. But, oh, the scowls. You could feel the tension between the two of them—like electricity. Snap! My daughters were like this growing up. It would be like waiting for a thunderstorm to break in the house. Dark, charged, and everyone just wanting the first loud crack of thunder to start and then things could blow over. I said to my wife, "Look, they are just like Sophia and Fiametta," and we chuckled a bit.

I gave both girls a glass of wine on the house along with some bread and oil. This olive oil is made by my brother-in-law. The best in the region, I tell you. I thought it would be nice to have them stay a bit longer. It is good for business to have beautiful girls sitting at your tables. And if they like our café, perhaps they tell their school friends, and all of them will come back later.

The blonde girl drank all her wine—whoop—in one big drink. Like life is short. The dark girl sipped hers, more careful. At first they were totally silent. Then the blonde one talked. My wife and I don't speak much English. My daughters are much better; they live in Florence and work in fashion—lots of English there. But me, not so much. I do know the blonde girl said sorry. This word I know in English. She said it several times. They went back and forth several times. I don't know what all they were saying, but even without language, you can feel the tension, no? I even said to my wife—"I bet you a boy is at the heart of this." I had of course no idea, but it seemed like that kind of fight. (*Thumps chest*) You can feel passion here, even if you don't know the language.

Their voices got louder, but not yelling. Then the blonde says something, and the dark-haired girl starts to cry. Then they are hugging. Boom. Storm over. (*Snaps fingers*) Now they seem like friends again. They finish their wine. They did not have more than a glass each. Not even a big glass. I told the police right after the accident, neither girl seemed drunk or angry anymore. They took the food and went back toward the

245

hotel. We heard the loud bang of the accident not even an hour later, but it wasn't until that night when some guests were in the café that we heard it was two American girls. I asked and they said yes, a blonde and a dark-haired girl. I told myself it wasn't the two beautiful young women, but I think in my heart I knew it to be true. Everyone is saying it was murder, a crime of passion, but I say they were not fighting when they left here. When they left here, all was well. I think it must be some kind of accident.

***

Media Statement from the Lawyers for Niccolo Landini
For Immediate Release
26 May

Our client Niccolo Landini would like to say first and foremost that he is greatly saddened by the death of Simone McIvory. Mr. Landini has cooperated fully with the police and their investigation, and has admitted having romantic relationships with that Ms. Jill Charron and Ms. McIvory. He regrets these actions, but we point out that no crime has been committed.

As to the rental vehicle that was used in the crime, Mr. Landini had no forethought or knowledge Ms. Charron planned to use the automobile. He rented the car with the intention of having the opportunity to speak with Ms. Charron and apologize. However, Mr. Landini did not see either girl in Montepulciano. He had parked the car near the hotel, but was under the impression that the students were out in the town.

Mr. Landini went for a walk to wait until later when the students were expected to be at the hotel. When he returned, the car was gone. He discovered quickly that it had been involved in an accident with two American girls. Mr. Landini knew that he had no knowledge of any crime, planned or otherwise, but he worried that if he admitted his connection to the car, the police would erroneously assume he was involved. He regrets not coming forward sooner.

Chapter Twenty-eight

The courtroom was a huge disappointment. Years of *Law & Order* watching had led me to believe it would be more imposing, or at least less like an outdated hotel conference room. It was small and there weren't any windows. The carpet was worn, and there was a large dark stain that I was pretty sure had been coffee near the defense table. Given that it was the halls of justice, you would have thought someone would have sprung for some steam cleaning.

I pulled on the neck of the shirt my mom had brought for me to wear. The tag itched. Evan wanted to make sure I made a good impression on the judge. I looked like one of those fundamentalist religious kids; all that was missing was hair straight down to my ass and a WWJD bracelet color-coordinated to my too-long floral skirt. I hated everything about the outfit, most of all the idea that I had to wear it. Was anyone really going to be fooled by a Peter Pan collar blouse and Virgin Mary baby blue cardigan?

I didn't want to be here. I wanted to be back at the hospital. I needed to talk to Dr. Weeks, but this appearance was mandatory, according to Evan. He said even though this wasn't an official trial, it would look bad if I didn't show up. The Italians weren't allowed to argue their case in our justice system. They'd successfully applied for me to be extradited. They'd already certified the record to the Secretary of State, who decides whether to surrender the fugitive to the requesting government. However, Evan had petitioned for something called a writ of habeas corpus as soon as the order was issued. Now it was up to the district court, and they could stay the order if they wanted.

Evan poked me under the table with his pen. This was my cue that I was doing something wrong—fidgeting, looking bored, scowling. One of the million things on the list he'd made when we prepped. He'd even included things like "pick at your teeth," like I had to be told how to have basic social skills. I forced my face into a bland smile and made sure I was sitting up straight and staring at the judge. I could feel the presence of my parents directly behind me. I could also sense the horde of reporters. They were forbidden from taking pictures during the hearing, but I knew they were recording everything, taking notes, hoping something would happen that they could talk about. Maybe some rampant tooth picking.

They would have been thrilled if they'd known the real news. I was starting to remember. Or at least I thought I might be having memories. There were flashes, images, like faded photographs. I could picture a hotel room with bright damask wallpaper and a glass of water balanced on top of the bedside table. There was a row of trees, cypress I think, lined up like lime Popsicles along a dirt road. A group of people all standing in front of an old building, arms around one another, mugging for the camera. A painting with a woman pleading on her knees in front of a solider wearing armor and a look of pompous arrogance. I sensed if I could just get the images in the right order, I could flip through them, like one of those homemade animation pads we'd made in eighth-grade art class. Put them in motion and see what was missing.

"Mr. Stanley," the judge said, "the court will hear you now on Title 18, Code 3184, in the case of Ms. Jill Charron." Despite the fact that I was knocking myself out to impress her, the feeling clearly wasn't mutual. The judge hardly seemed to notice me, and she sounded bored. She rarely looked up from her desk and kept scribbling something on the paper in front of her. For all I knew, she was working on a crossword.

"Your Honor," Evan said. He stood and buttoned his suit jacket. "You will see in our documents that the Italian court has failed to meet the standard for compelling evidence. Their request for extradition is nothing more than a fishing trip."

The two Italian detectives screwed up their faces. My hunch was they were trying to figure out what fishing had to do with anything. Detective Marco looked like he hadn't shaved in a day or two. They must have been frustrated with how things were turning out. Just a few days ago I was public enemy number one, a murderous slut, but now things were changing. Instead of just one or two blogs where the media company had placed the story, now there were at least a half a dozen talking about me as someone who was being framed for a crime. An innocent. The video of the police mishandling the evidence had been viewed more than 350,000 times since the media company had posted it on YouTube.

Evan was still talking while walking back and forth in front of the empty jury box. He seemed to be making his case to the crowd in the gallery instead of the judge. He ticked off the mistakes the Italian police had made. I knew they were listed in our petition to the court, but I supposed repeating everything was part of the process.

I focused on the images that I'd remembered, trying to see if there were any new ones. This morning I'd woken up with a crystal clear image of Simone sitting across a small table from me. We each had a wineglass in front of us; her face was serious. I wanted to reach through the image and hear what we were talking about, but there was nothing. It was a flat image. No sound, taste, or noise.

Evan sat down. He poked me with his pen, and I smiled up at the judge as if I were a beauty contestant in the bikini portion of the contest. A look that I hoped said, *Sure, I've been stripped bare, but I don't mind you seeing me like this. Heck, I like it. Stare away! I've got nothing to hide.*

"The court will review this petition," the judge said, standing. Everyone scrambled to his or her feet as the bailiff instructed us to all rise. The judge was gone before most of them were able to stand. A few people were murmuring, and I knew they were wondering if that was it. I was glad Evan had warned me that there wouldn't be an immediate decision. The secret to avoiding being let down is to keep your expectations low.

My parents were suddenly at my side. Mom rested her arm on my shoulder as if she could protect me from the crowd of reporters.

"How do you think it went?" my dad said, his voice low so no one around us could listen in.

"Good," Evan said. "Judge Rendahl can be a hard read, but her history shows her to be a stickler for people dotting their *i*'s and crossing their *t*'s. She's not going to like the Italians' sloppy work. She's got zero patience for that kind of stuff—that's going to be in our favor. Plus, with public opinion swinging to our side and questions about why the Italians didn't look more closely at Nico, I don't see her ruling for extradition. She won't want to be the one to send an innocent American abroad."

"Then Jill could come home?" my mom asked.

Evan nodded.

"And then this will be all over," she said.

Evan packed up his briefcase. "I don't know about that. The Italians may push forward with a trial. You need to prepare yourself for that. Even if this ruling goes our way, it doesn't mean that it will end right away."

My dad cursed under his breath.

"Mr. Stanley?" a reporter asked. "You said you had something for us?"

Evan nodded. He motioned for my parents and me to follow him into the hall where the reporters could turn on their cameras. I'd known this was coming, Evan told us it was time to make a formal statement. My knees felt like they'd turned to oatmeal.

As soon as we stepped outside, I blinked. A bank of lights shone directly in our eyes. It was like center-stage kind of bright. I paused, but my dad had his palm pressed into my back pushing me. I stood next to Evan, with my parents directly behind me. I didn't know what to do with my arms. I knew Evan wouldn't want me to cross them, but they felt heavy and meaty just hanging at my side. I settled for lacing them in front of me—maybe people would think I was praying.

"If everyone will be quiet, we'd like to make a statement," Evan ran his hand quickly through his hair. He had a game show host smile. "The Charron family is pleased with how our petition to the court went today. We have faith that the U.S. justice system will be fair and balanced. They will see that what happened in Italy was a tragic accident and will not want to compound one tragedy with another." Evan motioned for me to step forward.

I took a step, and my parents moved so I had one on either side of me, like the granite lions outside the library. I took a deep breath. I was holding my prepared speech in my hand. I'd read it at least a hundred times. Last night I'd done it in front of a video camera so Evan could point out any possible errors or weird facial tics. He was rabidly insistent that I not read it too fast, or too slow, and that I keep a bland expression, not happy, not too sad. I was striving for as middle of the road as I could make it. I hadn't wanted to bring the paper with me—I thought it made me look rehearsed—but Evan said he'd seen too many people lock up once the cameras were on. He told me to think of it as a security blanket, and I had to admit now that I was glad I had it.

"Thank you for letting me make a statement," I said. "I'm leaving my legal situation in the hands of my lawyer, but I wanted to speak about what's gotten lost in the coverage of this case. My friend Simone." My voice cracked, and I froze for a second. I took a deep breath and looked back up. I spotted Evan's secretary, Molly, standing at the back. Evan had promised she would be there to give me someone to look at, someone who would be friendly. She smiled and winked.

"Simone and I have been friends since fourth grade. And in that time, we did millions of things together—we had sleepovers, we went to camp, we learned to swim—and when she backed her parents' car into the garage, I was at her side when it was time to confess. We also had fights, as friends do, but one thing never changed—we loved each other. Simone was, and always will be, my closest friend. I look forward to the court finding in my favor so I can grieve her in private."

I paused. My dad tensed, ready to leap in and finish my statement if I couldn't hack it. I cut him off before he could say anything. Evan was going to freak, but I was going off script. Now that I had everyone's attention, I had to say it. The image I'd had this morning of Simone and me together cemented what I'd wanted to believe all along. I hadn't done anything.

"You know I lost my memory in the accident. But one thing I know is that I did not hurt Simone, that I couldn't have hurt her." A tear ran down my cheek, and the snap of cameras echoed back at me like muted applause. "I'm so sorry that this accident happened, and if I could go back in time and make it turn out differently, I would. I wanted to convince all of you, but now I realize that Simone, wherever she is, knows the truth, and that's what really matters."

I stepped back. I could hear Evan let out a relieved sigh. Then I remembered the last line of the statement. "Oh, and I wanted to thank the staff at the hospital and my parents for their unending support during this difficult time."

Evan clapped his hands together. "Okay then, that's our statement for today. Thank you all for coming."

***

"How did you feel things went?" Dr. Weeks asked.

"Pretty good," I said. "The statement to the press went better than I expected." I flushed. I felt absurdly proud of myself, like I'd won regionals in debate or gotten an A on an AP physics exam. "I didn't forget any words," I said. "The aphasia's almost all gone."

She smiled. "You should thank Deena," she said, mentioning my speech-language pathologist. "And give yourself a pat on the back too. You put in a lot of effort."

"I won't ever forget what you've done for me," I said.

"All in a day's work," she said. She tossed the rubber-band ball that had been on her desk and caught it. "Now, why don't you tell me why you wanted to see me so badly?"

I lowered my voice. "I'm starting to remember."

Dr. Weeks nodded for me to continue.

"Nothing really specific," I admitted. "But images, stuff from Italy. There had been a few things earlier, but now it's happening a lot."

"Are you sure you aren't having false memories, perhaps something someone told you about, or pictures you've seen?"

I shrugged. "I'm pretty sure they're real."

"The thing to remember is that it is going to be very hard for you to know if they are real or not. I'm not saying that they aren't—or that they are—but simply that I want you to be cautious."

I turned what she said over in my mind. "But that's the thing, right? I won't ever know for sure, unless I discover that I kept some kind of diary the whole time."

"Even then you couldn't be sure," Dr. Weeks said.

"Why?"

"You have no way of knowing if you wrote the diary with the goal of being completely honest with your feelings, or because you wished you felt that way, or because you suspected someone was reading your diary and you wanted them to find it."

I rubbed the bridge of my nose. "You have a way of complicating things that I thought were straightforward."

She shrugged humbly. "It's a gift."

"I get that I can't know for sure, but these *feel* real," I said.

She smiled. "Then I'm happy for you."

"One of my memories is of Simone," I said. "I can tell in that moment that things are okay. I didn't hate her." The words I'd been saving up came out in a rush, tumbling over each other. "I don't know how to explain it, but I can tell by how I feel when I think of that one memory. I wouldn't have hurt Simone over Nico. I didn't care that much about him. I *know* it."

Dr. Weeks reached over and took my hand. "Take it easy."

I stopped talking and took several deep breaths to try to calm myself down.

"I am happy you're getting some of your memories back and even happier if what you're remembering is giving you some feelings of peace and resolution."

"I know I've always said that I knew I didn't do it, but the truth is . . ."

"You were afraid that you might have," she said, finishing my sentence.

I nodded. Relieved that it was out there. Like I'd spat out a cancerous tumor, a wet, pulsing grey mass.

Dr. Weeks stood and came around her desk. "Come here," she said. I stood, and she hugged me. "I always knew you didn't," she said softly.

"How?" I asked.

She smiled. "I could just tell that's not who you are. But what's more important is that you've realized it."

"I think it's going to be okay," I said. I felt almost scared saying it aloud. Hoping I hadn't jinxed myself.

"I think so too."

Chapter Twenty-nine

***Justice for Simone* Blog**

Lately all the media has to talk about is that Chilly Jilly might be innocent, but if she's so innocent, why did her family have her flee Italy before an investigation could really happen? How does Jill explain the note she wrote to Simone that basically states she wanted her dead?

Fact: Jill's fingerprints are on the knife that was used to stab Simone. Not Nico's.

Here at *JFS*, we're not sure what we make of Nico's sudden admission that the car was his—but we are sure that we don't buy his story that he never even talked to either Jill or Simone after he was fired. He was involved in the accident, no doubt about it—but Jilly's no innocent. What do you think?

Comments:

Pixydust9: Chilly Jilly wanted to get rid of Simone and she convinced Nico to help her. She's like some kind of femme fatale.

Betty4just: I call bullshit on his whole story.

Murderfan22: What if Nico was waiting for them by the hotel when the girls returned from the café? Maybe he planned to kill both of them and Jill was trying to escape when the accident happened.

Kgrendds: OMG, what if Jill had been trying to save Simone?

Betty4just: If that was her plan she did a pretty shit job of it. No way she's innocent.

Dreamgurl: I think Nico did it and the Italian cops are framing Jill because she's an American. They'd like nothing more than to drag down the USA, even if they have to go after an innocent girl to do it. I don't trust the Italians. Wake up people, foreigners hate Americans. If you think they're not that corrupt then you haven't been paying attention to the news.

***

Police Statement from Isabella Forni, Local Resident, Montepulciano, Italy

Florence Police Department
Original transcript in Italian, translated to English by Stoker and Mills Translation Services, New York, New York

I saw this man (*points to photo of Niccolo Landini*) on April

28. I work at the bakery that is across from the hotel where the Americans were staying. He parked his car in the loading zone and then walked away. I didn't see him talk to either of the American girls, but he was here. Then I was busy in the back, getting an order ready. Later, when I looked again, the car was gone.

***

Postcard from Simone McIvory to Tara Ingells, dated 28 April

I would say I wish you were here, but I wouldn't wish this trip on anyone. It sucks. I wish I wasn't here. I wish I wasn't anywhere.

Si

***

Excerpt from Police Interview with Tara Ingells

Date: 27 May
Time: 15:00
Present: Tara Ingells, Jennifer Ingells (Tara's mother), Detective Linda Winston, Detective Jonathon Reid
Transcript to be provided to Italian police

Detective Reid: Why didn't you hand over the postcard to authorities when you were initially interviewed?

Tara Ingells: I didn't think it was important. In fact, I didn't even get it in the mail until a few days after the accident. I'd already met with you guys. I guess it took a while to get to me because of being so far and stuff.

Detective Reid: Is that the only reason you didn't turn it in?

Tara Ingells: I thought people might use it to say Jill was making Simone unhappy, and I knew that wasn't it. I keep telling people that they were best friends, but everything keeps getting twisted around, like, sometimes stuff is true, but then it's not at the same time.

Detective Winston: Why bring the postcard forward now?

Tara Ingells: There was a thing on the news yesterday that Simone's stab wounds wouldn't have been enough to kill her. Whatta you call it—superficial. Is that true?

Detective Reid: We can't confirm any details.

Tara Ingells: Well, the thing on the news is that she had only one really nasty cut on her arm and then one on her side. The news lady said it was, like, the accident that really killed her.

Detective Reid: Again, we can't confirm any of the details.

Tara Ingells: I don't want to hurt Simone's family.

Jennifer Ingells: Tell them what you told me.

Tara Ingells: I wondered if anyone considered the idea that maybe Simone stabbed herself?

Detective Winston: You think it's possible Simone was attempting suicide?

Tara Ingells: Not really wanting to die or anything, but Simone could be sort of, you know, dramatic.

Detective Reid: Stabbing yourself is more than a bit dramatic.

Jennifer Ingells: She tried this once before.

Tara Ingells: Mom!

Detective Reid: I'm sorry. Mrs. Ingells, can you clarify what you mean by "she tried it before"? Are you saying she stabbed herself?

Jennifer Ingells: No, just that she attempted suicide. Simone supposedly took a bunch of sleeping pills a year ago.

Tara Ingells: Not that many. I don't even know if she really took them—she just told me that she did. Simone had something going on with her parents. I don't know what it was, but she was really upset about it. She took the pills to sorta get their attention and make them stop fighting. Like I said, she never really wanted to die. I didn't know about it when it happened, just after she told me. She wasn't upset. More like proud that her plan worked.

Detective Reid: So you think it's possible this was an attempt to get Jill's attention?

Tara Ingells: Maybe. If Simone did try to kill herself and Jill tried to stop her, that would explain why her fingerprints were on the knife. I bet Italy doesn't have 911, so maybe Jill was just trying to drive her to a hospital.

Jennifer Ingells: I've been watching the news coverage nonstop since this whole story broke. I heard about it being this Nico fellow's car. My theory is that Simone found out he was there to get back together with Jill, and she snapped—pulled this suicide stunt. Nico freaked out and refused to help, so Jill took the car and then there was the accident.

Detective Winston: Okay, let's slow this down. Did Simone ever directly tell you that she wanted to kill herself?

Tara Ingells: No, but the postcard message seemed weird, especially after I heard about the cuts.

Detective Winston: Did Simone and you have any phone calls while she was in Europe?

Tara Ingells: No. I think their phones didn't, like, work or something over there.

Detective Winston: Were there any other emails or correspondence between you and Simone or Jill other than those we've already reviewed and this postcard?

Tara Ingells: No.

Detective Winston: So you have no direct knowledge of what happened between Jill and Simone?

Tara Ingells: No, but I'm telling you, Jill wouldn't kill Simone over some guy.

Detective Reid: Okay, thanks for bringing this forward. We will share this with the Italian detectives on the case.

Tara Ingells: Is this going to help Jill?

Detective Reid: I'm sorry, but we can't really comment on the case.

Tara Ingells: Will I get the postcard back? It's the last thing I ever had from Simone.

Detective Winston: We will put in that request.

Interview Ends

Chapter Thirty

I yawned, trying to decide if I was too tired to take a shower before going to sleep. I pushed open the door to my room and shuffled in. Using crutches to get around was like a nonstop spin class. By the time the day was over, I'd be coated in a thin layer of sticky sweat and torn between wanting to wash it all off and wanting to collapse directly into bed.

"Hey," Anna said.

I jumped. I hadn't realized she was in the room. "Any reason you're sitting around in the dark?" I asked her. Things between us were still awkward and overly polite. I wanted to fix that, but I didn't even know how to start.

"No. Just thinking," Anna said. "I guess I didn't realize it had gotten so dark."

I flicked on the light next to my bed and the fluorescent buzzed to life. I wondered if I could get the cast off early. My leg itched all the time now, like I'd slathered it in honey and stuck it in an anthill. It took all my self-control to keep from grabbing a wire hanger from the closet and shoving it down the side of the cast until I could reach just the spot. The only thing that prevented me was a horror story from one of the occupational therapists about someone who did that and developed a massive infection, complete with maggots. I peeled off my hoodie and caught a sniff of myself. Shower.

"I need to talk to you about something," Anna said.

"Sure." I stepped into the bathroom and pulled my hair up into a loose bun.

"It's sorta important."

My stomach clenched. I wasn't sure I was up to a big clear-the-air discussion. If she wanted to pound on my emotions, we'd need to wait until I had a nap at least.

I took a deep breath to ground myself. "What did you want to talk about?"

"I found out who your blog troll was." Anna's voice was calm, as if she was announcing something mundane, like there was a slight chance of rain tomorrow, or the cafeteria had oatmeal cookies.

This was a million miles away from what I'd thought she might say. I'd left my crutches by the bed, so I hopped double time to her bedside. "Who is it?" I knew Evan had said that any troll wasn't relevant to the investigation, but he might be wrong. I felt a rush of adrenaline. It was as if I could see a sliver of future opening up. Somehow, knowing who the troll was would put more of the puzzle together. I didn't know how I was so sure—but I could feel it.

"I'm not sure you'll want to know," Anna said.

She was so serious. It must be someone I knew. "I want to know," I insisted.

"The thing is, people do things for all sorts of messed-up reasons, and once you know something, you can't unknow it," she said.

"Tell me."

"Maybe we should both talk about it with Dr. Weeks tomorrow. You know, in case you need to process it with someone." Her hands twisted. "Except I'm not sure if we should tell her everything."

I stared at her. *Process it?* When had she started with the psychobabble bullshit? If she hadn't wanted to tell me, then she shouldn't have brought it up. Anna had her hands in fists in her lap. She was really stressed.

Fuck. It was my dad. That's what she doesn't want to tell me.

I blinked fast to keep from crying. Why else would she be that worried about telling me? I realized I was holding my breath and forced myself to inhale deeply. I think I'd known on some level that it was possible. My dad had always thought my blog was stupid. He never said it directly, but he was clear that he thought everything I posted on there was naïve and that I didn't really understand how the world worked. I snapped my attention back.

"—think if you've waited this long—" Anna was saying.

"I want to know," I said, cutting her off. "I have a right to know. I'm not going to freak out."

Anna sighed. "Okay, but sit down."

I dropped onto the edge of her bed and nodded for her to continue. I practiced the serious, nonhysterical, accepting face I would make when she told me.

"My friend Tomas is the one who checked into it. He sometimes sets up fake free Wi-Fi sites, like in coffee shops, because he can skim people's passwords and stuff." Anna looked at me. "He's not stealing from just anybody, just people

267

who look like they've got a bit to spare."

I rolled my eyes. "I'm sure he's a regular Robin Hood. Spit it out already."

"I'm telling you this so you understand he's a tech genius. He didn't make a mistake—he knew what he was doing. And the other reason I'm sharing is because Tomas was real clear he doesn't want to be messed up in this at all. If anyone asks, he's going to deny he had anything to do with getting you this information."

"No one else is going to care who it is," I said.

"It was Simone," Anna said.

All the air evaporated from my lungs, making a giant crater in the center of my chest.

"That's impossible."

Anna passed me a sheet of notebook paper. "Tomas figured that the troll set up a dummy account so they could post under that name—VoxDude. Most people figure that's enough to keep them anonymous, but if they post from the same computer as their regular account, the IP address is the same."

I stared down at the paper. It had a bunch of numbers on it. It might as well have been in Greek.

"The reason Tomas wanted access to your email accounts and other commenters was to see if there were any matches. And there was one." Anna's finger tapped the paper. "That's the IP address of Simone's email and the comments she left on the blog under her own name." She tapped farther down the page. "And that's the IP address of your troll."

"They're the same," I said, stating the obvious. Anna nodded. I stood up quickly.

I hobbled as fast as I could into the bathroom and puked. It felt like my stomach was tearing free from my body, flesh ripping. I stood panting over the bowl, half expecting to see my guts floating on top of the water. When I was sure nothing else was going to come up, I spat, trying to clear the sour bile out of my mouth.

Anna was in her chair at the door. "Are you okay?"

"No," I said simply. I spat again. My leg was throbbing. I'd put too much weight on the walking cast. I flushed the toilet and stumbled over to the sink. I swished water around in my mouth and leaned down, stuffing my head under the tap.

"Do you want me to get one of the nurses?"

"I'll be okay. Just give me a second."

Anna rolled back out, leaving me alone. I stared at myself in the mirror. I'd discussed the troll for hours with Simone. She'd slept over countless times, and we'd lain in the dark and talked about it.

"But why? This trolling happened almost a year ago. Simone and I were getting along fine then. Nico and the trip weren't even on the radar yet."

Anna snorted, broadcasting her view that clearly we hadn't been getting along fine. She'd seen the troll comments.

Is it hard being as stupid as you? Why didn't evolution take you out?

With all your money couldn't your daddy buy you any common sense?

Feminist is just another word for ugly bitch who can't get a guy.

Why do you have to have your huge nose in everything?

I'd always known Simone didn't see the point of the blog, but I hadn't realized that she thought it was stupid. That *I* was stupid.

Simone had been the one thing I had been certain I could count on, and now I wasn't sure she'd even liked me.

I hopped back into the bedroom. I didn't want to take a shower anymore. The idea of it exhausted me. Blinking seemed like too much work. I dragged myself into bed and pulled the covers over my head, curling into a fetal ball.

"Do you want to talk?" Anna asked softly.

"No."

Outside our room I could hear people bustling about. They'd been showing a movie in the common area, and it must have broken up. People were milling around in the halls, repeating jokes from the movie. Laughing.

"She might have had a lot of reasons for doing it, you know," Anna said.

I kept the blanket over my face. "You mean other than that she hated me."

"Maybe she was jealous. Or maybe she wanted to feel like you needed her, so she created a crisis."

"Sure." My voice came out flat.

"I'm not going to tell anyone," Anna said softly.

I stared up at the ceiling and realized the importance of her words. This was a motive. I might not kill Simone over a guy, but over finding out that she would do something like this . . .

"This would have given me a reason to have done it," I said.

Anna reached over and yanked the blankets away from my face. "Look at me." I rolled over so we were eye to eye. "I don't know if you did it, but I'd get it if you did."

270

My heart was racing. It felt as if it was going to burst out of my chest and onto the floor. I started shaking.

"Listen, all I'm saying is that finding out your best friend lied to you? Said those shitty things? That would make anyone snap. There'd be some who would say she had it coming."

"The cops won't say that. They'll send me to jail." The idea of spending years, decades, in a tiny cell, thousands of miles from home, reared up in front of me, blocking out all other thoughts. My shaking increased.

"You can't tell them about this." Anna's voice was stern, like a parent chastising a small child. "Do you get that? You can't tell a soul. Not even Dr. Weeks. I want to trust her, but the fewer people who know, the better."

I propped myself up on my elbow. "You can't be serious—I can't keep something like this to myself."

"Yes you can, and you better. There are only three people who know this—you, me, and Tomas. Tomas isn't going to say anything. He's got his own shit on the line. He isn't going to risk his own ass. He won't tell. And I won't either."

"But the police could find out on their own. If Tomas can figure out this IP address thingy"—I waved my hand, the explanation she'd given having already disappeared from my mind—"then surely a bunch of trained cops can do it. I should tell my lawyer at least so he can decide what's the best thing to do."

"The cops aren't looking into it. You shut that blog down at the beginning of the year. No one has connected the blog and what happened in Italy. And for all you know, it's not connected. There's no way to know for sure if Simone confessed this to you on the trip or if you found out some other way. It might mean nothing. Keep your mouth shut, and no one will know."

I put my weight on my bad leg, using the pain to ground me. I felt like if I let go of the covers, I would float away. "I don't know if I can do that."

Anna swung her body out of bed and into her chair. She rolled over so she was inches from my face. "Listen to me. You need to do this. You need to toughen up right fucking now."

I started to cry harder. I covered my eyes. Anna yanked my hands away, holding them down.

"You don't have the luxury of falling apart. Shit is turning around for you. You tell people about Simone being your troll, and it won't matter if you did it or not. People will assume you did. You have no idea what jail is like. However bad you think it is, it's a thousand times worse. And it will go on forever, not just while you're locked up. You'll have kissed your fancy college education goodbye. Even once you get out, try getting a job with a felony murder conviction. And you want to get married? What kind of person wants to marry someone who did time? Besides, you'll be too old by the time you get out to have kids. We're not talking about doing a stint in jail—we're talking about the entire rest of your life."

"But what about Simone's life?"

"She's dead. Nothing you do now is going to bring her back."

"I don't know," I hedged.

"Then listen to me. I do know. You forget we ever had this conversation. You forget it ever happened at all."

I searched her face. "Do you promise you won't tell?"

She met my gaze and didn't look away. "I promise."

If Anna told the media about this, they'd pay her. I didn't know how much, but I was willing to bet it would be a lot for that kind of exclusive. The police might even pay her; there could be a reward for proof I was involved in the crime.

"Why?" I asked.

"Because I'm your friend." She gestured around the room. "Because we had this together."

Chapter Thirty-one

It was a kitchen. Simone and I were making sandwiches. Side by side. Partners in culinary crime. I was slicing tomatoes. The knife piercing the flesh, sliding through effortlessly, a smear of juice and clots of seeds left behind on the counter.

We were talking about prom. We were going to go with a group of friends, no guys. Girls gone wild.

"We should think about getting dresses here. I feel sorry for every other girl at the dance, because we're going to look amazing," Simone said.

"It doesn't have to be a competition," I said. "Women should support one another, not tear one another down."

"Spare me the feminist lecture," Simone said. "The only women who avoid competition with other women are the ones who know they'll lose. And that's not us—we're going to look great." She pulled some bottles of water out of the tiny fridge and added them to the cooler. "Do you think we'll have enough if we bring one bottle a person, or should we bring a few extras?"

Her words bounced around in my head. That was the last comment my troll ever left on my blog. *The only women who avoid competition with other women are the ones who know they'll lose.* I'd read it and been so frustrated. The troll never stopped, and I hadn't been strong enough to keep fighting. I gave in. I deleted my blog. Just like that. The realization it was Simone fell into place with almost an audible click in my head.

"You left that message," I said, putting together the facts. The truth of the statement seemed obvious now that I'd said it aloud. I felt almost lightheaded, my nerves prickling up and down my spine. Simone knew me better than anyone. Each barbed comment had hit home because Simone knew where to strike. Why is it they say that you always hurt the ones you love? Because you know exactly how to do it.

Simone opened her mouth to argue, but she couldn't. She seemed to shrink as if her bones were deflating. Her eyes darted around the small kitchen—she wanted to escape, but I blocked the door.

"Why?" I croaked.

She stuck out her chin, defiant. "I didn't leave the first couple of comments," Simone said. "That was someone else. But they said what I was thinking, so then I started and I just kept doing it."

"You couldn't tell me to my face?" I asked her, my voice rising. "If you thought what I said was that stupid, then you should have said something. You didn't have to hide behind a fake name."

"I tried to tell you what I thought," Simone said.

I shook my head. "No, you didn't. Not really. Sure, you said a few times that you didn't get why I liked it, that you found blogs boring, but you wrote those things to hurt me."

"You had no business writing about all that stuff," Simone said.

"Excuse me?"

Who the hell did she think she was? Maybe she would have been okay if I'd asked her permission before I hit Publish. She thought everything I did had to have her personal seal of approval.

"What the hell do you know about hardship?" Simone fired back. "Armed with your daddy's credit card in your nice house and your plans to go off to Yale. People like you love to take up this cause or that cause." Simone chucked an apple into the cooler. "It's all such bullshit. A way to feel like you're doing something without having to make any real effort. I made those comments to knock you down a peg. You only act like you care because it lets you feel like you're a good person."

I don't think it—I am a good person. Simone was the one who laughed at people behind their backs, not me. She loved being God, deciding who deserved her approval and who would be a social outcast. My only mistake had been sitting silently by her side. I'd thought being there kept me safe. I'd been a coward.

"You don't know anything about it," I said. "You don't have to experience something to care about it."

"You know what you never got? Just because you have an opinion doesn't mean you have to share it. You're always the one with your hand in the air." Simone mimed me bouncing with my arm in the air, begging to be called on. "You know you have the right answer. You just have to share it in class because you want the rest of us to know how smart you are. It's not about being right; it's about all of us being so freaking impressed that once again the great Jill knows all. That's all your blog was, another chance for you to show off."

I drew back. "Oh, you'll have to forgive me for caring about something more important than what Kim Kardashian wears to Fashion Week. Or let's see, what else consumes your brain power?" I ticked off reasons on my fingers. "Major life choices like if you should put a streak in your hair, or if your jeans look good, or world events like if One Direction is breaking up—"

Simone jabbed a finger in my face, cutting me off. "See, it's shit like that. You think you're better than me. You always have. You sit there silently judging me, feeling superior."

My face broke out in hives. "That is not true. Don't make your insecurity my fault."

"I am not insecure," Simone said.

I threw my head back and laughed. "That is such a lie. I didn't used to get it, but I do now. Everything about you is insecure. All of your 'look at me, look at me' is about misdirection so that no one notices that you're just not that interesting. Maybe you're like your mom and worry that your daddy doesn't love you enough either, or maybe you just need everyone to approve of you all the time. Perfect example—the thing with Nico. You couldn't stand that he picked me and not you."

Simone shook her head. "I knew you wouldn't be able to forgive me. You can't let anything go. You'll be bringing this up ten years from now. It's always about being right for you. You're always the victim, the one we should feel sorry for. Look at how you're still pissed at your dad. He left your mom, but you were always more angry about how it impacted you. How poor sad Jill got left behind."

"Do not drag my dad into this," I said. "And don't try to turn this around. I could have gotten over things with Nico, but not this. I will never forgive you."

"So your stupid blog meant more to you than your Italian boyfriend?" Simone shook her head. "That is messed up."

"You know what's messed up? You. You don't even know how to be anyone's friend. All you want are fans. People to follow you around to make you feel better about yourself. That's what I did for years. Trailed behind you, telling you how awesome you are. Our friendship worked as long as I was there to clap for every tiny thing you did and not ask for any attention for myself. You couldn't stand that I was doing something." I cocked my head as if I were straining to hear something. "Maybe you need all that applause so you don't have time to realize that you haven't done shit with your life and you probably never will."

"Shut up." Simone shoved me hard. I stumbled back into the counter, the granite top digging painfully into my back.

"For someone who felt free leaving all sorts of comments about my life, you sure as hell aren't good at hearing a little feedback about your own," I said. "I guess maybe you're the one who isn't up to any real competition. The truth is you're the pathetic loser, and you can't stand it."

Simone lashed out to slap me. I went to block the hit, but the knife I'd used to slice tomatoes was still in my hand. The blade slid through Simone's skin, unzipping it from the center of her palm down into her wrist. When she pulled her arm back, the knife slid against her hip. I felt her flesh give way, resistance at first, but then cutting faster. Blood welled up, coming thick and fast. It splattered down onto the tile floor. Thick quarter-size drops. It sounded almost like rain.

Then the dream shifted gears, and we were in a car. I cursed when the side of the car scraped a wall as I rounded a corner.

"Watch where you're going," Simone barked.

"I *am* watching." I ground the gears as I eased around another turn. The knife rolled across the backseat, and I wondered why I'd even bothered to bring it. It had seemed important at the time. I braked hard when we came face-to-face with another car, throwing both of us forward against our seat belts. The other driver rolled down his window and started yelling and shaking his hands.

"Jesus, what now?"

"I think I'm going the wrong way—this is a one-way street." I craned my head around, trying to make sense of the road signs. I could feel my blood pressure rising. More than anything, I wanted to get out of the car and just walk away. Disappear.

The other driver was still yelling. He gestured that he wanted me to reverse down the road I'd come up. I swallowed hard. There was no way I'd be able to do that. The driver honked.

"Do something," Simone said.

My teeth clenched. I got the car in reverse, but made it only a few feet before there was a crunch as the rear bumper hit the corner of a building. I put it back in first, but then it stalled.

The other driver shook his head and yelled a few more choice comments. He expertly backed up, leaving enough space that we could move past him and then turn right onto another road.

"Do you even know where you're going?" Simone asked.

"This will get us there." I forced myself to relax my shoulders. "I know where I am now."

"Go faster," Simone demanded. She squeezed the towel that was around her wrist, and it gave a wet squishing sound that made me nauseous. There was another towel pressed against her hip, but that was bleeding more slowly.

"You're going to be okay," I said. I gripped the steering wheel tighter and tried to focus on the road.

"You're going to be in deep shit," Simone said. "Everyone thinks you're Mother Teresa." She pitched her voice high and mimicking. "Jill is *so* smart and kind. Why, that girl is going to change the world."

"I didn't mean to hurt you," I said.

"Let's see what everyone thinks of you now."

Adrenaline flooded my system. "It was an accident—you came at me so fast. I didn't mean—"

"Spare me. You better believe your family is going to pay for me to be better than fine. So I left a few comments on your stupid blog. Look at what you did!" Simone shook her arm in my direction, and a small drop of blood from the saturated towel flew up and hit my cheek. I flinched as if it were acid.

If Simone told on me, I was going to be in trouble. Real trouble. Even in the best-case scenario, Ms. Ochoa was going to send me back. Immediately. I wouldn't be able to finish the program.

Rage washed over me. Simone had ruined the entire trip. I hadn't even wanted her to come. The trip was supposed to be *my* experience, *my* adventure. I was the one who wanted to see Italy. Who actually cared about its history and art. She only came because she hated the idea of me having something she didn't. If Simone hadn't come, everything would have been different. I could have been with Nico—a wonderful, romantic once-in-a-lifetime fling. It didn't matter that we wouldn't have stayed together forever, but it should have been something that I could look back on with affection. I was entitled to have this trip be a great memory, and Simone had ruined every last bit of it. Just like she ruined my blog. Just like I was realizing she'd ruined everything.

And it wasn't just destroying Italy. Simone would make sure everyone at school knew what happened. She'd wander the halls with her arm in a sling. There would be whispering and people nudging each other when I went by.

"Please don't do this," I said.

"You're the one who stabbed me," Simone replied.

I bit back my irritation. I had to make Simone see reason. "I know you love drama, but you get that this is serious, right?"

Simone narrowed her eyes. "Did you just call me a drama queen?"

I clenched the steering wheel. I shouldn't have used those words. They were the truth, but Simone was in no state to hear them. There was no doubt in my mind that she was already casting herself in the role of tragic victim in a Lifetime movie of the week. "If you tell people this was on purpose, I'm going to get in serious trouble."

Simone was silent.

"It could keep me out of college. You could ruin my entire life." I tried to keep my voice even, to make Simone see the situation objectively, but my heart was racing, picking up speed.

"Now who's being the drama queen?" Simone wasn't even looking at me. She stared out the passenger window as if she were on a tour.

"If you tell people it was an accident, I'll make it up to you," I said. I hated myself for making the offer, but desperation was creeping up on me. Eating away at the corners of my awareness. We would be at the hospital soon. I didn't have time for Simone to have one of her sulks. It was always my responsibility to make things right between us. For years, whenever we had a fight, I was the one who'd had to stitch things back together. To woo Simone, no matter who was really at fault. As if her friendship was a gift that she was bestowing on me.

What was Simone going to want to make this situation go away? I had no doubt that it was going to cost me, and not just money. Simone would bring it up over and over. She'd act like it was a joke, but it would have that undercurrent, that bad taste in the background. She would mention it when she wanted something. She wouldn't have to ask; she would just hint around until I gave her what she wanted.

My hands were gripping the steering wheel, tears running down my face.

"Stop crying," Simone said. "I'm the one who's hurt."

"Please don't tell," I asked again.

Simone shrugged as if she couldn't be bothered to answer. There was a tiny hint of a smile on her face. My breath was coming short and fast.

"Please," I repeated. The word felt foreign in my mouth. Almost as if it had texture, like sucking on a large plastic Lego brick. Unyielding. Poking.

Our car passed another sign, blue with a large *H* and the letters *OSPEDALE* below. We were closer.

"Please," I begged. It reminded me of when Simone and I were kids and we would repeat a word over and over until it began to sound like gibberish, shedding its meaning.

Simone still didn't answer.

Either Simone would tell and I would be in huge trouble, or she would keep my secret but then hold it over my head, using it like a weight to push me into whatever she wanted. I'd never be free of her.

Another sign came up, indicating a big curve ahead. I reached for the gearshift to slow the car. The view of the valley opened up in front of me. My heart spasmed. I loved it here. I really loved it.

Screw her. I wasn't leaving.

My foot jammed on the gas; the engine roared and the small car pushed to its limits.

I heard Simone yell out, her hand reaching, scratching at me, trying to grasp the steering wheel. Scrabbling for purchase.

I didn't look over. I kept my foot on the gas and my gaze straight ahead.

We hit the stone wall at full speed. The car seemed to scream out in pain as the metal was ripped from the side and then we were airborne.

I gasped. We were flying. It was so beautiful. I could see for miles.

***

I sat bolt upright, a scream on the verge of tearing free from my throat. I grabbed the edge of the bed to remind myself that I was here in the hospital, not in the car. I looked over at the clock, 3:48 in the morning. Anna was sleeping on her back, the blankets rising and falling on her chest. I made myself match her slow breath until I had the panic under control.

The dream had been so real. I took a sip from one of the water bottles the nursing staff left by all the bedsides, but my hand was shaking so badly I spilled half of it down the front of my T-shirt. Anna snorted, her breath slipping into a snore. She shifted silently and drifted back to sleeping. She was right. Nothing good would come of telling anyone about what I'd learned about Simone, or about this dream.

I shook my head as if to clear the fog. I had to be honest with myself, if no one else. Telling people about my dream wasn't what scared me. What scared me was the idea that this wasn't a dream. That it was a memory. It seemed too vivid, too clear to be a dream. But there was no way I could know for sure. I'd learned enough in rehab to know that this could have been nothing more than a nightmare based on my discussion with Anna.

I could talk to Dr. Weeks about it, but that came with risks. She believed in me. This dream might not change anything, but it might. It might stick in her head, needling her, raising questions. She might feel that she needed to talk about it with someone else. Maybe even the police. What if there was some detail in the dream that could be checked out, verified? And things were changing. People were starting to believe I was innocent. Not everyone, but more and more. Perhaps enough to tip the balance.

It was possible I never knew Simone had been my troll. Heck, it was possible Tomas was completely wrong about the whole thing. Nothing against Anna, but it wasn't like she had trusted this question to a professional computer engineer. This guy most likely learned his technical skills by taking apart stolen Xboxes and stealing school computers. He could be wrong. It wasn't like I could take the information to anyone else to verify—but that didn't mean I had to take it as fact.

I'd never seen myself as the kind of person who would hide from the truth.

But if my dream was accurate, it had started as an accident. Simone had as much involvement as me. After what she did—in some ways she owed me. Simone didn't want a best friend; she wanted a minion. When I hadn't toed the line, she'd tried to take me down a notch, teach me a lesson. Whatever reason Simone had, or gave herself, it didn't excuse what she did. She had hurt me. Maybe she hadn't meant it to be as bad as it was—but I hadn't meant to hurt her either.

You could see it as the whole thing balancing out.

Chapter Thirty-two

It was a different courtroom, but it looked exactly the same as the first one. It made me uneasy, almost like déjà vu.

"All rise," the bailiff called out, and there was a scrape of chairs and rustling as everyone stood.

Judge Rendahl took her seat, her robe billowing, like a crow settling its wings.

"We're here today to discuss the appeal to the extradition request," Judge Rendahl said. "I understand Detective Alban has requested to make a statement?"

Evan shifted in his seat. This explained why we'd had to come back to court. He'd told me that typically the judge would issue her ruling without us having to meet again. He'd said there was no reason to worry, but I could see the look he gave my parents. He thought the Italians might have won and I was going to be taken into custody.

I'd refused to wear the outfit my mom brought. If there was going to be an arrest, then I wanted to go in my own clothing, not dressed like a puritanical librarian. We'd fought about it. I knew she thought I was being unreasonable, but none of it mattered. The judge had already made a decision. If I showed up in an angel outfit complete with feather wings, it wasn't going to change her mind.

I wondered what else the Italian detectives had found. I was certain they weren't here to repeat what they'd said a million times before. They must have some new evidence. Or perhaps a witness.

The media expected me to be arrested. They'd shown up early, rustling and pushing toward the front like eager puppies. They'd called out my name when we walked up the stairs to the courthouse. I'd practiced my look in the mirror in the bathroom before we'd left. I couldn't scowl, or I'd look mean. I couldn't smile—in case it came across as taking things too lightly. I couldn't cry—that would make me look guilty, as if the weight of my sin was wearing me down. The goal was to look neutral. A dispassionate observer.

The media didn't scare me anymore. They were swinging to my side. They were prepared to be outraged on my behalf. They wanted to be upset, to take up my cause. Being arrested wouldn't be the end; it would be the beginning of the next stage. The Italians wanted control. They didn't want to have to bow and scrape to the American system. They wanted me in their court, but that didn't mean they would win. Of course there were at least a few people who wanted me to go down. The *Justice for Simone* website was still calling for my blood. They didn't think much of the video from the police or the people saying there wasn't enough proof. They said they didn't need proof. Where there was smoke, there was fire. I was guilty. They'd want a front-row seat for anything that happened in Italy.

Detective Alban stood. "I thank the court for this indulgence."

I could hear the whir of cameras behind me. They'd been allowed in the courtroom today. A line of them, an honor guard along the back wall.

"Before Your Honor rules, the prosecutor in Italy has requested that I speak today," Detective Alban said.

I took a slow breath in. When he announced the condition of my arrest, I didn't want to give him the pleasure of seeing me break. I practiced the visualization I'd learned with Dr. Weeks. I pictured my veins filled with cool water and imagined it traveling through my body, slowing my heart and breathing.

"We believe that Ms. Charron has not told the true story. We are not medical doctors, so it is outside our expertise if Ms. Charron really cannot remember or if she is choosing to not remember." Detective Alban paused. If he thought I was going to break down and blurt out a confession, he would wait a long time.

Detective Alban continued. "Our court system has determined that there is insufficient evidence to prosecute Ms. Charron. In recent days, several other credible causes for the accident have been raised. As a result, the death of Ms. McIvory has been deemed an accident. We are dropping all charges and, as a result, also our application for extradition."

I heard my mom cry out. There was a loud murmur from the court audience, and Judge Rendahl slammed her gavel down on her desk.

"Order in this court," she demanded, and the chatter stopped. Detective Alban was already sitting, tapping his papers into order and tucking them into his folder.

Had I heard him correctly? My efforts to keep control were failing. My hands started shaking, and the tremors traveled up my arms into my core. I could feel myself vibrating. They were dropping the charges. They were dropping the charges. They were dropping . . . the charges.

Evan reached over and squeezed my forearm.

"What—" Every word I could think of was gone.

"Hang in there," Evan said. He stood. "Your Honor, in light of the revelations from the Italian court—"

Judge Rendahl waved him off. "No need for a speech, Mr. Stanley. Given that the application has been dropped, there is no ruling from this court. Ms. Charron, you are free to go."

The word *free* bounced around my head. Even the idea of it tasted delicious. I stood along with the rest of the court as Judge Rendahl exited.

As soon as the door to her chamber closed, my parents surrounded me, a family hug. My mom was crying, big, sobbing tears. My dad kept thumping me on the back murmuring, "That's my girl, that's my baby girl."

Evan stood next to us. He had his hands on his hips, his pelvis jutting forward, like he was about to lean his head back and howl his victory to the sky.

"Is that it?" I asked, my voice quaking. It didn't seem possible it could be over that quickly, just disappear in a poof. Like popping a nightmare balloon. I could feel laughter bubbling up inside me, but I wasn't sure if it was okay to let it out.

Evan threw his arm around me and hugged me. "That's it. It's over."

My knees melted, and if Evan hadn't been standing next to me, I would have crumpled to the floor.

"Hey, now, take it easy." Evan guided me back into my seat. "Take a second to get your legs under you."

The bailiff was clearing the court, but left us alone. My dad turned on his phone and called my stepmom with the news. My mom couldn't stop touching me, petting my hair, running her hand down my arm, or kissing my temple. It was as if she thought if she didn't make contact, then I might disappear.

"If you're up to making a statement, that would be great," Evan said. "If you think you're not ready, that's okay too. There will be a lot of opportunities." He glanced at my dad. "I'd suggest that you might want to think about letting my firm negotiate the deals."

"Deals for what?" Dad asked.

"The media will likely pay for exclusive interviews—20/20, Dateline. They've been nosing around already, and this ruling will bring them out in droves. There's also a good chance of a book deal, maybe a TV movie based on your story. The fees would likely cover your costs, and you'd have enough left over to make a dent in that college tuition."

I felt a prickle of excitement. The money didn't excite me, but the image of a book jacket with my face on it floated in front of me. A chance to tell my story, or at least a version of my story.

"Today has been a lot. If you feel you're not ready, we can do a short written statement later," Evan said.

"No, I want to say something," I said.

***

Less than a half hour later, we walked outside into the bright sunshine. Evan stepped to the front and smiled at the squadron of microphones in front of him. He'd taken time to slick back his hair. He was going to miss the spotlight, but the fact that I'd gotten off was going to work well for him. A feather in his cap. He raised his hand to make sure he had everyone's attention.

"Now, we're not going to answer questions, but Jill does have a statement to make." Evan stepped back and motioned for me to take his place.

The chatter of camera shutters sounded like a swarm of bees. I glanced down at the paper I'd scribbled on to make sure I remembered each bulleted point. I said a silent prayer that my aphasia would stay away.

"As you can imagine, I am very grateful for today's announcement, and I look forward to returning home and to my family. I owe a huge debt of gratitude to the entire staff of St. Regis Rehabilitation Hospital—in particular Dr. Weeks—for their support and guidance during this difficult period of my recovery. I also wish to thank Evan Stanley for his help." I turned and smiled at him, and he nodded with an aw-shucks-type gesture. "Most of all, I need to thank my parents and stepmom, whose faith in me never wavered and gave me strength to keep going. I couldn't have done this without them."

Mom sniffed loudly, and I could tell she was trying everything to hold it together. The reporters were all nodding and smiling at me. They loved me. Just a week ago, they'd been ready to stone me in the street, but everything was different now. Now I was innocent.

"I'm looking forward to taking the next steps in my life. I will never forget Simone. I learned so much from her." My voice shook, and I looked down at the paper again. The quaver was faked, but I could tell from the audience reaction that it was perfect. It was what they wanted.

"I'll remember her always." I touched my chest lightly, as if I had a piece of her tucked into my heart for safekeeping. The rustling clicking of cameras erupted again, catching the perfectly formed tear that hovered for a dramatic second in my eye and then fell.

A wave of questions rushed up at me. Each reporter screaming out louder than the next to be heard.

Evan stepped in front of me and waved them down. "We won't be taking questions at this time." He gestured for me to walk back into the courthouse. I stopped at the top of the stairs and looked back, letting everyone get one more shot. I'd learned more from Simone than I was going to admit.

I hadn't chosen for it to end this way, but now that it had, I was going to take a lesson from her book. The ends justified the means. A girl does what she has to. This was how it had turned out, and it would have been foolish for me to not take advantage of it. It's what Simone would have done. I'd gone to Italy because I wanted my life to change. And it had. In a way I'd never imagined. And I hadn't lied to the reporters. I was carrying a bit of Simone with me. I'd learned what she'd tried to show me all the time. That there is no black and white justice—there's what people need to do to survive.

The corners of my mouth curled up. And who knew? Maybe my memories weren't even accurate. Dr. Weeks would tell me that the brain can do amazing things. Either way, it didn't matter. The truth—and how I chose to tell it—was now up to me.

Acknowledgements

First, thanks to you for picking up this book and giving it a read. Feel free to write your name in here and point it out to your friends and family. A writer without readers is a lonely creature.

This book wouldn't exist without my agent Barbara Poelle, who encouraged me to write it and wasn't afraid to push me to make it better. I would lavish her with spendy handbags and eternal gratitude any day. I am truly fortunate to have her in my corner.

Writing may be a solo sport, but publishing takes a team effort. I am grateful every day that my editor, Sarah Landis, embraced this project and made me a part of the HMH team. Sarah moved mountains to get this book ready and I am forever grateful for her ability to bend deadlines using only the power of her mind. Thanks also goes to Ann Dye, Lisa DiSarro and Linda Magram in Marketing, Meredith Wilson and Karen Walsh in Publicity, Amy Carlisle in Managing Editorial, Mary Wilcox, editor-in-chief, Betsy Groban, publisher, Marie Gorman, Sales, and Christine Kettner, Design. And for a cover to die for, hugs and kisses go to Erin Fitzsimmons. For all things foreign, I have relied on Heather Baror-Shapiro, who has been nothing short of amazing.

I am lucky to have the best friends and family, so thanks to all of you for the support and laughter. I couldn't do it without you. Especially my parents, who were, if possible, more excited than I was about this book. Extra thanks to Kelly Charron, Joanne Levy, and Denise Jaden, who read early versions of this, helped to brainstorm plot holes, and cheered me on to the finish line. To David's Tea, who supplies me with the caffeine needed to get through a day – thank you a million times over.

I need to thank my husband, Bob, for travelling with me to Italy and standing by while I researched Jill's journey. I owe you another trip, this time without constant notetaking. For not thinking my fascination with making stuff up is crazy, I will always love you. Lastly, thanks to my dog Cairo, chewer of shoes, digger of holes, and constant writer companion.

Eileen Cook

Eileen Cook is a multi-published author, with her novels appearing in eight different languages. Her books have been optioned for film and TV. She spent most of her teen years wishing she were someone else or somewhere else, which is great training for a writer. Eileen lives in Vancouver with her husband and one very naughty dog, and no longer wishes to be anyone or anywhere else.

Follow Eileen, her books, and the things that strike her as funny at www.eileencook.com or on Twitter: @eileenwriter

HOT KEY BOOKS

Thank you for choosing a Hot Key book.

If you want to know more about our authors and what we publish, you can find us online.

You can start at our website

www.hotkeybooks.com

And you can also find us on:

We hope to see you soon!